Debonair in Death

A *Murder, She Wrote* Mystery

Debonair in Death

A *Murder, She Wrote* Mystery

A NOVEL BY JESSICA FLETCHER & TERRIE FARLEY MORAN

Based on the Universal television series created by
Peter S. Fischer, Richard Levinson & William Link

BERKLEY PRIME CRIME
New York

BERKLEY PRIME CRIME
Published by Berkley
An imprint of Penguin Random House LLC
penguinrandomhouse.com

Copyright © 2021 by Universal City Studios LLC
Murder, She Wrote is a trademark and copyright of Universal Studios.
All rights reserved.

Library of Congress Cataloging-in-Publication Data

Names: Fletcher, Jessica, author. | Moran, Terrie Farley, author.
Title: Debonair in death / a novel by Jessica Fletcher & Terrie Farley Moran.
Description: New York : Berkley Prime Crime, [2021] |
Series: A Murder, she wrote mystery
Identifiers: LCCN 2021018993 (print) | LCCN 2021018994 (ebook) |
ISBN 9780593333624 (hardcover) | ISBN 9780593333631 (ebook)
Subjects: GSAFD: Mystery fiction.
Classification: LCC PS3552.A376 D44 2021 (print) |
LCC PS3552.A376 (ebook) | DDC 813/.54--dc23
LC record available at https://lccn.loc.gov/2021018993
LC ebook record available at https://lccn.loc.gov/2021018994

Printed in the United States of America
1   3   5   7   9   10   8   6   4   2

This is a work of fiction. Names, characters, places, and incidents either
are the product of the authors' imaginations or are used fictitiously,
and any resemblance to actual persons, living or dead, business
establishments, events, or locales is entirely coincidental.

Shannon Larkin Moran
best daughter-in-law ever

Debonair in Death

A *Murder, She Wrote* Mystery

Chapter One

Jessica, I really think you should let me fluff up the top." My favorite hairdresser, Loretta Spiegel, used her fingers and the handle of a round-headed brush to push my ash blond hair about an inch higher than I normally wear it. Then she turned the easy-to-rotate salon chair I was sitting in from right to left and back again so I could view it from all angles in the mirror in front of me.

"No, thank you, Loretta. I am happy with my hair the way it is." Then I added, "At least for the time being," to soften the blow.

Loretta and I had some version of this same conversation nearly every time I came in for a trim. She kept trying to make what she called "small changes" to my hairstyle, which I was sure would eventually lead to major changes. My short hair, layered with just enough waves to have an agreeable, feminine look, suited me perfectly. I found it easy to manage, a boon when I am traveling, what with book tours, research trips, and my favorite jaunts—visits to family and friends. Although I resisted every suggestion Loretta made, that never stopped her from making them.

Loretta pulled a long, pointed stainless steel hair clip off a cardboard placard that was standing upright on her countertop and snapped it open to section off the side of my hair she was ready to cut. "If you say so, Jessica, but I wish you'd let me make a small change here and there. I think it would give you a more modern look."

My longtime friend and neighbor Ideal Molloy was tucked under a pink domed hair dryer a few feet behind us. She was wrapped in a kimono-style smock, her dark hair covered with rows of plastic curlers and a bouffant hairnet. Ideal raised her voice as if not sure we could hear her over the whirring of the dryer. "More modern. That's exactly right, Loretta. Thank you."

Coreen Wilson, the salon's manicurist, had worked as Loretta's assistant since she was a student in high school. Now she stood in front of Ideal, holding open a plastic nail polish display case filled with inch-high bottles of lacquer of every color of the rainbow, along with a few odd shades I couldn't identify. Coreen ran one hand through her honey blond curls while she waited patiently for Ideal to look over the entire selection and then choose her usual deep red polish. She'd said it so many times, even I knew the name—Dark Cherry. So when Ideal veered off, we were all taken by surprise.

"Loretta, that's exactly what I want. A more modern look for my fingernails. Maybe this time I'll even do my toes. Should I go with royal blue or stripes, or something bolder? Every time I thumb through a magazine, I feel frumpy when I look at the models. To tell you the truth, I am sick of red, red, red all the time."

Loretta caught my eye in the mirror and gave me a quick wink. I answered with a smile. Neither of us said a word to Ideal, who turned back to examining the box filled with polishes. My money was still on Dark Cherry.

"Coreen, you're the one who would know—how are the young girls coloring their nails? Not the teenyboppers—I mean the college girls, or even the mid-twenties crowd."

I watched their reflections in the mirror. Coreen was as hesitant as Ideal was insistent. Coreen was barely in her twenties and probably thought of Ideal as motherly, if not grandmotherly. I'm sure she was having a tough time visualizing Ideal as a trendsetter. I could see she was having difficulty hiding her grin while she tried to come up with a suggestion that would mollify Ideal and, hopefully, not look ridiculous on a woman of a certain age.

I could almost see the lightbulb flash over Coreen's head when she thought of something that might do the trick. "Here's what I think, Miss Ideal. Since your hands look so pretty with the deep red polish you get every week, you might want to keep the same color but jazz it up by adding sparkles on the tip of one nail. I can tell you for sure that look is extremely popular with, ah, girls my age."

Coreen held up two bottles from the nail polish case. Rays of sunlight beamed through the front window and bounced off glittery silver sparkles in one bottle and shimmering gold sparkles in the other. "Take a look, Miss Ideal. You can pick."

Ideal pondered for a moment and then agreed. "That sounds like a good start. If I like it, we can go bolder next week. First, I have to decide which finger I want to sparkle and shine." Ideal held out her hands, examining them critically. "How about my left ring finger? I've been divorced for so many years, the tan line from my wedding ring is long faded. Metallic sparkles will perk it up. Jessica, what do you think? Silver or gold? Which would you do?"

As someone who likes her nails to be neat and unobtrusive, I wouldn't opt for either one. While I was trying to think of a diplomatic answer the front door opened and drew everyone's attention to our local Realtor, Eve Simpson, who began complaining before the door shut behind her.

"Wouldn't you know it? That would be my luck. I was on my way here for my weekly hair appointment—I'm not late, am I, Loretta?—and I stopped at the post office to mail some brochures about the Barkley house to a few of my out-of-town prospects. You know the house I mean—that gorgeous two-story with the wraparound porch near the cliff top. The one with the stunning view of the water. I'm positive it's going to go superfast, and for top dollar, too. Anyway, Debbie promised me the brochures would be on their way to Boston in this afternoon's mail. Then, when I turned to leave, who do you think was walking in as I was walking out?"

We all knew that when she was in midstory Eve's questions were nearly always rhetorical, so we silently waited for her to continue, and in less than two seconds, she did.

"I've been dying to run into him casually, to have the opportunity to strike up a more private conversation, if you get my point. But not today. And certainly not when I look like this."

Eve stopped to take a breath and look around the room, wide-eyed, as though she was expecting wails of sympathy from every corner. But since we actually had no idea what she was talking about, no one said a word. When she crossed her arms and began tapping her toe, Loretta took the hint.

"Who did you meet, Eve? Who is this Adonis who has you so bothered?"

"Who do you think? Who have I been trying to wangle a few private moments with for months now? The handsome, distinguished, and so very cultured Nelson Penzell. You all know him. He owns La Peinture, down on the dockside. Naturally, we all must admire a man who uses the French language to name his shop. I did hear that he was a college professor at one time—he probably taught art history or romance languages. He is *très* Continental."

She pulled the black cloche hat off her head and dropped it on a chair alongside her purse. "And here I am *avec des cheveux en désordre*. Couldn't I have met him later today, after Loretta works her magic, when I will look totally stunning? Of course not. He held the post office door for me, and smiled rather warmly. And he ensured that the door was less than fully open so I was able to brush his arm ever so lightly as I walked through—you know, a signal of interest. But I'm sure it was all for naught. How could he possibly realize how attractive I am? There I was with my hair a complete mess, and wearing that silly hat that barely hid my untidy hair."

She might have believed she looked awful, but I thought Eve looked absolutely perfect, as she always did. She was wearing a light gray fitted jacket with notch lapels over an emerald mock turtleneck, and tapered black slacks that complemented her trim figure. Her expertly applied makeup added subtle color to her finely chiseled features. And other than a strand that moved slightly out of place when she pulled off her hat, her light brown hair didn't look as if Loretta needed to do a thing.

"Eve, take it from me: You shouldn't waste your time on that Nelson Penzell. He may be good-looking, but from what I've heard, he's a real playboy. The love-'em-and-leave-'em kind." Ideal's conversation generally centered around the up-to-the-minute recipes she'd discovered on the Food Network or her frustration with her latest craft project, so I was surprised to hear her pass along cutting-edge romantic gossip.

But Eve simply waved her off. "Nelson Penzell is a cultured gentleman, and we are extremely lucky to have him as a part of our community. Why, as soon as he bought a partnership in that slovenly tourist trap Angus Michaud unimaginatively named the This and That Shop, Nelson turned it into a quality establishment. Within weeks he'd upgraded it to an art emporium I am proud to recommend to my new householders as they begin decorating their Cabot Cove homes. Angus still has some of his touristy junk for sale, but I guess Nelson felt that couldn't be helped."

Ideal, who generally retreated as soon as anyone disagreed with her, stuck to her guns. "You may see him as a classy businessman, and you may be right, but when it comes to his personal life, well, according to the ladies in my ceramics class, he is—"

Eve wasn't having any. "Oh, them! Ideal, who would pay attention to anything those old biddies have to say?"

I suspected Coreen was trying to make peace when she interrupted. "I do Mr. Penzell's manicure every week, and, well, he's always on time and a good tipper . . ." She trailed off when she saw the look on Eve's face.

Eve's jaw dropped, her eyes popped, and her tone rose to manic. "Coreen, what are you saying? Are you telling me I've been in danger of having Nelson Penzell walk in here to get his nails done when I am sitting under the dryer looking exactly the way Ideal does? Good grief, why didn't anyone warn me before now?"

Ideal pushed the dryer away from her hair and stood up, hands on her hips, ready to do battle. "Eve Simpson, exactly what is wrong with the way I look?"

Loretta leaned in and whispered, "Jessica, I'll be right back."

She quickly moved into the middle of the room and held her hands up as if she were surrendering, when in reality she was taking charge. "Ladies, we're all friends here. Can we please stop the bickering? Coreen, why don't you put out a plate of those doughnuts I picked up at Charlene Sassi's bakery this morning? Ideal, Eve, can I offer you a cup of coffee?"

Ideal was instantly diverted. She licked her lips and asked, "Are any of the doughnuts chocolate crème?"

In contrast, Eve ran her hands over her waistline and said, "Only coffee for me. Black, thank you."

While pouring coffee into oversized pink mugs decorated with pictures of blow-dryers, scissors, and curlers, Loretta said, "Eve, I can promise you will never run into Mr. Penzell here."

Eve's tension began to dissolve. "Thank you, Loretta. I knew I could count on you to handle the scheduling with discretion so I don't have any, er, embarrassing encounters when I am not at my best."

Loretta laughed. "Eve, I don't have to do a thing. When he first moved to Cabot Cove, Mr. Penzell dropped by and asked if he could arrange for a weekly manicure at his home. When he saw that I wasn't keen on his request, he offered his shop as the site and threw in a ten percent 'travel bonus.' Coreen and I talked it over and we agreed to accommodate him."

But Eve was taking no chances. "What about when he gets his hair cut? Don't tell me he goes to the barbershop. Why, every man in this town comes out of there with a flattop straight out of the nineteen fifties."

"Not a problem. He still travels to his stylist in Portland. From the look of him I would say he makes the trip at least once a month."

Loretta came back to my chair, picked up her scissors, and mumbled so only I could hear, "Crisis averted."

Ideal nibbled on a chocolate crème doughnut held carefully between her thumb and index finger to avoid smudging her nail polish. She watched as Eve settled into a chair and opened the latest copy of *Vogue*.

"Eve, you have such great taste." Ideal began with flattery, as though their mini altercation hadn't happened less than five minutes ago, then got to the point. "What color looks better with red? Would you say silver or gold?"

"Every year I decorate my office Christmas tree with silver twinkle lights and red ornaments, if that is any help," Eve answered, then quickly buried her head in the magazine to show she was still miffed.

Happy to have the decision made for her, Ideal stretched her left hand toward Coreen and said, "Silver."

The front door opened again and a young woman dressed in jeans and a bright green Celtics sweatshirt hesitated in the doorway, then walked to the desk and looked around uncertainly. Her bright blue eyes met mine and she gave a tentative smile, which widened when I smiled back.

Loretta said, "Give me a minute, Jess." Then she asked, "Can I help you?" as she walked to the counter.

"Yes, ah, hi." She curled an unruly lock of ginger hair around her finger. "As you can see, I'm in need of a trim. I was wondering if you'd have an appointment available later today or perhaps tomorrow."

Loretta glanced at the appointment book that lay open on the desk. "We are a little busy right now, but how about after lunch—say, two o'clock? Name?"

"Erica, Erica Davenport."

"I'm Loretta, and I will be doing your cut. If you'd like a manicure while you're here . . ."

Erica shook her head. "I'm embarrassed to admit I bite my nails. I keep promising myself that I'll quit, but so far, no luck. My dream is to have perfectly manicured nails, but I haven't gotten the discipline yet."

"You're in the right place. While I am cutting your hair, our manicurist can give you a few tips on how to conquer the nail-biting habit. Free of charge."

Erica laughed. "As long as it doesn't involve that evil-tasting stuff my mother used to slather on my nails when I was in junior high, I will be grateful for any advice."

"Terrific." Loretta handed her an appointment card. "We'll see you at two."

Erica began turning toward the door and then stopped. "One more thing . . . Could you tell me where I might find a shop called La Peinture? I know it's somewhere in town."

Eve's head snapped up and her copy of *Vogue* slid onto the floor.

Loretta answered, "Sure, honey. You know where the wharf is? Where all the boats are moored?"

Erica nodded.

"Right along the dockside there are a number of stores, Mara's Luncheonette being the most popular. A few doors down from Mara's you will find La Peinture. You can't miss it. There is a huge painting of a storm-tossed trawler in one window and some toy-sized boat models and touristy knickknacks in the other," Loretta said.

"Thank you. I'll be back this afternoon." And Erica practically flew out the door.

"Well!" Eve bent to pick her fallen magazine. "What could she possibly want at La Peinture? She doesn't look the type to be able to afford high-end art."

"Maybe she's a friend of Angus Michaud or, more likely, Nelson Penzell. Maybe they're dating." Ideal's innocent tone was belied by her devilish chuckle.

"Don't be ridiculous. She's a mere child," Eve insisted. "A man of Nelson's taste would clearly prefer a more mature, experienced woman."

Fortunately for us all, a timer bell dinged and Loretta told Coreen it was time to take the curlers out of Ideal's hair.

Saved by the bell, I thought.

Chapter Two

The next morning I awoke to one of my favorite perks of living on the Maine coast in late September—a flawless autumn day.

I belted my robe over my pajamas, opened the back door, and stepped outside. For as far as the eye could see, the sky was bright blue, interrupted here and there by soft, billowy clouds puffed like down pillows. I took a deep breath. The air was pleasantly cool and clear. I thought I detected a tinge of woodsmoke, which made me wonder if my neighbor Maeve O'Bannon was making hearth bread. The modern kitchen in her nearly two-hundred-year-old house still had an ancient fireplace, with iron rods that crisscrossed the firebox and acted as a brace for a flat iron pan suspended on thick chains. The setup allowed her to "bake" bread over burning pine logs. Maeve has told me more than once that when she was a child her grandmother taught her how to cook over an open flame and helped her memorize the recipes she still uses all these decades later.

The thought made my stomach growl, reminding me that I was meeting Seth Hazlitt, my close friend and our town's most popular doctor, at Mara's Luncheonette down on the dockside for breakfast. I hurried upstairs, showered, and jumped into a pair of jeans. I tied the sleeves of my blue pullover around my neck, on top of a plaid man-tailored shirt. If a chill hit the air, I was ready.

It was a perfect morning for a bicycle ride as I pedaled along the streets of Cabot Cove. Fall foliage was almost upon us. Leaves were beginning to turn, with wide swaths of gold peeking through the green in the old beech trees I passed, while the tall oak trees displayed splashes of crimson and orange. On every block a friend or neighbor called out, "Good morning," and I waved a greeting as I rode by.

As always, I couldn't suppress a smile when the harbor came into view. Most of the sturdy fishing boats and the narrow lobster boats, which the locals call peapods, had already gone far out into the Atlantic Ocean. By this time of morning the crews were hard at work. Even so, there were dozens of pleasure boats dotting the harbor. I could see tiny pontoons and skiffs and mid-sized powerboats securely tied to the dock cleats. Several of the extra-large slips reserved for yachts were empty, but I did notice one yacht, at least a sixty-footer, that had the name BREW'S BABY stenciled on the bow.

All along the wharf there were people carrying out the daily chores that came along with boating and fishing—cleaning, loading, unloading. Two men I recognized as shipwrights from the boatyard were gesturing animatedly as they inspected the hull of a sailboat. The man they were talking to didn't look at all happy. I supposed he was the owner and the needed repairs were going to cost a pretty penny.

I propped my two-wheeler in the bicycle rack at the north end of the dockside and walked past three or four storefronts. When I reached La Peinture, remembering Eve's frenzy yesterday at Loretta's Beauty Parlor, I automatically glanced through the window, and the shop looked deserted.

I opened the door of Mara's Luncheonette and was immediately caught up in familiar sights, sounds, and smells. The round stools that lined the long counter were filled with shopkeepers and recreational fishermen who were gossiping and joking like old friends. At the far side of the counter thin coils of smoke rose from the grill, accompanied by the sizzle of bacon and sausage. Both smelled delicious. Mara gave me a wide smile and held up a coffeepot. I nodded yes and she pointed to Seth, who was sitting at a table in the middle of the room with his back to me. I could see that he was tapping his fingers on the Formica tabletop, a sign that he considered me to be late. I came up behind him, slid into the chair to his left, careful not to catch my sleeve on a tear in the vinyl seat back, and said, "Good morning, Seth. Isn't it a magnificent day?"

"Ayuh, we don't get many days like this, but when we do, 'magnificent' is the word. Woman, you're late. I have patients who'll be lining up in my office in less than an hour, and I'd planned on a leisurely breakfast. Completely unrushed." His blue eyes peered over the top of his horn-rimmed glasses as he waited for my reaction.

I knew better than to let his teasing rattle me. "Well, then, I hope you ordered your breakfast."

"Sure did. Ordered mine and yours as well. Two short stacks of Mara's blueberry pancakes, along with real maple syrup. I never understand why anyone orders that sugar-free stuff. What is the point?"

"Now, Seth, as a doctor you know very well that there are some people who can't have syrup, can't have sugar."

He harrumphed. "Well, then, those people likely shouldn't be eating blueberry pancakes. My guess is they should be the folks who order two poached eggs and decaffeinated coffee."

Mara came along with the coffeepot to fill my cup and refill Seth's. "Two short stacks of blueberry pancakes coming right up. Is that okay with you, Jessica? Doc Hazlitt ordered for you both a few minutes ago."

"Exactly what I am longing for, a taste of your championship blueberry pancakes," I replied.

Mara's blueberry pancakes won prizes in county fairs all over the state of Maine, and lately she had branched out into Vermont and New Hampshire, taking home ribbons and trophies from both states. During the height of the Maine blueberry season, which coincides closely with tourist season, we locals would have to get up extra early if we didn't want to wait on line for a table at Mara's. Fortunately, both seasons were dwindling to an end and life was getting back to normal here in Cabot Cove. Of course, the "leaf peepers," as we called the tourists who come to see our amazingly colorful fall foliage, would begin arriving soon.

Mara came back and set down two plates, steam rising from pancakes dotted with succulent blueberries. She pulled a bottle of maple syrup from her apron pocket and deposited it on the table about an inch from Seth's hand. "Here you go, Doc. Delivered yesterday. You can do the honor of opening the bottle."

"Thank you, Mara. Jessica, would you look at these pan-cakes?" Seth dabbed a pat of butter on the top of his stack, and then drowned everything in the fresh maple syrup that Mara regularly ordered from a farmer up near Bangor. "Nice and hot, and that's the way I like 'em."

Mara and I exchanged a smile. Seth said the same thing every time he ordered blueberry pancakes, which was practically every morning we had breakfast at Mara's.

Just over my shoulder a mobile phone rang, and then I heard someone mutter, "What now?"

I glanced and saw Angus Michaud, co-owner of La Peinture, sitting at the counter. He was dressed in his usual jeans and a sturdy but ancient pair of Timberlands. He was one of the very few customers of Mara's who tucked a napkin in their collar, in his case the collar of whatever he was wearing under his navy blue windbreaker.

"Can't a man have breakfast in peace?" he snapped into the phone.

I could only hope he wasn't talking to a customer.

"What is? When? Today? Can't you ever take care of any-thing?" He listened for a minute, said, "Oh, all right," then shoved the phone in his pocket.

He swiveled his seat and scanned the counter, tables, and booths as he called, "Mara? Mara?"

She came out from the kitchen, her arms loaded down with plates of pancakes, and said, "In a minute, Angus."

True to her word, she was back in a jiffy. "What do you need?"

"What I need is a new business partner, but I will settle for you wrapping up the rest of my breakfast to go. And do me a favor: Add a couple more sausages—they were extra tasty this morning."

Mara took two sausages off the griddle, wrapped them in foil, and put them in a hinged cardboard food container.

Watching her transfer the remains of his breakfast from plate to container, Angus said, "I'll tell you one thing, Mara. You were smart to open this place on your own. Business partners are like a five-hundred-pound weight around your neck. No getting out from under."

He grabbed his breakfast leftovers and charged toward the door, bumping against Seth's chair as he went.

Seth stared after him with raised eyebrows, and then turned back to me. "Well, I'll be . . . Here I thought the partnership of Michaud and Penzell was doing so well, for all they gave the This and That Shop a silly French name."

I nodded. "I thought so, too, but we can't be sure that it was Angus's partner on the phone."

"Jessica, didn't you hear Angus congratulating Mara for keeping her business solo? Sounds to me like he is sorry he didn't do the same. I thought they had worked out an arrangement: Nelson Penzell handles the expensive items and Angus remains in charge of the more affordable, touristy fare."

"Good morning, Seth, Jessica." Ryan Hecht stood resting both hands on the vacant chair opposite mine. Tall and clean-shaven, with closely cropped dark hair, Ryan wore a conservative three-piece pin-striped suit and looked every inch what I'd always known him to be: an extremely trustworthy accountant. He nodded toward the door that Angus had slammed shut. "Seems obvious Angus and Nelson aren't managing their separation of duties as well as they'd hoped."

Mara stopped by our table with a coffeepot. I quickly put my hand over my less-than-half-full cup, but Seth gratefully took a refill.

While she poured, Mara said, "All I can say is that Angus and Nelson fight like an old married couple. Pick, pick, pick—and always about money. Nelson tries to keep his private business private, but, well, Angus . . . This episode was one of the many examples of his inability to control his voice or his temper."

"Shame, that," Ryan's wife, Julie, a business-savvy fund-raiser who worked with many of the nonprofit endeavors I supported, chimed in. "We had planned to stop in La Peinture after break-fast. My sister, Marcy, and I recently moved our father into a nursing home."

"Oh, I'm sorry that's become necessary," I said. My sincerest wish was that my nephew Grady and his wife, Donna, would never have to make that decision for me.

Ryan tried to put his arm around Julie, but I noticed she moved slightly away from what I thought was a comforting gesture. I guessed she was still feeling too guilty to accept any solace for what she had been forced to do.

Julie went on to explain, "Dad couldn't manage by himself anymore. At first we had a part-time caretaker, but when it became evident that he needed help brushing his teeth and cutting his meat . . . And he had a number of falls. It was only a matter of time until he hurt himself seriously. Marcy and I both have demanding jobs, and she lives all the way down in New Hampshire, right outside of Manchester. We really had no choice.

"The one thing Dad really misses is the sea." Julie's chocolate-colored eyes moistened and she quickly blinked before tears could form. "Ryan had the idea that we should buy him a true-to-life seascape. If we hang it in his bedroom, he can visit the waterfront whenever he likes."

I nodded. "That's a wonderful plan." I wanted to encourage Julie's confidence that she was doing as much as she could to make her father comfortable in his new surroundings.

"It's a plan we are going to have to put on hold for a day or two," Ryan said. "After listening to Angus's carrying-on, well, this probably isn't the best time for us to pop into the This and That Shop for a painting."

"Ryan, really? The store name changed months ago. It's La Peinture, which is French for 'the painting.' It shouldn't be that hard to remember," Julie scolded.

Ryan chuckled sheepishly. "It's not hard to remember. It strikes me as an awfully phony masthead for a store that sells model boats and jigsaw puzzles of purple lupine flowers dotting the fields and byways of Maine. Almost as phony as that Nelson Penzell."

Julie gave him a light tap on the arm. "Hush. We can't have anyone overhear a prominent accountant making fun of a local business owner. That could hurt your business more than his."

"Julie's got a right pertinent point there, Ryan," Seth said in the tone he used when he was half serious, half teasing. I was one person who knew that tone well.

Julie offered Seth a grateful smile. "Thank you. Well, we have to run along, but I hope I will see you both tomorrow at the committee meeting for the renovation of the children's wing at Cabot Cove Hospital."

I said, "Absolutely. We wouldn't miss it. I am anxious to see what Dr. Leung and the hospital administrators have in mind."

After they left, Seth took a long sip of coffee and then said, "I see you got a haircut. So tell me, what is the latest news from gossip central?"

Seth was right on that score. Loretta's was second only to Mara's when it came to spreading the latest facts or fantasies throughout the Cabot Cove grapevine. Our local newspaper, the *Cabot Cove Gazette*, had a difficult time keeping up.

"Pretty much same old, same old, but if you run into Ideal Molloy, be sure to compliment her on her left ring finger."

Seth looked startled. "Don't tell me she's run off and gotten engaged or married or some such foolishness."

I laughed. "Nothing that drastic. She added a touch of sparkle to her manicure and is quite pleased with herself. Oh, and a young girl came in to make an appointment. Maybe up from Boston. As I recall, she was wearing a Celtics sweatshirt. Got everyone's curiosity riled."

"I'm not surprised. Doesn't take much to get those gals a-wondering. Pretty redhead, about five feet six and one hundred twenty-five pounds or so. That would do it." Seth gave me a Cheshire cat grin.

"You know who she is!" I leaned closer, ready for him to spill the beans.

"If you must know, her name is Erica."

"I know that. She had to give it to Loretta when she made her appointment. Now tell me how you know her."

"Lavinia Wahl tripped a couple of weeks back while docking her sailboat. Broke her leg in two places. I kept telling her she was too old to handle a thirty-foot sailboat on her own, but you women don't listen." Seth waggled a disciplinary finger in the air, intended for all the patients who ignored his warnings.

It was as though he was trying to irk me. "I *know* all about Lavinia's leg. Tell me about Erica."

"Nothing to tell. She's Lavinia's grandniece on her sister Laverne's side, and she's come north to help out. Lavinia is so awkward using crutches, I had to confine her to a wheelchair before she fell and broke another bone or two."

"Well, that will be a big disappointment to the girls at Loretta's. No big mystery after all." I sighed.

But I had spoken too soon.

Chapter Three

We left our usual tip on the table and settled up our breakfast bill with Mara at the cash register.

"How is that arthritis doing?" Seth asked as Mara handed him his change.

"Much better, thank you, Doc." Mara held out both hands so he could take a quick look. "That ointment you have me rubbing on morning and night really does the trick. Look at my thumb joints. Redness is nearly gone, and so is a lot of the stiffness."

Seth held the door open for me, and as I passed through I said, "I feel so lucky to live in a place where I know everyone and everyone knows me. That is one of the comforts of small-town life."

"Ayuh, and another comfort is that I can walk from breakfast to my office in less than five minutes. And back again for lunch if I so choose." Seth patted his ample waistline. "I forgot to look at the chalkboard to check Mara's lunch specials."

"Oh, Seth, we've barely finished breakfast," I clucked.

"Now, Jess, you know there's nothing wrong with planning ahead." Seth steered us toward the bicycle rack where I'd left my two-wheeler. "I see you rode your trusty steed into town."

"I did. I have some errands to run. I love the Nantucket basket that Grady and Donna gave me for Christmas last year. It's deeper than my old basket, so I can get more shopping done without worrying how I will get everything home. Not to mention the leather straps are super sturdy."

We had almost reached La Peinture when the front door suddenly opened and a woman dashed out to the curb and leaned against the light post. I recognized her ginger hair immediately. Loretta had done a good job of taming the curls yesterday afternoon, but the color was unmistakable. It was difficult to see her face because she was sniffling and holding a tissue up to her eyes.

Always the gentleman, Seth stepped closer and said, "Erica, are you all right?"

She looked at us, surprised at having been noticed. "Dr. Hazlitt, how nice to see you. Silly me. I banged my toe on the front door of that store"—she waved in the direction of La Peinture—"and it stung so bad, I started to cry like a little girl."

"Do you want to come to the office and let me take a look at it?" Seth asked.

The way Erica blanched at Seth's obvious concern made me realize that whatever the cause of her tears might have been, it had nothing to do with her toe. There was something else going on.

The door to La Peinture opened and Nelson Penzell stepped out. He was a handsome man, probably in his mid-forties, with tawny-colored hair and deep hazel eyes. According to the rumor mill, he was the only dockside shopkeeper who habitually wore a suit and tie. His shirts were always crisp white, with long sleeves to show off elegant cuff links. At this close distance, I could see the edge of one of today's gold cuff links peeking from under the sleeve of his navy blue pin-striped suit jacket.

He'd lifted his arm as if he was about to wave hello to us when his eyes lit on Erica, who called out, "Sonny. Sonny, wait. I only want to talk."

Nelson ignored her, turned on a dime, and went back into the store. I could swear I heard the door lock click. Erica froze in place. I was surprised to hear her call Nelson "Sonny." Was that his nickname, and if so, how did she, a stranger in town, know it?

Seth seemed not to notice anything out of the ordinary and said, "My car is parked by my office, but I'd be delighted to walk over to get it and drive you to your aunt's house. Keep you off that foot."

Erica looked as though she was about to cry again and shook her head, ginger curls dancing in the sunlight. She thanked Seth politely before she hurried off in the direction of Lavinia Wahl's house.

We watched her walk away, and then Seth said, "I guess the toe wasn't all that serious."

I shook my head. "No, it wasn't."

I am sure Seth thought I was agreeing with his estimation, when in fact I was wondering how he could be so dense. Clearly it was Erica's heart that had been stubbed, not her toe.

We said our good-byes and Seth headed off to cure whatever ills his patients might present this morning while I pedaled over to Charlene Sassi's delightful bakery, where each day she baked assorted breads and sweet treats in the store's cavernous kitchen.

By the time I was a half block from the bakery I could smell the heavenly scent of the delicacies fresh from her oversized ovens.

I parked my bike next to the wide glass window filled with a display of cakes, pies, and pastries sure to attract passersby. When I opened the door, the shop bell jangled cheerfully above my head. Charlene was hovering over the computer on her side of the counter while clasping a telephone receiver to her ear. She rolled her eyes and held up an index finger, signaling that she would be only a minute or two. She began tapping a few keys on the computer and said, "Yes. As I told you, I do understand."

She grimaced, which let me know she was not happy with whatever she was hearing from the person on the other end of the line. "Of course. I guarantee your order will be ready on time."

Charlene hung up the phone and turned to me. "That was Jeremy Brewington placing an order for rolls and scones that he wants at eight o'clock tomorrow morning. He repeated it three times. 'Eight o'clock sharp!' He's such a bossy fussbudget. He's the kind that, because he owns the biggest yacht in the harbor, thinks he can talk to folks any way he wants." She shuddered. "I'm glad he doesn't come around often. A pleasant customer like you, Jessica, is far more my cup of tea. How can I help you today?"

"I want to place an order of pastries, doughnuts, and muffins for the Friends of the Library meeting. A little birdie told me Doris Ann is having a special birthday this weekend, a number worth commemorating. Here, I wrote all the details down." I passed a piece of paper over the countertop.

Charlene scanned it quickly and said, "No problem. Do you want a few candles to put in the muffins? You know, so she has something to smile at while everyone sings."

"Singing? In the library? Now, there's a thought." I laughed. "But yes, why not?"

"I'll have your order ready an hour before the meeting starts. You can pick it up at your convenience," Charlene said.

I smiled. "Perfect. And I'll take a loaf of rye bread with me now."

The shop door opened and in walked my good friend and our town sheriff, Mort Metzger, looking somewhat the worse for wear.

"Hey, Mrs. F., how goes it? Charlene, if you have any hot coffee left, I'll take a container and a couple of buttered rolls."

"Coming right up, Sheriff. I just made a fresh pot a few minutes ago." Charlene got busy behind the counter.

"Mort, you look extremely haggard this morning. Were you on duty overnight?"

He took off his tan Smokey Bear hat and ruffled his graying hair. "You don't know the half of it. We had two break-ins on high-end boats last weekend. When the first owner filed a complaint, we investigated and saw lots of damage to the furniture. Mattresses overturned, chair legs broken, that kind of thing. I suspected some underage kids used it as a hiding place to drink a few beers. Looks to me like they wound up drinking too much and got carried away."

I nodded. "I would think the same thing."

"Anyway," Mort continued, "a couple of hours later, in comes Jeremy Brewington, and he is raging like a bull. Someone broke into his yacht that same night, ransacked the place, and stole— get this—more than three thousand dollars from his 'petty cash' drawer. I ask you: Who keeps that kind of money lying around on an open boat he's berthing in a public wharf? I don't care how rich he is—Brewington must have a few loose screws to do that."

Charlene rolled her eyes and muttered, "I'll second that." Clearly she'd had enough of Mr. Brewington for one morning.

Mort went on. "For the past few days Floyd, Andy, and I have been taking turns watching the dock overnight. So far, we haven't gotten a nibble, but I'm sure that as soon as we stop watching, the perps will be back in action. Hitting *Brew's Baby* was too lucrative for them not to want to take another stab at it."

Both Floyd McCallum and Andy Broom, Mort's longtime deputies, were unquestionably trustworthy, so I was sure that as a team they could keep the burglars at bay, but I wondered how long they could continue spending all night staring at the boats in the harbor.

I asked, "Have you talked to Walter? What does he say?"

Walter Hendon had been the highly respected harbormaster in Cabot Cove for decades. I never met a soul who didn't admire the way he was able to keep the docks running smoothly. He even appeared to have a knack for settling the countless squabbles between the fishermen and lobstermen, who earned their living on the sea, and the recreational boaters. It seemed to me he would take whatever steps necessary to quickly curtail a problem as serious as break-ins and burglaries.

Mort said, "Walter is doing his best, but the security company that handles boatyards, harbors, and the like is headquartered in Portland, and they claim to be having trouble finding trained and bonded workers who are willing to travel to Cabot Cove. So until Walter can get some help, the Sheriff's Department is on the case, which is why I am going to chow down these rolls, guzzle this coffee, and hit the sack."

Charlene said, "Er, Sheriff, I didn't realize you wanted decaf. Let me swap out that container for you."

"Thanks, but no, thanks, Charlene. After the night I had, I could chugalug an entire jar of whole coffee beans, grind 'em between my teeth, and still pass out as soon as my head hits the pillow."

Even as exhausted as he was, Mort glanced in the reflection of the front window while he put his hat back on. When he was sure he looked every inch a top-notch lawman, he said good-bye and headed for home.

I waved to Charlene and followed Mort out the door. My next stop was the post office to pick up some stamps. When Debbie noticed I had a couple of Priority Mail boxes tucked under my arm she said, "If I had to guess, one of those boxes will be back here before long and on its way to your New York family."

I told her she was absolutely right. It always amused me that she identified friends and family by where they lived. She might not remember that Grady was my nephew but she would never forget his zip code. I guessed it was an occupational idiosyncrasy, similar to how when Mara was describing someone but didn't know his name, she'd say, "He's a lobsterman. Comes in for breakfast—black coffee and a double order of pancakes, side of sausage."

My final stop was at the Fruit and Veg. I was running low on salad greens. And since, here in Maine, we were now in the heart of apple-picking season, I was hoping to find apples from a nearby orchard. I loved nothing more than nibbling on an apple fresh from the tree. A few feet inside the front door two wooden produce baskets were brimming with colorful red apples, some tinged with green, some with yellow. One basket was labeled

FRESH FROM ANDROSCOGGIN COUNTY, while the other was FRESH FROM CUMBERLAND COUNTY. I was in apple heaven.

I bagged a half dozen apples and then went off to round up some garden-fresh lettuce, arugula, and watercress. Nearby I found a container of goat cheese, brined and cured at a local farm. When I got to the checkout line, I noticed small bags of sweetened cranberries nestled alongside the candy bars and chip bags the management put there to tempt hungry shoppers. They would make a tasty and colorful addition to my lunch salad. I added a bag of cranberries to my groceries on the conveyer belt just as the belt began to move.

I was still unpacking my groceries when there was a knock on my kitchen door. I signaled Maeve O'Bannon to come inside. As soon as she opened the door the smell of fresh-baked bread wafted through my kitchen.

"Here you go, Jessica. I've been baking all morning. Poor Lavinia Wahl is housebound for a while, so I thought I would make her some soda bread. Remembering that soda bread with extra raisins is your all-time favorite, I baked you a wedge." She handed me a warm bundle wrapped in a cloth dish towel.

I opened the dish towel and inhaled deeply. "This bread smells heavenly. I stopped at the market and brought home fresh salad ingredients and goat cheese. Your soda bread will be the perfect dessert for my lunch."

"Well, I hope you enjoy it. Now I better get over to Lavinia's while her bread is still warm."

Maeve reached for the doorknob but stopped when I said, "I met Lavinia's niece this morning, down by Mara's."

"Erica, yes. Lovely girl. Come up from Boston to help out." Maeve took a step closer to me and lowered her voice, as though there were prying ears hiding in my dining room. "Sad story there. Lavinia told me Erica had her heart broke by a scoundrel a few years back. Some teacher at her college. Don't they have rules about that? He should be horsewhipped for playing with the heart of a young girl. No fool like an old fool, I always say. Well, I have to run. Enjoy your lunch."

After I finished sorting my groceries, I spread my calendar on the dining room table. The synopsis for my next book was due on my editor's desk in ten days and I'd been mulling ideas, had even done a bit of research, but I'd yet to put a word on paper. It was definitely crunch time. I looked at the calendar. The only absolute must-dos were tomorrow's fund-raising meeting for the children's wing at Cabot Cove Hospital, and the Friends of the Library meeting a few days later. Somewhere along the line I needed to stop at Charles Department Store to buy a birthday present for Grady's wife, Donna. Other than those things my time was my own.

I tapped my computer to life, confident that I'd be able to get a crackerjack synopsis written and off to my editor with time to spare.

Meeting my deadline was soon to become the least of my problems.

Chapter Four

The next morning Seth picked me up at quarter to ten and we drove the short distance to Cabot Cove Hospital. Dr. Gregory Leung, deputy administrator of the hospital, was in charge of the project to modernize and redecorate the children's wing. When he called and asked me to join the committee he explained that, besides matching the highest medical standards, his goal was to make the children's floor comfortable, entertaining, and fun for children and their parents, whether they were dealing with an appendectomy or a chronic illness. I questioned how a hospital stay could ever be entertaining or fun, and Dr. Leung assured me that if I came to the meeting I would find out.

When Seth and I arrived, Dr. Leung was deep in conversation with a young woman. Her brown hair was highlighted with pink strands and woven into a thick braid that reached nearly to her waist. She was wearing a denim jacket over dark yoga pants and a crop top that matched the pink in her hair. Dr. Leung greeted us and said, "This is Rosie Santangelo, who teaches arts and crafts at the Memorial Hall Community Center. Rosie is planning an array of projects that will help us provide the fun you were wondering about, Mrs. Fletcher."

"I'm happy to meet you," I said to Rosie. "I look forward to hearing about your ideas."

"I'm so excited to be part of this. When I was nine I spent several days in the hospital—broken collarbone, fell off my bike. All I remember is a gloomy room where I was all alone except for the few hours each day my parents were allowed to visit. My sister was only seven, so the hospital didn't permit her to visit me at all." Rosie's eyebrows tightened at the memory.

"When I heard this modernization was going to include a family room and an art room, I jumped at the chance to become part of it." Rosie smiled. "I have so many ideas bubbling around in my head. I can't wait to get started."

Seth said, "Ayuh, I remember the dark old days of medicine, and I for one am glad they are gone. The last thing patients need is a depressing atmosphere while they are trying to get over what ails them."

"Rosie, your enthusiasm is contagious. Now I'm truly glad to be part of this committee," I said.

"What did I tell you, Mrs. Fletcher?" Dr. Leung said. "We have quite a creative team, and I am glad you are part of it."

"Doctor, please call me Jessica."

He smiled warmly. "And I'm Gregory. Why don't we all have a seat?" He indicated the oval conference table where several people were sitting and chatting among themselves.

Susan Shevlin, my favorite travel agent, who is also the wife of

Cabot Cove mayor Jim Shevlin, came into the room a minute or so behind Julie Hecht. I introduced them to Rosie, and we all found our way to the conference table. Rosie sat next to Dr. Leung's assistant, and they immediately began to confer in low tones. I suspected Rosie was gathering courage for her presentation.

Dr. Leung passed out a brief written agenda. "As you can see, our first item is to determine if there are other community members who could contribute their expertise to our committee or any subcommittees. I'd be happy to invite them to join us."

Susan Shevlin said, "I do have a friend—he's not from Cabot Cove but he doesn't live too far away—who might be a good fit. He is an amateur magician . . ."

"That's the kind of suggestions we're looking for. He'd be a perfect addition to the entertainment subcommittee." Dr. Leung indicated his assistant. "Please give his information to Marge before you leave. Jessica, I hope that you will participate with that committee, coordinating story hours and the like."

Before I could agree, the conference room door slammed open and a voice behind me said, "Sorry I'm late."

Dr. Leung said, "Ah, Nelson, so glad you could join us. Does everyone know Nelson Penzell, owner of the art shop La Peinture?"

There were some murmurs and a few people nodded. Nelson walked past two side-by-side empty seats and squeezed into a vacant chair next to Rosie Santangelo.

Dr. Leung moved the agenda along with practiced ease, but I was distracted by something else going on. Nelson Penzell leaned repeatedly toward Rosie, sometimes whispering, often brushing his arm against hers. At one point he pressed his shoulder into hers and she, in trying to move out of his way, bumped into Marge, who said, "Ouch," and began rubbing her elbow.

While everyone else at the table looked toward Marge, I kept my eye on Nelson and was taken aback to see him cast a self-satisfied smile around the table.

Rosie apologized for jolting Marge, who replied, "Entirely my fault. I banged my elbow on the table's edge."

Dr. Leung quickly regained control of the meeting. He asked Rosie to talk about her plans for the art room and the family room. She had clearly given them a great deal of thought and had planned projects for various age groups, including dividing two sections of the family room into video game centers, one for younger children and one for teenagers.

That led us to a conversation about whether we should be sacrificing what some committee members thought was valuable medical space and let it be used for arts and crafts, games, and the like.

And then someone brought up the expense. "Should we really be spending money on entertainment when it might be better spent on medical equipment and supplies?"

Dr. Leung let the conversation flow for a few minutes, and then assured everyone that the renovation was designed to increase the number of beds in the children's wing rather than decrease it.

He continued. "Julie Hecht will be heading up the fundraising subcommittee, and once she outlines her ideas I am sure your concerns will be addressed. Julie, if you would."

Julie said, "I have given this a lot of thought, and I think we need two fund-raising tracks. I'm sure there are many people who would be more than willing to donate to a fund that will renovate and modernize the children's wing. We can dazzle those potential donors with displays of the latest—that is, the latest medical . . ." Julie faltered, seemed flustered for a moment, and then quickly recovered. ". . . the latest in medical equipment specifically for pediatrics."

From where I sat she seemed to be staring at Nelson Penzell, who was casually resting his arm on the back of Rosie's chair, while Rosie had hunched over the conference table as far away from his arm as she could get. I thought it was an uncomfortable scene, and I supposed Julie thought so, too.

Julie composed herself and went on. "There are other donors who would be very excited to contribute to making the hospital as cheerful and as sunny—yes, I said 'sunny'—as possible. I suggest we have a renovation track and an entertainment track so donors can choose the track they prefer or contribute to both."

Several committee members spoke in support of the idea, and Julie seemed pleased when two people volunteered to join the committee.

After we heard a few more reports, Dr. Leung passed out assignments and announced the next meeting date, which I was pleased to note was nearly a week after I had to submit my synopsis.

As soon as the meeting had closed, Seth said, "Jess, would you mind waiting for a few minutes? I need to speak to Gregory about a patient."

"No problem at all. I'd like to find out more about Rosie's plans, and then I'll wait for you outside. I could use a breath of fresh air." But when I looked around the room, Rosie Santangelo had disappeared. So had Nelson Penzell. I wondered if that was a coincidence. I looked for Susan and Julie, but they were gone as well, so I waved good-bye to the few remaining committee members and left.

Once outside I pulled out my cell phone to check for any messages I might have missed. But when I turned the phone on, the bright noontime sunshine made it impossible for me to read anything on the screen. There was a tall, stately maple tree about ten feet away and I moved into the shade it provided. Instantly I saw that I had three text messages. I was about to tap on the first but stopped when I heard a familiar voice.

"That was some display you put on at the meeting. What do you think you're doing? Do you have any idea how hurt, how embarrassed, I was? You were all over that little hussy." Julie Hecht sounded close to tears.

My first thought was that she, too, had retreated to a shady spot to check her messages, so I almost dropped my phone when I heard Nelson Penzell answer aloud and in person.

"Rosie is no hussy. She's a nice kid and a talented artist. Honestly, Julie, if I act the happy bachelor in public, isn't that safer for us both? For our reputations? You know in a small town one bad word can kill your business and mine."

"You are worried about our *business* reputations?" Julie sounded confused.

Nelson's response confirmed my feeling that her confusion was exactly what he was going for.

"We both have to earn a living. Better remember, baby, *you* are the one who is married. How many clients do you think your husband would lose if it got around town that he couldn't keep track of his own wife? How could anyone trust him to keep track of their money?"

Julie's voice softened. "Oh, Sonny, Sonny darling, I'm sorry for doubting you. Of course, you're right. We have to be careful in public. And you flirting with that artist is the perfect cover for us. No one in that room would think we were anything more than colleagues."

Well, there's one of us who knows differently now, I thought. And Julie used the nickname Sonny, just as Erica had. Odd.

"Jess? Jessica?" Seth was calling me from the doorway. "Oh, there you are."

I hurried to head him off before he could walk over to where I was standing. No need for him to hear Julie and Nelson Penzell's intimate conversation.

"Woman, what on earth were you doing under that tree?"

"I needed a shady spot to check my phone messages. And you and Gregory Leung? Did you solve all of the world's medical mysteries?"

"Nothing mysterious about it. I merely wanted to know if he was able to take on a new pediatric client. A patient of mine is taking temporary custody of a minor relative from out of state while the child's mother is undergoing serious cancer treatments. The child has asthma, and it's too soon to know how the medical bills will play out under either MaineCare or CHIP—you know, the Children's Health Insurance Program."

I nodded. "And Gregory said not to worry about his fee, to have the child's guardian make an appointment for a checkup."

"Yes, that's exactly what he said. How did you know?"

"Gregory Leung has a kind face, which usually reflects a kind heart." I linked my arm through Seth's. "You will be happy to know that I have some of Maeve O'Bannon's homemade soda bread left over from yesterday. Can I interest you in a slice along with a nice hot cup of Irish breakfast tea?"

"You can indeed, especially if you have a tub of sweet butter to slather on the bread." Seth was rarely one to turn down any snack; that he might refuse some homemade bread was never a serious possibility.

After finishing the last crumb of Maeve's soda bread, Seth left for his office and I began tidying the kitchen. I was still aghast at the conversation I had overheard between Julie Hecht and Nelson Penzell. Julie and Ryan seemed to have such a strong marriage. And from what I could surmise, Nelson Penzell was definitely striving to be a "player," as one of my writer friends called the men in her books whom I would describe as womanizers. Why Julie would risk her marriage with such a decent man for a fling with an obvious cad was a mystery to me.

Well, there was no point in getting my brain fried by what I'd overheard. More pressing issues needed my attention. I opened my notebook and hit the power button on my computer. I reread what I had already written and immediately caught an idea that didn't fit with my overall story line. Yesterday I thought it would make a wonderful thread if woven through a larger story, but, sadly, today I realized it simply would not fit in this one. I did a quick cut and paste of that section of the synopsis and put it in the computer file I called "Future Ideas." *Maybe the next book.* I laughed to myself. *Or the book after that.*

I had developed a strong and smart female protagonist in her early thirties who was a doctor by profession. The murder victim was one of her former medical school classmates who had recently moved to the doctor's city and gotten privileges to work in the same hospital. My problem was that I couldn't decide who my killer would be. There were several candidates. I tried out one, a doctor who had been skipped over for a prime spot at the hospital, and then I tried the murder victim's ex-husband. Neither was quite right. Frustrated, I leaned back in my chair and rubbed the back of my neck. My entire body was stiff as a board. I glanced at the bottom-right corner of the computer screen. Five o'clock. I realized I hadn't moved in hours.

I got up, put on the kettle, and did some stretches while I waited for it to whistle. Then I poured the boiling water over oolong tea in my small blue ceramic teapot. I let it steep for a few minutes while I chomped on one of my fresh apples and marched around the kitchen.

My short break was invigorating, and I threw myself into the synopsis with some creative ideas that I hoped I would still believe were worthwhile when I came back to the synopsis tomorrow. Insights and concepts were flowing so fast I could hardly keep up. My doorbell rang, jarring me away from the break room of Mother of Mercy Hospital in Philadelphia. I looked around and was surprised to see dusk settling in outside my window. Before I could get out of my chair, someone began banging fiercely on my door.

What on earth?

I ran up the two steps to the foyer and heard Loretta's voice, shaky but loud.

"Jessica! Jessica! Please, you have to help."

She was pummeling the door so hard that when I opened it she nearly fell inside. I steadied her by holding on to both of her arms.

"What is it? What has you so upset? For goodness' sake, come inside. Let me make you a cup of tea."

"No time. We have to go." Loretta pulled away from me and yanked my gray wool jacket off the coat-tree. "Put this on."

I took a step back. "Loretta, what—"

"It's Coreen. She's been arrested for murder."

Chapter Five

Murder? Coreen? That wasn't possible. But I knew this was not the time to ask questions. I shrugged into my jacket, snatched up my purse, and followed Loretta to her ancient red Mustang, which she'd left idling at my front gate.

I buckled my seat belt and crossed my fingers, hoping that Loretta would be able to concentrate on the road ahead. It wouldn't do for us to crash into someone's garden fence while we were on our way to rescue Coreen, or whatever Loretta imagined we were doing. Once we pulled away from the gate Loretta became calmer, as if driving was something she could control, so she gave it her full attention. That certainly put my mind at ease.

I held my questions until we pulled into the parking lot of the Sheriff's Department. As soon as she turned off the ignition, I tugged on Loretta's arm. I was determined to get some details before we went inside.

"What happened?" I demanded.

"Here's what I know. Sheriff Metzger called me at home and asked me to come to his office. He said there'd been a murder and he had Coreen in his office, but he didn't come right out and accuse her. But, Jess, why else would he keep her there? He did say she was hysterical and he wanted me to help calm her down. I thought you could convince him that Coreen had nothing to do with whatever has happened. You know that, don't you, Jess?"

I was deep in thought. How could Coreen possibly be involved in a murder, much less commit one? She was a sweet, naive young woman who tried to be as helpful as possible to everyone she met. I believed her even, friendly temperament was an asset to Loretta, especially given the brashness of some of the clientele that frequented the beauty parlor.

"Perhaps Coreen witnessed something tragic," I said. That was one interpretation of Mort's comments that I could offer Loretta, and it seemed to be the likeliest scenario to me. "Let's go inside and straighten this all out."

Loretta flung open the door to the Sheriff's Department and we were both surprised to see Mort Metzger pacing back and forth directly in front of us. He was so close that I thought he was lucky the door hadn't hit him.

"Mrs. F.! Both your house phone and your cell keep going to voice mail. I was ready to send Andy over to check on you." Mort's voice conveyed a mixture of annoyance and relief. "I'm glad you're with Loretta. I need you both."

I knew this wasn't the time to explain that I'd muted my house phone and turned off my cell phone because I was working on my synopsis and trying to avoid interruptions. *Now,* I thought, *there is a plan gone terribly awry.*

"Mort, what happened?" I looked around the empty office. "And where is Coreen? Loretta told me you said . . ."

Mort gestured toward the cells. "She's in there. I gotta tell you, Coreen is incoherent. We've barely been able to get a word out of her. She just keeps crying and staring into space. I sent for Doc Hazlitt. He's with her now."

Loretta was having none of it. "You locked her in the cells? Mort Metzger, what is wrong with you? No wonder she's upset. I demand you release her—"

Mort cut her off. "Loretta, we didn't lock Coreen in a cell. It happens that, at least so far tonight, the cells are unoccupied. I sent Doc Hazlitt and Coreen in there for some privacy so Doc could examine her. With all the blood, I wanted to be sure none of it was hers, and maybe—I don't know—Doc can give her a pill or something to calm her down."

Suddenly we heard a mournful wail from behind the door to the lockup. I assumed that it was Coreen's. She sounded frantic.

"See what I mean?" Mort said. "Whatever happened between her and Nelson Penzell, Coreen is nowhere near ready to be interviewed."

"Nelson Penzell? You mean Angus Michaud's partner in the old This and That Shop?" I was stunned. Until Eve came into Loretta's the other day raving about his charms, I barely knew the man existed. Since then, however, he wasn't just on my radar; he'd crashed right through the screen and was demanding my attention wherever I went.

The front door opened and Deputy Andy Broom began reporting to Mort before he was fully in the room. "Sheriff, the forensic team—"

When he saw Loretta and me standing next to the counter, he

clamped his mouth shut and raised a questioning eyebrow to Mort.

Mort nodded. "It's okay, Andy. They're here to help."

Andy walked over to the coffeepot, and looked disappointed when he found it empty. He began filling the pot at the water-cooler while he spoke. "Well, he hasn't been dead long. And, like you thought, the candlestick definitely could have been the murder weapon. We'll know conclusively after the autopsy."

Colonel Mustard in the gift shop with the candlestick floated through my mind totally unbidden and I quickly pushed it away. Whatever was going on here was undeniably not a board game.

"Mort, Loretta and I are both totally dumbfounded. We really need to know what happened. And how in heaven's name is Coreen involved?" I asked.

He led us to his desk and picked up a memo pad. "Have a seat and I'll tell you what we know. It appears that earlier this evening Coreen came out of"—he glanced at the pad—"La Peinture, a dockside store that backs on the wharf. It's a few doors from Mara's."

"We know where it is." I tried to keep my voice patient, but I wished Mort would get to the crux of the matter. What had happened to Coreen?

"Walter Hendon was standing in front of his office, getting a breath of fresh air, when, as he described it, he heard woeful screams for help. He ran from the wharf around to the shops. Coreen was standing in front of La Peinture and her screams had morphed to a low wail. Walt said she was swinging her head wildly from side to side, looking for anyone who could come to her aid. When she saw Walt, she ran to him, sobbing the word 'dead' over and over again. Her hands and clothes were covered with blood, and so was the unwieldy brass candlestick she was holding."

"Oh my stars," Loretta blurted. "Thank goodness she had the candlestick to fight off her attacker. Think of what might have happened."

"That's one way of looking at it." Mort's tone was drier than sand, and he had his "I'm all business" face on, so I wasn't expecting him to support Loretta's theory.

He took a deep breath and went on. "According to Walt, he tried to find out why she was so upset, but he couldn't get Coreen to say anything worth hearing. She was able to point to the inside of the store. By that time he had his arm solidly around her, but when he tried to walk into the store she began hyperventilating and pulled back so strongly that Walt gave up and called me."

Andy put an oversized mug of coffee on Mort's desk and asked if Loretta or I wanted a cup, but we were both too jittery to even consider caffeine.

Mort continued. "When Andy and I pulled up, Walt immediately waved us inside the store, so I knew that a sobbing, bloody Coreen was not the worst thing we were going to find on the site. We didn't even have to cross the threshold of La Peinture. Right from the doorway, with that huge chandelier brighter than the Times Square ball on New Year's Eve, we could see the body of a man lying facedown on the floor, a few feet past that fancy archway Penzell contracted Tom Middleton to construct last year. Fake columns with gold trim." Mort frowned and shook his head as if the gaudy addition were more upsetting than the murder. "Anyway, we were nearly twenty feet from the body, but we could tell by the way the blood was pooling, radiating from his matted hair, that someone had beaten the victim's head in with an extremely heavy object. Right, Andy?"

"No doubt about it." In spite of the grim circumstances, Andy was proud that their initial observations were proving to be correct. "After watching the techs do their thing, I guarantee we'll have expert confirmation as soon as the forensic paperwork is done."

"And Coreen?" Loretta asked.

Before Mort could answer, the front door banged open and a human hurricane blustered inside. Jeremy Brewington was at least six and a half feet tall and what my mother used to call as broad as a barn door. His yellow rain slicker was old and torn, with patches of gray duct tape covering a tear near his right-hand pocket and another by his shoulder, but he protected his feet with top-of-the-line XTRATUF insulated fishing boots.

"Sheriff Metzger"—Brewington pronounced Mort's name as if he was giving a direct command—"I warned you."

Mort stood and tried to stare down Brewington as best he could. "Mr. Brewington, I am assisting these ladies at the moment, but if you have a seat, Deputy Broom will be happy to take your information."

"Deputy? Why would I talk to a deputy when you are standing in front of me? You should know by now, I do everything top dog to top dog. I require your undivided attention, and I require it now."

I could see Mort was losing his patience, but he gritted his teeth and made every effort to speak respectfully. "I'm afraid I will be tied up for a while, so if you would care to wait—"

"Metzger," Brewington barked, "what kind of town are you running here? Crime is rampant. The thieves are at it again. Someone was nosing around on *Brew's Baby* tonight. My deck furniture was tossed around, and there are scratches on the brand-new locks I had installed on the cabinets in the main salon and the master suite. Luckily they didn't steal anything this time, or, I promise you, there'd be murder to pay."

"Mr. Brewington, we've already had one murder tonight and that has my undivided attention, so if you'll have a seat . . ." Once again Mort indicated the waiting room chairs.

I could tell that Jeremy Brewington was not a man used to being silenced, but Mort Metzger had clearly one-upped him. Brewington opened his mouth, but not one sound came out. Then he waved his hand in the air as if chasing a pesky fly.

"Murder? There's been a murder?" he managed to say as he leaned one arm heavily on the counter. "May I ask who the victim is, or should I say, was?"

"No harm in telling you. I am sure that one half of Cabot Cove has been phoning or texting the other half to tell them that Nelson Penzell was murdered in his store earlier tonight." Mort began rubbing his hands together as if his announcement would end the conversation and Brewington would take his leave, recognizing there were more important things at hand than scratches on a cabinet lock.

Brewington's face turned ashen. "Murdered? In his store? Right here in Cabot Cove? Tonight?" He appeared so shocked, so overcome by disbelief, that I half expected him to finish by demanding, "Are you sure?"

Andy Broom hurried around the counter and offered to assist

him to a seat, but Brewington shook him off. "No, I can see you're busy. I'll come back tomorrow. All I need is a report for the insurance company. Tomorrow."

I couldn't help but notice that he wobbled, unsteady on his feet, as he headed out the door.

Loretta said, "He certainly took the news hard. Mr. Brewington tends to stay away from the locals. Doesn't think we are classy enough, I suppose. I wonder how he knew Nelson Penzell."

Mort said, "Not sure that he did. City folks that come up here expect Cabot Cove to be a haven of tranquility and are shocked when the smallest crime happens. A murder will put them over the edge every time. Don't forget I'm a Brooklyn boy; I know the type."

Andy said, "Oh, they knew each other all right. I was on patrol a couple of weeks ago and I got a call to quiet down a shouting match in the parking lot of the Hill House. There the two of them were, hammer-and-tonging it, Jeremy Brewington and Nelson Penzell."

That took us all by surprise. I couldn't help but ask, "Did you happen to learn what they were fighting about?"

"Oh yes, ma'am." Andy puffed out his chest. "They were so intent on their argument that they never even noticed me pull into the parking lot. I had to flash my turret lights twice to get their attention. That made them both clam up, but not before I heard Brewington say, 'Don't forget it's my money we're talking about.' Or something close to that."

Loretta heaved a loud sigh to bring us back to our immediate problem.

Mort took the hint. "Andy, stick your head in the back and see if Doc Hazlitt can come out here for a minute. If he can, you stand by the door so you can keep an ear on Coreen while we talk to Doc."

It'd been a good long while since I'd seen Seth as tired as he looked when he came through the door from the cells. He lowered himself slowly into a brown leather chair and tilted it back until the chair's front legs lifted and his head rested on the wall behind him.

"Obviously Coreen has been through a major trauma. She needs rest and care. If I had my druthers I'd admit her to the hospital, but when I mentioned it she began to hyperventilate so deeply that, well, I dropped the idea."

Mort leaned forward and propped his elbows on his desk. "Doc, what I really need to know is, when can I talk to her?"

Seth shook his head. "That's hard to say. Maybe a day or two."

Mort popped straight up. "A day or two. I can't wait, Doc. I've got some serious questions. And, at least for now, it seems like Coreen is the only person who can answer them."

"Well, I'm sorry, Mort, but that's the best I can do. I gave her a light sedative to help her sleep tonight, and I can reevaluate her condition first thing in the morning. You might want to give her some extra blankets. It's getting chilly in the cells."

"Oh no. You're not keeping her here. She's coming home with me. I'll put her in my guest room and Doc can see her in the morning." Loretta slapped her hand on Mort's desk for emphasis. Then, as if she realized she'd overstepped, she added, "And if that's a nonstarter, you can arrest me now, because I am not leaving this building without Coreen. I'm more than happy to sleep in the cell next to hers, with or without blankets. Your choice, Sheriff."

For a brief second Mort looked as though locking up Loretta would suit him perfectly, but then he stood, hoisted his belt, and glanced at Seth. "What do you think, Doc?"

"I can tell you that Coreen is in no condition to be interviewed by you. If nothing else, the pill I gave her would render anything she said in the next eight hours or so inadmissible in court, so I don't see the harm in every one of us getting a good night's sleep."

Mort said, more to himself than to us, "Well, I could have Floyd set up a fixer—you know, park in front of Loretta's house for the night."

Now Seth was irritated. "I told you, I gave the girl a sedative. She is going to sleep all night. Don't waste your deputy's time." He turned to Loretta. "I am only a few blocks away. If she gets at all fretful or fussy, give me a call. I'll come right over, no matter the hour."

"You've got to be more specific, Doc. A day or two won't cut it. When might I be able to have an honest-to-God interview with Coreen? Nothing she said tonight made any sense at all."

"I'll examine her in the morning and give you a call to let you know when she is well enough to be interviewed. Best I can say for now. I might need a hand getting Coreen into Loretta's car."

"Andy can help you, and then he'll follow Loretta home and help her get Coreen settled."

Andy touched two fingers to his forehead in a brief salute and escorted Loretta to the cells. Within a few minutes they returned with a dazed but ambulatory Coreen. Loretta and Andy each held one of her arms, Seth close behind.

Coreen gave a half smile of recognition when our eyes met; then her eyes closed and her knees buckled. Loretta and Andy helped her straighten. And they all managed to get out of the front door into the cool night air.

Seth stuck his head back through the doorway. "Jess, I'll be back to drive you home."

I waved my thanks, secretly grateful to have some conversation time with Mort. I was sure Coreen wasn't guilty of murder, and I was eager to hear Mort's theories about the case.

Chapter Six

Mort topped off his coffee cup and motioned to the watercooler. "You turned down coffee earlier, but how about a nice glass of cold water?"

I accepted gratefully.

"You've been unusually quiet all evening, Mrs. F. Still, knowing you as I do, I'm sure you have a question or two."

"As it happens, I have been wondering if anyone else was around when Walt found Coreen outside La Peinture," I answered. "It was reasonably early in the evening. Mara's was still open. Didn't anyone see or hear anything?"

"If anyone did, they're not saying. We couldn't find a single witness. Mara's was open, but there was a heated discussion going on about a couple of players on the Maine Mariners."

Mort correctly read the blank look on my face and quickly explained. "Do you remember the Portland Pirates moved to Massachusetts and changed their name a few years back?"

That rang a bell. "Yes, I do recall. So, the Mariners are that newish franchise based in Portland. The team plays in a midlevel league; I can't quite remember the name, but I know they're not in the American Hockey League."

"That's right. They play in the ECHL, which used to be called the East Coast Hockey League. Anyway, the debate about the Mariners got louder and the debaters were becoming unruly. It turns out that about the time Coreen let out her loudest screams, Mara was banging two skillets together to, as she said, 'regain order' in the luncheonette."

"I see. An episode like that would keep all of Mara's patrons rooted in their seats. Not a soul would leave until they were sure the drama was completely over. No one would want to miss a word. After all, today's debate is tomorrow's gossip."

"That's for sure," Mort agreed. "And by then Walt had arrived and Coreen was reduced to crying and sobbing. The sound wouldn't have been heard by anyone more than a few feet away. So, Mrs. F., you see my predicament. Coreen is both my only witness and my only suspect. So until I can interview her . . ." He trailed off.

The door opened and Seth popped his head in, then said, "If you are ready, Jess . . ."

And before I could signal that I would be right there, he closed the door again.

While I gathered up my things, Mort said, "I guess Doc is afraid that if he came inside, I would hassle him to give me early access to Coreen."

"Oh, Mort, he's just tired. We're all tired. Now, I'll get out of your way. I expect you still have a ton of paperwork to complete. Try to get a good night's sleep."

He gave me a weak smile. "I don't see much sleep in my immediate future, but thanks for the thought."

I climbed into Seth's car, and before I could ask him how Coreen was doing he said, "Coreen was all settled in Loretta's spare bedroom by the time I left. Young girl like that, snores like a horse. I'll have to get her into the office for a checkup when all this is over. Might be sleep apnea."

"So you think she's innocent? That Mort will soon be able to cross her off his suspect list?" I asked.

"In your mystery-writer mind it's always about the crime, Jess. But I'm a doctor, not a judge. In my bailiwick, her health comes first and foremost. Even if Coreen winds up over in Windham at the Maine Correctional Women's Center, she should have a doctor check out that snoring."

The idea of Coreen in prison seemed preposterous to me and I said so.

"Ayuh, I would agree with you, except I seem to remember that over the years you have known some extremely likable people who turned out to be murderers. I've even known a few of 'em myself. That's the trouble with people: They are too darned unpredictable," Seth said. "The real question is, who would snap and murder Nelson Penzell? I'm willing to bet there are quite a number of possibilities. I happen to know he had quite a reputation with the ladies."

"Seth! How on earth do you know that?" I was amazed that he was fully aware of something I'd only recently discovered.

"Let's put it this way: My patients like to gossip, especially if they hope it will distract me from figuring out they haven't been following my orders. Doesn't work, though." Seth chuckled.

"And you kept that idle talk to yourself? Didn't bother to

share with me? What kind of friend are you?" I tried to sound stern but there was no fooling Seth.

"Woman, if you spent more time here in Cabot Cove and less time visiting old friends or wandering to book conferences, you'd be up on things here at home," Seth teased.

"Oh, you blame my travels for everything from burned-out lightbulbs to my smoke detector beeping when the battery runs low."

"Well, when you are away, how can you be sure I routinely check your house if I don't let you know about the things gone wrong?"

Seth pulled up in front of my walkway but declined to come in for a snack, a sure sign he was, indeed, worn out.

I unhooked my seat belt and reached for the door handle, then said, "There is one more thing. What do you really think happened between Coreen and Nelson Penzell?"

Seth pondered for a long minute. "With what we know about Nelson Penzell's, shall we say, proclivities, do you think it's possible that he made advances or harassed Coreen in some way and she got frightened and responded too forcefully? Could she have grabbed the nearest weapon and brained him?"

"I can well imagine Nelson making the advances, but the Coreen Wilson I have known since she was a teenager is too timid to do anything more than cry and beg him to leave her alone," I said.

"To be honest, that's my impression as well," Seth said.

I stepped out of the car and leaned my head in to say one last thing. "Do me a favor, please. After you see Coreen in the morning—"

"Call you. Will do," Seth said. "Now let me get home and catch some shut-eye. Before we know it the rooster will be crowing, and I have a heavy patient load tomorrow, not to mention I'll have to continue to hold Mort at bay until I'm sure Coreen is well enough to be interviewed. Get a good night's sleep, yeah?"

I hurried down the path to my front door, unlocked it, turned, and waved to Seth, who then sped away.

While I was gone, my computer had put itself into sleep mode. I closed my notepad and straightened the research papers that were scattered about the tabletop. I knew I was too stressed to get my head back into the story line I had been trying to develop when Loretta came to tell me the news and ask for my help. Best let working on my synopsis go until the morning.

I was far too wired to so much as get ready for bed, so I set the kettle on the stove to make a large mug of chamomile tea. While I waited for the water to boil I canceled the automatic voice mail and cleared the messages from both my house and cell phones.

Mort had left four messages, two on each phone, and there was a hang-up call on my cell, which, according to the caller ID, was from Loretta's phone number. The final message on my house phone was from Evelyn Phillips, longtime editor of the *Cabot Cove Gazette*.

"Jessica, call me back as soon as you get this. You won't believe what happened."

I hit the delete button. Unfortunately I did believe what had happened, but rather than speculate about the murder with Evelyn, I planned on sipping my restful cup of chamomile and going straight to bed.

My phone jangled and startled me awake. It wasn't even five thirty. My mind was so fuzzy, I first thought it must be Evelyn, since I hadn't returned her call last night. Her reputation as a sharp-eyed newspaperwoman rested largely on her ability to persist until she got the information she needed. I reached for the phone, prepared to tell Evelyn this wasn't a good time, that I would have to call her back later in the day.

"Jessica, are you awake? I've been waiting for the lights to come on." It wasn't Evelyn Phillips on the line. It was an extremely distraught Eve Simpson.

"Lights? Eve, what lights are you waiting for?" I wondered if we were in the midst of a power outage, but when I reached for the lamp on my night table it lit brightly.

"Your house lights. I thought surely you would be awake by now. Sitting in my car, I've been barely able to sleep a wink."

"My house lights? Eve, where are you?"

"I'm parked in front of your house. Jessica, something terrible has happened. Have you heard? It's Nelson Penzell. He's . . . he's . . ."

By now I was sitting on the edge of my bed and sliding my feet into my well-worn slippers. "I know. Eve, come to the kitchen door. I'll make coffee."

I'd unlocked the back door and was adjusting the burner under the coffeepot when Eve came inside. She was clasping a raspberry-colored shawl tightly around her upper body. When she loosened her grip on the shawl, I could see it covered a very dressy black satin suit. Her mascara was smudged from under her right eye to a sallow cheekbone, where her usual plum-colored blush had worn off. She looked as though she'd been up all night, which, I supposed, she had.

I put one arm around her and guided her to the living room. "You look half frozen. Here, please sit down." I led her to the couch. An orange and yellow ripple afghan I had crocheted decades ago hung in its usual place, covering the headrest of my recliner. I held it out to Eve, and she quickly burrowed underneath it.

"Thank you, Jessica. I drove up to Bar Harbor last night to attend an awards party for some Realtors who'd reached various industry sales milestones. A long and tedious trip, I know, but so worth the connections I was sure I could make. *Voir et être vu*— See and be seen—I always say."

"You must be starving," I said. "Would you like a piece of toast? Or I can boil some eggs."

"I couldn't possibly eat. Black coffee would be divine." Eve kicked off her spiky high heels. "Would you mind if I curled my feet on the couch, under the afghan? There's not much circulation left in my toes."

"You do whatever makes you comfortable. I'll be right back." I left Eve to settle herself among the overstuffed cushions. I came back to the living room carrying a large tray containing my white china coffeepot, with matching sugar bowl and creamer, along with two coffee cups and a small plate of wafers.

While I was gone Eve had taken her compact out of her purse, and she was trying to erase her mascara smudges with a tissue, which she soon tossed on the table. "Hopeless. I guess I'm no longer young enough to get away with an all-nighter and still look fresh as a daisy in the morning."

I knew it would normally be better not to inquire how Eve had happened to be out all night, but the past twelve hours had been far from normal, so I asked, "Eve, how is it you came directly here from the party in Bar Harbor?"

"During the presentations and the speeches I put my phone

on mute. My ringtone is soft and professional, but it wouldn't do to have my phone interrupt the proceedings. I'd be mortified," Eve explained. "So when Ideal called . . . well, her call went to voice mail and I never noticed it."

That still left quite a time gap between the awards dinner and this morning. "And when did you finally realize that Ideal had called?" I approached the missing time cautiously. With Eve there was always the chance that her response would include activities I'd rather not hear about in detail.

"Some of the highfliers were hosting an after-party for the awards committee and the recipients and a few select attendees. I'd apparently made quite an impression, because Jonathan Kimbrough, president of the Maine Realtors Association, personally invited me to the soiree. How could I refuse?"

In all the years I had known her, the idea of Eve refusing an invitation to any sort of social gathering had, quite frankly, never crossed my mind.

"It was a lovely affair. I'd exchanged business cards with nearly everyone, pleased with the contacts I was making, when a dashing man I'd noticed much earlier in the evening approached and introduced himself to me. Clark Geddings had come all the way from Boston specifically to meet Realtors who sold properties in towns where his clientele desired weekend and summer homes. He was extremely excited when I mentioned Cabot Cove. Unfortunately, he had run out of business cards. I didn't want to miss the opportunity, so when I gave him my card I also passed him my phone so he could put his name and number in my directory. That's when I noticed I had a message." Eve stopped and sipped her coffee.

I wasn't sure if she'd paused for dramatic effect or if she merely expected me to ask the obvious question. In case she was waiting for me, I obliged. "And when did you listen to the message?"

"Of course, I didn't play it in front of Clark, and thank goodness for that. Whatever would he have thought about Cabot Cove if I had? When it was appropriate for me to slip away, phone numbers exchanged and all that, I went to the restroom, which, fortunately, was empty, and I played Ideal's message. She told me that Nelson was dead, Coreen was in jail, and you and Loretta were on the case."

"And did you call Ideal back to see if she had an update?" I asked.

"Oh, I couldn't. By then it was past two o'clock. I knew she'd be out like a light. I scratched my original plan of stopping at a motel for the night and decided to drive straight home. It was after four thirty when I pulled into my driveway. I hadn't even turned off the ignition when I realized there was no point in my trying to get any sleep, so I pulled right out again. I drove to the Sheriff's Department. Floyd McCallum was the deputy on duty, and the only thing he would tell me was that he couldn't tell me anything. I decided you were my only hope of getting accurate information."

Eve hesitated, then looked me straight in the eye. "Tell me the truth, Jessica. Why did Coreen kill Nelson Penzell?"

"Oh, please, Eve. We both know Coreen well enough to be sure that she couldn't possibly harm another living creature, much less another human being," I said. "Don't you remember the time Loretta had a mouse problem at the shop? Coreen talked her out of using poisonous bait and into buying catch-and-release traps by promising she would take the traps to Camden Hills State Park and release the rodents there."

"I do remember. I can't even imagine driving to the park with those creatures in my car. Suppose they escaped and found a home in my upholstery?" Eve shuddered. "Still, Coreen did keep her word, and I suppose she saved their lives when she set them free. So perhaps you are right. Anyway, tell me whatever you know so I can make up my own mind."

Eve listened attentively while I sketched out the occurrences of last evening as I understood them.

"So Coreen hasn't been arrested. She's staying at Loretta's."

"Yes, for the time being, and she is under Seth's care. We'll see what today brings."

Eve was mulling over everything she had just learned, and I was sitting quietly, waiting for her next question, when my doorbell cut through the stillness and startled us both.

Chapter Seven

What now? I thought as I hurried to the front door. I should not have been surprised to see Evelyn Phillips leaning against the doorjamb.

"Morning, Jessica. Don't you ever answer your messages?" Her short gray hair was a bit more tousled than usual. Her jeans were rumpled but her plaid flannel shirt and brown quilted vest looked fresh. She peered over my shoulder and saw Eve on the couch, sipping from a cup. "Ah, I see coffee is served."

I opened the door wider. "Come on in. I'll get you a cup."

When I got back from the kitchen with a cup and saucer for Evelyn, she was seated in my recliner and saying, "So you weren't even in town when the murder happened. Darn shame. You'd make a fine witness."

Eve preened at the compliment.

I poured coffee for Evelyn and set the cup in front of her.

"Everyone knows the *Cabot Cove Gazette* reports the news as accurately as we can," Evelyn said as she added a teaspoon of sugar to her coffee. "So I don't understand why Mort Metzger is playing cat and mouse with me. He won't return my calls, and here I am with a deadline and no story. Last night Ideal Molloy was able to tell me the sheriff called Dr. Hazlitt over to the jail to look after Coreen, but the doc is stonewalling me, too."

"It's possible that Mort and Seth don't have any information to give you. Mort may not have examined all the evidence yet. As for Seth, Coreen is his patient, so he is prohibited from saying anything about her condition to anyone," I said. "Besides, I'm sure you would rather print actual facts than suppositions."

Evelyn tugged on the long chain that hung around her neck until the wire-framed eyeglasses that were anchored at the end were in her hand. Then she perched the glasses on the tip of her nose, reached into her cavernous tote bag, and pulled out a pen and an old-fashioned stenographer's pad. "Jessica, you know as well as I do that there are truths and there are theories, and folks are happy enough to read both so long as we tell them which are which. Now, I need you gals to tell me what you know."

Eve said, "What can I possibly tell you? I was out of town."

"But that doesn't mean you haven't talked to your friends, like Jessica here. Maybe you can come up with an idea or two about what happened in the This and That Shop."

"La Peinture," Eve corrected automatically.

"See what I mean? You know more than you might think." Evelyn was pleased to get such a quick response.

I decided that the easiest way to end this was to tell Evelyn a few details and send her on her way. "Here are the particulars as I know them. Norman Penzell was found dead in his shop by

Coreen Wilson and Walter Hendon. Sheriff Metzger is waiting for the coroner's report to verify the cause of death. The circumstances did look suspicious, but the death could have been accidental."

I added that last tidbit in the hope that it would tone down the news coverage, but Evelyn shook her head. "Nope. It was murder. That's been all over the radio since well before midnight. Wouldn't surprise me if the big-city newspapers were all over this story in a few hours. And I need to have the jump on them. Thanks for the lead, Jessica. I'll be on my way."

Evelyn pulled off her glasses, let them drop back to her chest, and tucked the steno pad in her tote.

"Lead? What lead?" I couldn't imagine what I had said that Evelyn didn't already know. I'd deliberately kept my description of events to the bare minimum.

"Walt Hendon. Didn't know he was on the scene." Evelyn hoisted herself out of the recliner and patted the headrest. "That's a comfortable chair. Once I retire I am going to be spending a lot more time in a nice, soft chair reading. One of my plans is to read all your books, Jessica, from the first to the latest. Now I get to them strictly catch as catch can."

"Retire? Evelyn, I can't imagine the *Gazette* without you. I'm sure you have plenty of good years left."

She gave a hearty laugh. "I hope I do, but I'm not sure that I want to spend them banging on people's doors at the crack of dawn, tracking down a story."

I closed the door behind her, and when I got back to the living room Eve was sound asleep on the couch. I turned off the lamp and went upstairs to get ready for the day.

I was drying my hair when the phone rang. I ran and caught the bedroom extension before the second ring, hoping the first jangle hadn't woken Eve.

Without as much as a "Good morning," Loretta ordered me to come to the shop right away. "Jessica, it's urgent. Please. Hurry."

"Loretta, Eve is asleep on my couch . . ."

"Leave her there. I called Demetri. He'll be at your door in a few minutes. I would have come myself, but I didn't know what to do with . . . Oh, please come. I'm at the beauty parlor." And the phone went dead.

Eve looked as though she would be asleep for hours, but in case she woke before I returned, I left a note on the coffee table.

Had to go out. Back soon. J

I walked past the computer and my research papers, thought about my synopsis, and sighed. *Soon,* I promised myself. Then I slipped outside, where Demetri was already waiting.

"Good morning, Jessica. You are out and about early this morning. Getting a new hairdo?" Demetri and his cousin Nick had been running their taxi service in Cabot Cove for so long that hiring them for trips large and small was like going for a ride with a family friend—chatty conversation and all.

"No, not today." I was hard-pressed to say why I was rushing off to Loretta's.

"That's good news. I think you look fine just as you are. Say"— Demetri's tone darkened—"did you hear the awful news? That artsy guy who worked with Angus got himself killed. What do you think about that?"

At that moment I wished I had thought to inquire about Demetri's son and namesake, which would have sent him gabbing on about how wonderful the young man was doing in all his endeavors, and we could have steered clear of the recent tragedy.

"I did hear. Terrible shame." I kept my comment short and my opinion to myself.

"He was a bit of a phony," Demetri opined. "But still."

Demetri pulled his cab right to the corner by the beauty parlor's front door. He jumped out and opened my door. "Here you go. Do you want me to wait or come back in a while?"

"To tell you the truth, I have no idea how long I'll be. I may stay in town for a few hours. I'll call if I need you again."

I handed him a few bills and he tipped his cap. "Thank you, thank you. I will take this right over to Charlene Sassi's bakery and see what specialties have come out of her oven this early."

Before I'd crossed the few feet from the curb to the shop entrance, Loretta pulled the door wide open. "Oh, thank goodness. Once I saw it, I had no idea what to do. Call Mort? Get Coreen? No. I decided the smart thing to do was to call you."

"Loretta, please, calm down. What exactly did you see?"

"I came in to call the clients who had appointments today so I could reschedule them. I'd made two calls and was about to make a third when a streak of sunlight began to shine through the window, and it caused a shimmer to bounce off that chair. Look." She pointed to the seat of a chair next to the domed hair dryers. "I didn't touch it. I thought the two of us should look at it. You know, we could back each other up as witnesses."

Witnesses to what? I wondered as I walked to the chair and bent over to look at a cell phone in a gold-tone case. There was nothing special about it.

Behind me Loretta said, "It's Coreen's. She must have forgotten it last night. Maybe it holds a clue of some sort."

A clue? I smiled to myself, thinking Loretta had been spending too much time watching those true-crime shows on late-night television. "Okay, let's see what we have here."

I picked up the phone and placed it on the counter next to Loretta, who said, "It should open as soon as you touch the screen. Coreen stopped locking her phone because she kept forgetting her code."

Loretta took a step back, as if she expected the phone to explode when I touched it.

Instead, as soon as my finger swiped the black screen, two adorable calico kittens rolling in a garden of pink and purple flowers came into view. I glanced at the icons and saw that Coreen had one voice message and a couple of unopened texts.

"I suppose we should bring this to Mort," I said.

Loretta reached out and covered the phone with her hand. "Oh no. Before we do that, shouldn't we know what the messages are? So we are prepared in case . . ."

"I suppose . . . Oh, what harm can it do? But once we check her messages, we will turn the phone over to Mort. Agreed?"

Loretta hesitated, so I persisted. "Loretta, if Coreen had her phone with her last night, we both know that Mort would have examined it closely, read every text, listened to every message, and requested who knows what information from her service provider."

"But Coreen didn't have the phone with her last night. Maybe we should return it to her. You know, respect her privacy." Loretta was wavering.

Rather than argue, I hit SPEAKER and we heard Coreen's friend Anna confirm a brunch date she and Coreen had scheduled for after church on Sunday.

"Well, nothing there for Mort to worry about." Loretta heaved a sigh of relief.

The texts were a different story. Both were from Nelson Penzell. The earlier one was a reminder of their appointment for his manicure last evening.

Loretta said, "Appointment confirmation. Ordinary business. Let's hope the other text is a cancellation. Something came up. Coreen shouldn't have been at the shop in the first place, but she never got the message."

Somehow I didn't think that was the case, but I never expected Nelson's final text to say: Let tonight be the night you call me Sonny.

"What does that even mean?" Loretta asked.

I was afraid I knew exactly what it meant, but I wanted to verify before I said anything. "Where is Coreen? Is she still at your house?"

Loretta nodded. "I left her there with instructions not to let anyone in except for Seth, who promised he would come over and check on her this morning."

"Good. Let's go see if she is in any shape to talk to us. I have an idea about what may have happened. We need to get our facts straight before she talks to Mort."

Loretta didn't question me. She simply grabbed her appointment book and said, "I can finish these calls from home." Then she flipped the OPEN sign that hung on the glass panel of the door to CLOSED and propelled me into her car.

"I hope Coreen's awake," Loretta fretted. "I can't wait to hear whatever it is you need to ask her. Tell me honestly: If her answers satisfy you, will that get Mort off her case?"

"I can't promise you that. But I am sure the closer we get to the truth, the better off we'll all be. Especially Coreen," I said.

Loretta pulled into her driveway and turned off the ignition. "Jessica, I can't tell you how much I appreciate this."

I patted her hand in what I hoped was a comforting gesture and opened the car door. Coreen might be able to clear herself of suspicion if she could give us enough information to point Mort in a completely different direction, although I really had no idea what direction that might be.

Loretta unlocked her front door, and we stood in the foyer, listening to the deadly quiet. I followed Loretta into the living room, and she walked to the staircase that led to the second floor. "Coreen was awake when I left. I hope she didn't go back to sleep."

"Seth did say the medicine he gave her was quite strong," I said.

Loretta climbed up a couple of steps and called, "Coreen? Coreen? Are you awake?"

We heard a door open, and Coreen came to the top of the stairs. Her hair was tousled and she was wearing what were probably Loretta's pajamas, since they were several sizes too large. She was barefoot and held a pair of blue snowflake-pattern Sherpa lined socks in one hand. "These were at the foot of the bed. Am I supposed to wear them? I can't find my clothes or my shoes."

She seemed completely baffled.

"Come on down and say good morning to Jessica." I'd never

heard Loretta speak in such a caring tone, especially not to Coreen.

When Coreen had half walked, half stumbled down the stairs, Loretta steered us to the kitchen. We sat around the table and Loretta asked, "Coreen, do you remember last night? After you put on a pair of my pj's, Andy packed your clothes in a big plastic bag and took them away so Sheriff Metzger could, er, have them cleaned."

That wasn't right. Why on earth had Loretta let Andy take Coreen's clothes? Of course I understood why Mort would want them. He was looking for whatever evidence he could find. Evidence of murder.

Coreen looked puzzled. "I guess I remember, sort of. Well, then, it's Sherpa socks for me. This wooden floor is cold. And I am awfully thirsty."

Loretta put the kettle on the stove and brought a pitcher of orange juice and glasses to the table. Then she began preparing her china teapot and cups and saucers.

I watched Coreen pull on the blue socks, and then she leaned back in her chair, hands folded in her lap, and stared blankly at the juice glasses. When I offered to pour orange juice for her she gave the briefest nod, but after I filled her glass she didn't touch it.

Loretta put the steaming teapot next to a plate of oatmeal cookies in the center of the table and asked with forced cheerfulness, "Do we have everything we need? Jessica? Coreen?"

I took the hint and said, "I have such a busy day ahead. A snack break is exactly what I need. How about you, Coreen? Try one of these cookies."

I pushed the plate in her direction, and she automatically took one and placed it delicately on the napkin next to her teacup. Her eyes roamed from me to Loretta and back again; then her shoulders relaxed and a tear slid down her cheek.

"I shouldn't have gone to meet him. I knew he wanted me to call him Sonny, but I went anyway. Now look how it all turned out."

Chapter Eight

Coreen buried her head in her hands and began to sob uncontrollably. I was afraid we were in for a repeat of last night, but Loretta surprised me. Instead of the doting-mother tone, she turned on the brusque employer-to-employee voice that I was used to hearing in the beauty parlor.

"Coreen, you know Jessica and I don't understand a word you are saying. How am I ever going to open the shop and take care of our clients if I have to stay here fussing over you? Just come out with it. What happened when you went to give Nelson Penzell his manicure last night?"

Coreen sat up straight and began to brush her tears away with the heel of her palm. "I'm sorry, Loretta," she said. "I'll try to do better."

"Good girl. Now, listen. Jessica is going to ask you some questions. I want you to answer as honestly as you can, and there will be no more crying in my house. Do you hear me?"

"Yes, ma'am." Coreen's pale face was contrite.

I was amazed that Loretta's change in voice and attitude did the trick. Mort and Seth could have saved themselves a bucketful of stress last night if only any of us had known that "Loretta the Boss" could snap Coreen out of her frenzy and bring her back to reality.

To give Coreen time to fully gain control, I deliberately reached for an oatmeal cookie and took a small bite. "Delicious. Did you bake these, Loretta?"

She laughed. "Charlene Sassi and I have a deal. She doesn't style hair and I don't bake anything. I bought these from her yesterday morning."

I asked as gently as I could, "Coreen, what did you mean when you said you knew Nelson Penzell wanted you to call him Sonny? What does that nickname mean to you? Or perhaps, what do you think it meant to him?"

At first I thought Coreen was ignoring my question, but eventually she looked directly at Loretta and began to speak. "You know he was a good tipper, right? I told you that months ago. That's why I went back even though he sort of hit on me the last time I gave him a manicure."

Then she turned to me, raised her eyebrows, and clamped her mouth shut, as if that explained everything.

I nodded as though she were making perfect sense. I took a sip of tea, patted my lips with a napkin, and circled back. "Could you explain 'sort of'? I'm not sure what you mean."

Coreen furrowed her brow as if she didn't quite understand what I was asking. Then she tried again. "Nelson Penzell kind of hit on me."

She picked up her glass and took a big gulp of juice, clearly satisfied that she'd told me everything I needed to know.

Loretta and I exchanged a look. We needed Coreen to move past making vague statements. "Sort of" and "kind of" would never help us discover what actually happened.

"If we forget about last night for a minute, can you tell me what happened the last time you went to La Peinture? You know, the time you actually gave Nelson a manicure," I asked.

Coreen sat stone-faced for a couple of moments. Loretta started wiggling in her chair. I could tell she was losing patience, but I hoped she would stay quiet. We'd probably learn more if Coreen came around in her own time.

At long last, she did.

"I used to meet Mr. Penzell in La Peinture every few weeks to give him a manicure, or what he liked to call 'a trim and a buff.' The store was always well lit. And sometimes we'd be interrupted by one of his clients, but I never minded because Mr. Penzell said my time was valuable and he tipped extra if I had to wait. Mr. Michaud was almost always in the store when I was there. I hated that he'd make fun of what he called Mr. Penzell's 'namby-pamby habits.' He'd even march back and forth in front of me, blowing on his fingernails and polishing them on his shirtfront. He was trying to get my goat. I guess Mr. Penzell didn't like it either. A while back he told me we would only make our appointments when he was sure Mr. Michaud wasn't going to be around. I appreciated that. After all, I am a professional, and Mr. Michaud was making fun of my job." Coreen looked to Loretta for approval.

When Loretta nodded in the affirmative, Coreen threw her shoulders back and sat up straighter, clearly proud that her defense of beauty culture had pleased Loretta.

"The next time I went to the shop, it was so peaceful without

Mr. Michaud around. I gave Mr. Penzell his manicure, we set our next appointment, and I left. Then . . ." Coreen picked up her cookie and took a bite. I expected she was getting to the difficult part and needed a second.

Loretta and I waited.

Coreen continued her story. "Two weeks ago I went to La Peinture to keep my regular appointment with Mr. Penzell, and"—she paused—"everything was different."

She took a deep breath and exhaled. "For one thing, except for a small lamp near the archway, the entire shop was dark. When I walked in, Mr. Penzell said, 'Ah, there you are. I was just brightening up the place.' And he lit some long taper candles that he'd set on the table where I usually put my manicure kit. I thought there was an electrical problem." Coreen held her hands outward, palms up, and gave us a sad, apologetic look.

"I would have thought the same thing," I said, hoping to give her enough support that she would feel comfortable continuing. I could pretty much surmise what happened next.

"I said that I might have a hard time doing his nails with so little light. I thought maybe we should move nearer to the lamp. That way he could put his fingers directly under the light. That's when things got weird. He said there was no hurry to do the trim and buff. He thought we should use our time to get to know each other better."

I heard Loretta murmur, "Uh-oh."

Now that she was finally able to talk about her experience, Coreen's words picked up in tempo and tumbled out. "He handed me a fancy stem glass of wine. I didn't want to insult him, so I took it. I couldn't work with a wineglass in my hand, so I put it on the table. He picked it up and tried to force me— Well, 'force' isn't the right word. He kept, like, pressuring me to drink the wine.

"Loretta, you know how you always say we have to be careful at work not to violate our clients' personal space? We never talked about what to do if a client violates *my* personal space. Mr. Penzell moved so close, I felt trapped between him and the table. Then he took my hand and said, 'Relax. Have some wine. Please call me Sonny. All my close friends call me Sonny.' That's when I got nervous. I told him we had to get right to his manicure because I had another appointment. And I called him Mr. Penzell over and over again. 'Mr. Penzell, can I have your right hand, please?' 'Mr. Penzell, is that nail short enough?' It was the worst manicure I ever gave anyone. Then I got out of there fast, but not before he paid me and added an extra-large tip. And as if everything that happened was perfectly normal, he insisted we schedule the next appointment for last night."

"Oh, Coreen." Loretta, back in mother-hen mode, pushed her chair back and leaned over to give Coreen a comforting hug. "Why didn't you tell me? I would have straightened him out for sure."

Coreen shrugged. "By the next morning I'd decided I was being silly. He didn't force me to do anything. When he knew I wasn't interested he didn't really push. So I figured it would never happen again. Besides, there were those generous tips. They would be hard to give up. I have rent to pay."

"That's quite understandable," I said. "I am wondering, though, about last night. Coreen, can you tell us exactly what happened last night?"

She dropped her eyes and began shredding her napkin. After a moment she shook her head and whispered, "I don't want to talk about it."

"Coreen, if you don't tell us, I am sure you realize that you will have to tell Sheriff Metzger everything about last night, and we won't be there to run interference. You'll be completely on your own. But if you tell us whatever you can remember now, maybe Jessica will be able to help you. It's possible she could ease the pressure when you have to talk to Mort." Loretta was not one to pull her punches.

Coreen hung her head, and her voice was so low-pitched that I had to strain to be sure I could hear every word. "I walked over to the shop, and got there right on time, but the entire front of the store was dark. I thought that maybe Mr. Penzell forgot we had an appointment, but when I got closer I saw light shimmering from deep inside. It wasn't bright enough for me to actually see anything. Then I noticed the door was open—not all the way, but a few inches, like someone left without pulling it shut."

Coreen reached for her juice glass, took a drink, and then continued. "I poked my head in the doorway and said hello in case there was someone inside. My eyes adjusted to the dark, and I realized the light I could see was coming from a couple of taper candles on the table in the back room. Someone had to be around. I mean, who would go out and leave candles burning?"

"No one would. At least, not on purpose," I said.

Coreen nodded her agreement. "That's why I walked inside. I knew there was that lamp by the archway, and I thought if I turned it on I could see my way to the table, blow out the candles, and leave Mr. Penzell a note to say that I was sorry I'd missed him.

"I switched on the lamp, and that's when I saw him. Although at first I wasn't sure who it was sprawled on the floor by the table. I could see it was a man and he was on his stomach, but that was all. I dropped my bag and ran closer, yelling, 'Are you all right? Do you need help?' But there was no answer.

"The circle of light from the lamp ended eight or ten feet from the man, so it was darker where he was, with only that little glow from the candles. I felt along the wall and found a light switch. When I flicked it the big chandelier flooded the room with light, and I screamed. The man on the floor wasn't moving, and his head was covered with blood, and one of the thick candlesticks was covering his neck, like someone had dropped it on top of him. I bent down to touch him—you know, shake his shoulder to see if he . . . if he . . . was okay. One of his arms was stretched out, and that's when I saw the cuff link. It was a gold disk etched with a lion's head. I'd seen it before, so I knew the man on the floor was Mr. Penzell. I shook him and I called his name over and over, but . . ." She trailed off.

"While I was shaking him, the heavy brass candlestick slid off his neck and startled me. I guess that must be when I picked it up. I don't remember. I do remember that I had blood smears on my arm, my hand, and the front of my shirt.

"I ran outside and yelled for help. That's when Mr. Hendon came. He was the one who called Sheriff Metzger. It all got really crazy and confused."

"And you didn't see anyone? Think carefully, Coreen. Did anyone pass you in the street as you walked over to La Peinture? Or was anyone going in or out of Mara's when you arrived on the dock?" I asked, knowing that any witness at all might be helpful.

"No. It was suppertime. I guess most folks were home. I wish I'd been home having my supper. Let somebody else find Mr. Penzell." Coreen shuddered involuntarily.

The sound of the doorbell startled us all. I knew it was probably Seth or Mort or both. When Loretta went to answer the door I said to Coreen, "If the sheriff or a deputy comes to talk to you, please stay quiet and let me do the talking."

I was fully prepared to shield her until I knew more, but I really didn't want to upset Mort, so I was relieved that the visitor was Seth.

He cocked an eyebrow at me, which as much as said, *I should have expected to see you here.*

Then he gave Coreen a robust smile. "Good morning, young lady. Have a good night's sleep, did you?"

She nodded but didn't say a word.

"Well, let's get a look at you. Loretta, is there a place where—"

Loretta cut him off. "Coreen, take Doc Hazlitt up to the bedroom you're using and let him check your blood pressure and the like."

As soon as we heard the door close upstairs, Loretta asked me what I thought about what Coreen had told us.

"I believe her. I believe every word. That goes without saying. Coreen wouldn't hurt a fly, much less a person, no matter what he tried to do to her. Plus, I am aware of several other people who had reason to be angry with Mr. Penzell. Was anyone angry enough to kill him? We'll have to figure that out."

Loretta clenched her jaw. "If I get my hands on the beast that put Coreen in this position . . ." She shook her head as if to clear it. "Anyway, what's the next step? What should we do now?"

We heard a door open, and Seth came downstairs. "Coreen is a lot better this morning. She's going to freshen up. She'll be down in a few minutes." He glanced at the table. "It seems that tea and cookies with you ladies has done her a world of good."

Loretta stood. "Have a seat. I'll get you a cup. Help yourself to a cookie. They're from Sassi's."

"Don't mind if I do." Seth sat down and turned to me. "This is a sticky one, Jess. I don't mind saying my heart goes out to the poor girl. Mort has called me twice so far this morning. He wants me to clear her for questioning and have Loretta bring her to his office. If I don't he is perfectly willing to come and get her."

"And? What is your diagnosis?" I asked.

"She certainly is in better shape than she was last night, both emotionally and physically. She's technically well enough to be interviewed. However, I do have a real fear that once Mort starts asking Coreen questions it will send her spiraling again. And what good will that do? Won't help Mort and certainly won't be good for Coreen."

Loretta put a cup in front of Seth and poured his tea. "It took a lot of coddling and cajoling to get her to speak to us this morning. I can't imagine she'd be able to talk to a man—any man, but especially one who might wind up arresting her."

"Ah, I see. I thought her being alone with Penzell at any time might have caused a problem," Seth said. "So, Jessica, what is the plan? You always have a plan."

"I do think that several things have to happen before Mort can interview Coreen. For one, she can't spend the day in Loretta's pajamas. We will have to get some of her clothes. For another, she absolutely cannot speak to Mort without a lawyer." On that point I was adamant.

Chapter Nine

Good heavens," Loretta said. "If she didn't do anything wrong, why does she need a lawyer? Oh, I get it. You are not talking about needing a lawyer because she's done something wrong. You're talking about a lawyer who can support Coreen when she talks to Mort. Maybe even prevent that conversation from happening."

None of us was aware that Coreen had come out of her room until she called from the staircase, "No lawyer. I can't afford a lawyer."

Loretta pushed her chair back and jumped up. She folded her arms and put on her sternest face. When Coreen got to the bottom step, Loretta was firmly in no-nonsense mode. "You don't worry about that, young lady. We'll pay him in haircuts and manicures if we have to, but you definitely will be represented by a lawyer, the best one we can find."

That was all it took. The dam burst and Coreen began crying

again. She flung herself at Loretta, who graciously opened her arms and patted Coreen's head reassuringly.

Coreen sobbed, "What would I ever do without you? I'd go to jail for fifty years—that's what."

Seth leaned over and whispered to me, "If I leave right this second I can honestly tell Mort that Coreen was in no shape to be interviewed when I left her. Good luck."

He picked up his well-worn leather medical bag and slipped away.

While Loretta got Coreen quieted down and settled at the table, I searched the directory in my phone for Joe Turco's number. I had visited his law office on Main Street for some legal work several times, but I didn't think that criminal law was one of his specialties. Still, he was a place to start.

Before I placed the call I said, "Coreen, I am going to call Joe Turco. Do you know him?"

She thought for a few seconds. "Yes. Well, I've never met him, but my friend Monica worked as a part-time receptionist in his office. She said he was a nice man and a good boss. Is he going to help me?"

"I don't know. I would like your permission to call him and ask him either to represent you or to recommend another lawyer, one who is more familiar with, ah, this kind of case. Loretta will rest much easier once we find a lawyer to help you."

Coreen asked, "How would a lawyer help me?"

"Well, think of it this way: A lawyer will advise you on how to answer Sheriff Metzger's questions," I said.

"Don't I just tell the truth?" Coreen's eyes went wide at the thought that she might do anything else.

"Of course, you will. You have nothing to hide, but sometimes everything depends on *how* you tell the truth. Perhaps the order of what you say will help the sheriff understand more easily, or there may be things that can be left out for time's sake. Believe me, Sheriff Metzger can become quite impatient if you ramble on and on. And if he tries to rush you along, well, the lawyer can insist that he allow you to speak at your own pace."

I could tell by the look on Coreen's face that I'd finally hit on a reason that appealed to her. She turned to Loretta, who said softly, "I think it is a good idea."

Coreen bowed her head, and when she raised it again she said, "Okay, make the call—I'm sure you are right. After all, you write books for a living, so who would understand the way words should be used better than you?"

I was dumbfounded that somehow in Coreen's mind everything I'd said about conversations with the sheriff appeared to be things she assumed I'd learned by writing books. Loretta actually snorted as she tried to stifle a laugh.

"The other thing we have to do is get you some clothes. Will you be staying here for another day or two, or do you think you are ready to go home?" As soon as the words were out of my mouth I realized I should have spoken to Loretta privately. Suppose she didn't want a houseguest for another night or two or three.

So I was relieved when Loretta said, "Coreen, you know you can stay here as long as you like, or I'm happy to drive you home, but Jessica is right. My clothes are several sizes too large; we're going to have to get you something to wear."

Coreen hesitated for a split second, and then said, "Would it really be all right if I slept here one more night? I won't be any trouble, and Dr. Hazlitt gave me a pill to take before bed to make sure I sleep without nightmares. I am so afraid of nightmares.

One more night. I'm sure I'll be able to go home on my own after work tomorrow."

I personally didn't think that Coreen would be able to manage on her own for several days, or even weeks, but before I could say anything Loretta jumped out of her chair. "Work. My appointment book. Where did I put it? I still have a couple of cancellation calls to make." And she ran out of the room.

Coreen munched on a cookie. "I think my appetite is coming back. Dr. Hazlitt said it would, but I didn't think it would come back so soon. He's a smart doctor."

"Yes, he is. And we will find you a smart lawyer. Is it all right if I call Joe Turco now?"

"Yes, I can see that is a good idea. I would like to have someone help me talk to Sheriff Metzger. He can be darn scary." Coreen shivered at the thought.

I'd never seen Mort as scary, but I could understand that from Coreen's vantage point he might appear so. I smiled and reached across the table to pat her hand. "I'm sure he can be, but he is a fair and honest man. You have nothing to fear."

I tapped Joe's number into my cell phone, and a receptionist answered on the second ring. I was disappointed when she told me that Joe was busy with a client, but she assured me that he would return my call as soon as possible. I tapped the END CALL button on my phone just as Loretta came back to the table.

"Well, that's taken care of, kiddo." She smiled at Coreen. "We don't have to go back to work until noon tomorrow. Would you like me to drive you home to pick up some clothes and whatever else you will need for the next couple of days?"

Coreen brightened, then looked down at the pajamas she was wearing. Loretta caught the uncertainty in Coreen's eyes.

"Not to worry. I have a superlong raincoat that will cover you right to your ankles. Besides, no one will see you. Once you jump out of my car it's only a few feet to your front door. Open the door and you're in."

Coreen panicked. "My keys! Where is my purse? My keys are in it. Oh goodness, did the sheriff keep them?"

"Calm down—didn't you see your purse? We brought it home with us last night. After Deputy Andy searched and returned it, I tucked it on top of the chest of drawers. Why don't you go look for it while I get the raincoat?"

Coreen clambered up the stairs and Loretta turned to me. "She is still very fragile. Would you mind coming with us in case she gets too difficult for me to handle alone?"

Since I had never seen or even heard of any situation that Loretta thought was beyond her capabilities, I quickly agreed.

Coreen's tiny apartment looked as I expected it would, neat and clean, with bright pink and red floral prints hanging on the walls and vibrant multicolored rag rugs on the floor. When Coreen went into her room to change into fresh clothes, I told Loretta that I hadn't had any luck reaching Joe Turco.

"Maybe we should stop by his office on our way back to my place. He might be free. If not, we can make an appointment," Loretta suggested.

I didn't even consider it. "I don't like the thought of anyone in town seeing Coreen going into a lawyer's office. Some of the more ferocious gossips will have her hanging from the gallows by lunchtime."

"True enough. As it is there are more than a few messages on the beauty parlor voice mail from people I've never heard of who are demanding 'emergency manicures' that must be done immediately. I mean, seriously, Jessica, do these people have no shame?" Loretta asked, although I was sure she knew the answer.

"Why don't you drop me near Joe's office? I can stop in and see if he's free. Then I'll call you and let you know how he can help," I said.

Coreen came out of the bedroom wearing gray and white running shoes, jeans, and a yellow cotton T-shirt. She was carrying a large tote with a radiant orange sun near the top and the words *Penobscot Bay* embroidered across the dazzling blue water that covered the rest of the bag. She looked much more like her usual self. And if the bounce in her step was any indication, she felt more like it, too.

"I just need to get my work smock and my jacket from the hall closet." She opened a door, pulled out her pink smock, and then stared. Her face clouded over. "I guess the sheriff kept my denim jacket. I'll take my ski jacket."

She put on a blue and white zipper jacket that looked both waterproof and toasty warm. Perhaps a little too warm for the day, but she left it unzipped and seemed comfortable.

We piled into Loretta's car and she drove along Main Street. Coreen never asked where we were going and we never said. Loretta pulled to the curb at the corner a few doors from Joe Turco's office. As I got out, Loretta told me to be sure to call her if I needed a ride home. I nodded, but I had other plans.

I stepped into Joe Turco's office. I'd always admired how attractively furnished it was. The desk, credenza, and bookcases were oak and the visitors' chairs were covered with a soft plum-colored corduroy. Professional but with a homey look. Whenever I had a meeting with Joe I stopped to admire the three pen-and-ink sketches of the harbor hanging above the credenza. He once told me that they were a present from a grateful client. His assistant, a young woman I didn't recognize, looked up and immediately said, "Hi, Mrs. Fletcher. I told Mr. Turco you called. He is anxious to speak with you. Would you like me to tell him you are here?"

I said, "Thank you. That would be fine."

She stepped through the doorway to Joe's inner sanctum and was back in a flash.

"Please have a seat, Mrs. Fletcher. He'll be right with you."

As I settled into a visitor chair, she said, "I'm Lena. I know who you are because I've read your books and your picture is inside the back cover. You look prettier than the picture."

I considered that quite a compliment, since my cover photo was at least eight years old. I am sure I blushed when I thanked her. It also reminded me that it was past time to call my friend and favorite photographer, Richard Koser, to make an appointment to have some new stills taken for future book jackets.

Joe Turco came bursting through the door from his inner office, all smiles and energy. It seemed like yesterday that he was a young lawyer setting up his practice here in Cabot Cove, and now I noticed some streaks of gray were lightening his dark hair.

"Jessica, come in. Come in. It's so good to see you. We seem to be breakfasting at Mara's at different times lately. I feel like I haven't seen you in ages."

He guided me to a black leather sofa and sat opposite me in a matching chair.

We chatted for a few minutes, and then he rubbed his hands together. "How can I help you today?"

"Actually, it's Coreen Wilson who needs the help."

Joe nodded, and then made a steeple with his hands and

rested his chin on his fingertips. He seemed to be pondering something, so I sat patiently and waited for him to speak.

At last he said, "Okay, I am not going to ask you any questions other than a personal one: Have you seen Coreen today, and how is she feeling? I heard she was totally out of control last night."

"She is doing better than I would have expected, considering it isn't even twenty-four hours since—"

Joe held up his hand. "Jessica, you know I do lots of estate work and real estate law. Civil litigation as well. I can't say I've never done a criminal case, but I can say that in this instance Coreen would be poorly represented if I took her case on."

His answer was not unexpected. I said, "I understand. I thought perhaps you could recommend someone suitable?"

He walked over to his desk and bent over his computer screen. I watched him scroll and then hit a button, and the printer roared to life. A page popped up and he handed it to me. It appeared to be a professional biography.

"I really think this attorney is a perfect match for Coreen. As you can see, her name is Regina Tremblay. It's possible she is in the middle of a heavy case and unable to take on anything else at the moment, but she is the first lawyer I would try to retain. She lives and works up Wiscasset way, no more than a fifteen-, twenty-minute drive, so meetings shouldn't be a problem. As soon as you leave I will give her a call, tell her what I surmise, and pass along Coreen's name and yours, along with your phone number. If you don't hear from her in an hour or so, feel free to give her a call." He scribbled something on a pad and ripped off the top page. "Here's her number."

I thanked him, and then added, "If Ms. Tremblay is unable to take the case, do you have a backup or two?"

"I know a couple of people, yes, but Regina has experience handling cases where women have been accused of assaulting men who were, shall we say, aggressive in their approach, so I think she's the best place to start," Joe said decisively.

It was becoming obvious to me that Nelson Penzell's reputation was widespread around town. I thanked Joe for his help, and he told me he wished Coreen well.

I stood on the sidewalk outside Joe's office wondering where to go next. I had a couple of choices, but I decided to walk over to Charles Department Store before I reported to Loretta and Coreen. If things were going to be complicated for the next few days, I'd better be sure I had a nice birthday present ready to send to Donna.

I had taken only a few steps when I saw Angus Michaud coming directly toward me. Instead of his usual sweatshirt and windbreaker he was wearing a white shirt and black tie with a navy blue sports jacket along with his usual jeans and Timberlands.

"Morning, Jessica." Angus touched two fingers to his eyebrow in a salute. "How is this morning treating you?"

"I can't complain, Angus. I was sorry to hear about the tragedy that befell your business associate, Mr. Penzell," I said.

He squirmed uncomfortably. "Ayuh, guess I should have known better than to partner up with a stranger come from away. Those flatlanders bring nothing but trouble."

"Perhaps you were lucky not to be in the store when it happened." I was looking for an alibi, if he had one.

"As it was, I wanted to work late. Had some new puzzles come in and I needed to fix up a display, but, well, Nelson was expecting a high-end client to look at some painting or another. He was always claiming he needed privacy with the high-enders, but I never saw that we made much money from them. So I stopped at Mara's for chowdah and went on home."

"Oh my, someone told me there was quite a to-do in the luncheonette about the Maine Mariners. Did you happen to hear it?"

"Walt Hendon mentioned it this morning. Apparently it's the latest gossip, along with Nelson, of course, but I missed the whole thing. I must have left before it started and was home in my easy chair watching the news while the hockey fans were yelling at each other. Well"—Angus saluted again—"I'll be on my way."

He walked past me and turned into Joe Turco's law office. I wondered what legal business he wanted to accomplish with the co-owner of his shop dead less than twenty-four hours. I would have to see what I could find out about their contractual agreements, and I knew Joe Turco would never break a client's confidentiality. I'd have to look for other sources.

I walked over to Charles Department Store to do some shopping and, if I was lucky, pick up a word or two of local gossip.

Chapter Ten

I know large chain stores abound in bigger towns and cities. In recent years a couple of the more well-known names had popped up along the highways outside of Cabot Cove, but a local family-run store like Charles Department Store, owned by the Ranieri brothers, provided the kind of friendly service that I could not get in any of those oversized stores where management thought I should rifle through the shelves searching for what I wanted and then process my own purchases on a self-checkout machine.

An elderly couple was leaving as I approached the main entrance. The gentleman tipped his hat, said, "Good morning," and held the door for me. I stepped onto the tan tweed carpeting and looked around. Soft indoor lighting ensured that everything was visible without glare or deep shadows. The restrained melody of a violin concerto I recognized but could not quite name floated gently through the air. I went directly to the women's department.

"How can I help you this morning, Mrs. Fletcher?"

Sally Thomson had been a sales associate at the store for so many years that I could remember when her iron gray hair was brown, often with blond highlights added by Loretta. She was an absolute wiz at helping me find just the right gift, no matter the occasion or the recipient.

"I am looking for an extra-special birthday gift for my niece Donna. She's hitting one of those round numbers, and I want to be sure to acknowledge it and her," I said.

"Oh yes, Grady's wife and young Frank's mother. How are they all doing down there in New York City?"

As I brought her up to date on the latest family news I could see that, although she was smiling attentively and commenting in all the right places, her mind was busily categorizing everything in stock, narrowing the list to perhaps two or three items from which I could choose the perfect gift.

Sally placed her hand on my arm to let me know she was ready to guide me around the store. "I'm going to assume that since it is a special birthday Grady will be sure to buy her a lovely piece of jewelry, so we won't bother looking in the jewelry department."

"You are something of a mind reader. Grady texted me pictures of two attractive bracelets he was considering."

"Do you know if he made a decision as to which one to buy?"

"He told me that, much as he liked the pearl bracelet, he purchased the entwined gold-and-rose-gold cuff, which he thought was more modern." I didn't add that I was pleased with his choice.

"Hmm, let me show you something really special." Sally stepped over to a counter and took a large white box from the top shelf behind it. "This is one of our newest items, and it is so delicate that we don't dare leave it on display."

When she opened the box and pulled back the cream-colored tissue paper Sally uncovered an alluring rose-gold-colored fabric. "This is an evening wrap made of silk, and you'll notice it is the exact shade of rose gold that is used in fine jewelry."

Sally unfurled the wrap carefully and passed it to me for closer inspection. "Do you see the flecks of gold woven into the fabric? How do you think this would look with the bracelet Grady bought for Donna?"

"Well, let's see." I pulled out my phone and scrolled through my texts until I found the picture of the cuff bracelet, with strands of gold and rose gold woven around each other. I enlarged the picture and held the phone in my palm. Sally draped the wrap over my fingertips.

"I should also tell you that this is part of a line of wraps and shawls that comes from an artist colony up by Millinocket. Much of the material is woven by local weavers, and some of the more intricate designs, like this, are made by a company located near Augusta, to keep them more affordable."

"This is absolutely gorgeous, and being a product of Maine artists is always a plus. Perfect. I'll take it. I'm sure Donna will love it."

Sally asked if I wanted the shawl gift wrapped and showed me several rolls of decorative paper. I selected silver foil with "Happy birthday" printed on it repetitively in English and a few dozen other languages. I knew my grandnephew Frank would enjoy trying to pronounce "Happy birthday" in Spanish, French, and other languages I didn't recognize.

"Gift buying again, Jessica? I'm glad we had something in

stock." David Ranieri and his brother Jim were the longtime owners of the department store, and they took pride in carrying a wide variety of household items, clothes, and gifts so their customers would have plenty of choices.

"You've never failed me yet." I smiled.

"We do our very best," David said, then changed the subject. "Terrible news about Nelson Penzell, isn't it? What is the world coming to? A man murdered in his own shop. Jim and I are talking about hiring a security firm for the store. Can you imagine? It's rare that we even have to deal with shoplifters, which are a common problem for many retailers, but murder? Well, it's unthinkable."

I tutted sympathetically, then asked, "How well did you know Mr. Penzell?"

"Not well. Not well at all," David replied. "Which is why I found it so surprising that he approached us about selling what he described as his 'upscale merchandise' from a space in our store. Sort of like a sublet, I suppose. He swore it would be extremely lucrative for us all."

"Really?" I was taken aback, although the more I learned about Nelson Penzell, the more I supposed that nothing he did should be unexpected. "And what did you and your brother think of the idea?"

"I was willing to consider it, at least momentarily, but Jim was adamantly opposed. He argued that we already had art and gift items in stock that were of better quality than the merchandise in the back room of La Peinture—you know, Nelson Penzell's domain."

"And did Angus Michaud know that there was a possibility that his partner would leave him high and dry?" I wondered.

David laughed. "Yes, in fact, he did. One morning, as I was going into Mara's, Angus was coming out. He wasted no time in telling me that he knew all about 'the flatlander's cheating scheme,' as he called it. He warned that Jim and I should be wary of dealing with a man who had an ironclad contract with someone else. Then he turned on his heel, marched toward his shop, and left me to assume that he was the 'someone else' and that he would resort to a legal battle if he found it necessary. That was enough for me to drop the idea entirely."

"I can see why it would be," I said.

Sally handed me a shopping bag with Donna's gaily wrapped present safely tucked inside. I thanked her, and then asked David if there was a quiet spot where I could make a phone call.

"Jim is interviewing prospective employees in our office, which is why I escaped. The atmosphere in the waiting room is palpably nervous, so I can't suggest that, but . . . let's see. Come with me."

I followed him into the household-linens department, and when we got to the rear wall David opened a brown door marked EMPLOYEES ONLY.

He ushered me inside the room behind it, glanced at the wall clock, and said, "I can't guarantee you'll have privacy for long, but you are more than welcome to use the staff break room, which seems to be unoccupied at the moment."

And he waved good-bye, shutting the door behind him.

I called Loretta, and she answered on the first ring. Without preliminaries she asked, "And?"

"We may have a lawyer. Her name is Regina Tremblay, and she's over in Wiscasset. Joe Turco says he thinks she will be a good match for Coreen. He is calling her now to explain the circumstances, and I will talk to her later to find out if she can help."

"And what if she declines? What happens to Coreen then?" I could hear the anxiety in Loretta's voice.

"Don't worry. Joe knows a few other possibilities. We'll find a lawyer." I tried to sound as reassuring as I could.

"I hope we find the *right* one."

"I totally agree. How is Coreen doing?" I knew it was important for us to monitor her emotional state.

"Her appetite is back. She made a sandwich with some leftover meat loaf I had in the fridge, and then ate an orange, followed by an apple. Right now she is looking at the television, watching one of those shop-from-home shows. This one sells jewelry, and Coreen is commenting along with the host like she's the top salesperson in Day's Jewelers in Bangor."

"Well, that sounds encouraging. She's doing much better than she was last night, or even earlier this morning." I was relieved. The calmer Coreen remained, the better equipped she would be to handle the difficult conversations I knew were ahead of her.

"Where are you, Jessica? Do you need a ride home?" Loretta asked.

"Not at the moment, thank you. I just finished picking out Donna's birthday present at Charles, and now I think I will walk over to see if Seth is finished with his morning appointments."

"Okay," Loretta said. "Just give a holler if you need a ride."

David was nowhere to be seen, so I asked Sally to thank him for allowing me the privacy of the break room, and I headed to Seth's office.

The morning had begun with fog covering the landscape, but a powerful sun had long since burned it away. As I walked along I passed neighbors who had nipped into town for a quick stop at a store or two or were out to enjoy the sunshine of an early autumn day in coastal Maine.

As we exchanged greetings I was surprised by how few people remarked on last night's tragedy, and how those who did comment said things like "Too bad that fella died—you know, the one from away." And then they talked about the weather and moved on. It seemed that Nelson Penzell wasn't well known by his neighbors, and I thought that alone should make it easier to narrow down the field of suspects and clear Coreen.

Seth was walking across the waiting room of his office with his jacket in his hand when I came through the front door. It was evident I'd startled him.

"Jess, you about gave me a heart attack." He placed a dramatic hand on his chest. "I've been overrun with walk-in patients and I was hoping to escape to Mara's for a leisurely lunch, so when the door opened I got angry at myself for not locking it right after Josie Cummings left."

I refrained from saying that doing without a meal or two wouldn't harm him in the least. Instead I offered, "I am in need of a ride home, and I do recall that I have half a roast chicken sitting in my refrigerator."

Seth's scowl turned to a smile. "What are you standing there for? Let's go."

I unlocked the front door of my house and led Seth inside. He hung his jacket on the coat-tree and said, "Mort called me twice since I first told him that Coreen was still too upset to be interviewed. I don't think I can fend him off much longer."

"It's possible you won't have to," I said with more confidence than I felt. "I stopped by Joe Turco's office earlier, and he recommended a lawyer who may be the right person to help Coreen. I am going to call her in the next few minutes."

"Not before lunch, I hope," Seth said. "My stomach is growling to beat the band."

I wisely decided to get Seth settled in the kitchen so that he wouldn't be hovering when I called Regina Tremblay. Otherwise I feared he would be circling around me, pointing to his stomach and making other signs of starvation as a means of rushing me off the call.

I said, "I suppose if you set the table I could rustle up enough food to keep you quiet while I make the call. Shall I put on the kettle or the coffeepot?"

"Well, if you have any left, I wouldn't say no to a cup of that black and green tea mix we had the other day. Don't know who thought of putting both in one tea bag, but I think it came out right flavorful," Seth replied.

Once I'd filled the kettle and set it on the stove, I took the chicken out of the refrigerator, cut some thick slices for Seth's sandwich, and tore a few pieces to put on top of my salad.

I tossed some mixed greens together with cherry tomatoes, carrot sticks, and a small sprinkling of goat cheese. I divided the salad into two bowls and added the shredded chicken and a few raisins to mine.

I put two slices of bread on a plate for Seth, hesitated, then added a slice for myself. When he saw the bread Seth sighed. "Is that Charlene Sassi's rye bread? This is indeed my lucky day.

Before you sit down, would you happen to have any mayonnaise?"

As soon as Seth was happily building his sandwich and sipping his tea, I went into the living room and called Regina Tremblay.

An efficient-sounding woman took my information and put me on hold until a pleasant voice said, "This is Regina Tremblay. How may I be of assistance?"

"My name is Jessica Fletcher, and according to Joe Turco you are the perfect attorney to help a friend of mine who is in grave difficulty."

"Mrs. Fletcher, I've been expecting your call. Joe Turco telephoned earlier, and he explained the bare basics of the, ah, situation. I would have to speak to the prospective client before I commit to representation, but I can arrange to do so later today or first thing in the morning, if you believe that is possible on your end."

"We can definitely arrange for a meeting. The young lady in difficulty is Coreen Wilson, and you can reach her by calling her friend and employer, Loretta Spiegel, who will gladly set up a meeting."

After I gave Loretta's cell phone number to Ms. Tremblay she said, "I'll be in touch with her soon. And when you see him, please give Joe my thanks for his expression of confidence in me."

I said I would gladly do so and hung up, satisfied that I had done everything I could do at the moment to help Coreen. Now I looked forward to enjoying a relaxing lunch with Seth.

"How'd you manage with the lawyer?" he asked after he finished chewing the large bite he'd taken of his sandwich at the exact moment I walked back into the kitchen.

"Her name is Regina Tremblay. She seems competent, and she

is interested in hearing more about Coreen's situation. I thought that was a good sign. Even though Joe told her what she called the 'bare basics,' she declined to jump right in and take the case, preferring to speak with Coreen before making a decision."

"Ayuh, sounds like she has a good head on her shoulders. And she can be the one to wrangle with Mort, which leaves me out of it." Seth was relieved enough to change topics. "So, tell me, Jess, how's the new book coming along?"

I pursed my lips, then said, "Well, I am having a great deal of difficulty getting the plot organized. My protagonist is a doctor."

"A doctor, eh?" Seth sat up a little straighter. "Is he modeled after anyone we know? Maybe a handsome gray-haired small-town doctor with sharp wit and an uncanny knack for diagnosis?"

"Actually, *she* is a big-city doctor. Philadelphia, as it happens. But perhaps you could help me. I have been considering using one of those large hospital machines as a murder weapon. I'm looking for something so heavy that if it fell on a person it could crush him. Does anything come to mind?"

"Well, I would think a gamma camera could do the job. Of course, they are so safe and secure that I don't know how you could possibly weaponize one, but I am sure Gregory Leung could tell you all about it. He's a specialist in nuclear medicine and understands the ins and outs of the gamma." Seth reached for the piece of bread I'd set out for myself. "I wouldn't mind a dollop of jam to make that last piece of bread taste more like dessert."

"Oh, Seth, didn't you have enough bread when you ate your sandwich?" I chided even as I went to the refrigerator to get his jam. "Strawberry or raspberry?"

"Raspberry sounds like it would hit the spot. And don't forget the butter, heah?"

I passed the butter and jam to Seth just as there was a sturdy rat-tat-tat on my kitchen door. I turned to see Mort Metzger looking at us through the glass pane in the top half of the door. And he didn't look happy.

Chapter Eleven

I waved to him to come and join us.

He looked at Seth, who was slathering butter on his bread, and said, "I saw your car outside, Doc. I thought we might have a little chat, seeing as how you seem to be doing your all-fired best to prevent me from interviewing Coreen Wilson."

"Mort, sit down—you look tired. Cup of tea? And I have some leftover chicken, if you'd like a sandwich, or perhaps a salad?" I knew I was babbling, but I hoped to distract him from jumping on Seth.

"Tea's not usually my drink, but since the kettle is on the boil I'll be glad of a cup," Mort said.

As Mort pulled out a chair and settled in Seth said, "Don't let her hide the rye bread from you."

I set a cup of tea in front of Mort, put two pieces of bread on a plate next to it, and pointed to the butter dish and jam jar. "Please feel free. Help yourself."

Mort took a sip of tea, and then said, "Nice as this is, Mrs. F., I'm not here on a social call." He turned to Seth. "Doc, why are you stalling me on Coreen? I have a dead body on my hands and you've put my only real witness in medical isolation. Mayor Shevlin is on the phone it seems like every ten minutes. He says the town council is in an uproar, not to mention the Chamber of Commerce and the Ladies' Auxiliary. I've got to come up with something fast. And Coreen is my only lead. I have to talk to her. I can't cut you any more slack."

Seth opened his mouth wide, took a bite of his bread and jam, and chewed slowly and deliberately while pointedly staring at me with a look that said, *He's in your ballpark now.*

"To tell you the truth, Mort, Coreen is conferring with a lawyer, and if all goes well they should be able to meet with you tomorrow at the latest," I said while I tried to gauge his reaction to the news.

No need for me to try to gauge; Mort showed us, in no uncertain terms, how upset he was.

He banged his hand on the table with such force that it made my tea splash the sides of my cup. "A lawyer? Isn't that great? And I suppose the lawyer will come up with some reason or another to keep Coreen away from me. Or worse, he'll bring her into my office but won't let her speak. Without talking to her, how do I solve my case? Jim Shevlin has already dropped broad hints about calling in the Staties from Augusta. How will that make me look? I need to be able to report that we're making progress and I need to report it right now."

"I suppose you've interviewed Angus Michaud," I said casually. "Was he any help?"

"Not really. Of course I spoke to him first thing, but he claims to have left the store early. I checked with Mara and she was able to back up the approximate time he stopped in for a quick bite. After that he was home alone. Widower, you know," Mort said. "The way Angus tells it, he and Penzell were sharing space but not sharing any actual business, so he couldn't even tell me much about Penzell's business life, and he claimed to know nothing at all about his personal life."

"Now, that is interesting," I said.

"Woman, what could you possibly find interesting in anything Mort just said? Sounds like a dead end to me." Seth picked up the last bit of bread and jam and put it in his mouth.

Mort reacted differently. He turned a curious eye to me. "Interesting? In what way, Mrs. F.?"

"Well, I happen to know that Nelson Penzell recently spoke to the Ranieri brothers about moving his wares into a section of Charles Department Store. When Angus Michaud found out, he approached David Ranieri and made a not-so-veiled threat of legal action. So I don't put much faith in Angus's claim that he and Penzell didn't have a formal business agreement."

"Okay, I grant you," Mort said, "that is somewhat interesting, but knowing crotchety Angus, isn't it more likely that he was bluffing about their arrangement because he didn't want to lose Penzell's share of the rent?"

"That is a possibility, of course. But as it happens, just this morning I ran into Angus. It struck me that he was dressed rather formally, at least for him. And where was he going? I watched him walk into Joe Turco's office. I suspect there would be legalities to consider if he and Nelson Penzell had more of a partnership than anyone knew."

Mort pushed his chair back and stood. "Thanks for the tea,

Mrs. F. I think it's time I have another talk with Angus. That'll give me something to tell the mayor. In the meantime, I'd appreciate your passing the word that I'll expect to hear from Coreen's lawyer soonest. I'd hate to have to show up at Loretta's or Coreen's."

Mort was barely out the door when my phone rang. I answered the kitchen extension and wasn't surprised to hear Loretta on the other end.

"Jessica, the lawyer called, and she's on her way to meet with Coreen right now. She explained that their meeting would be private. Knowing how busy you are, I hate to ask, but I could use a friend to sit with me so I don't go insane thinking the worst while I wait for them to be finished. I'd be happy to pick you up." Loretta sounded desperate, which was not like her at all. The Loretta Spiegel I had always known could robustly tackle any problem, wrap it in a bow, and put it behind her. She was back in mother-hen mode, more worried than I had ever heard her. How could I refuse?

"Of course I can come. I'll be there shortly. Seth is here, and he'll be able to drop me off."

Seth was putting his dishes in the sink. "I heard, and I'm happy to drive you. Where are you going? Or should I guess? Loretta's house?"

I hurried to put away the leftovers and wipe down the table. "Yes, if you wouldn't mind. I've never heard Loretta so distressed. She wants me to wait with her while Coreen meets with Regina Tremblay. You know it's not like Loretta to ask for help."

"Ayuh, that's true enough. As her doctor, I have a hard time getting her to take over-the-counter medicines when something ails her. And she fights the idea of prescriptions as if they were arsenic." Seth grimaced at the memories of doctor-patient battles he and Loretta had obviously had in the past. "I'll just stop in to check on Coreen, and I'll have a surreptitious look at Loretta while I'm there. It wouldn't do for one or the other to have a fit of nerves with only you to look after them."

Rankled, I was about to object to his implication that I couldn't handle any crisis that might occur, but he offered me a toothy grin and a broad wink.

"Oh, Seth, you find humor in the oddest things. Now, let's get going before I have a conniption. I guarantee you won't find that funny."

After he had a brief conversation with Coreen, whom he pronounced to be in fine fettle, Seth told Loretta to call him immediately if she felt the need for any reason, and he went back to his office.

Coreen said, "Mrs. Fletcher, I want to thank you for finding Ms. Tremblay to help me. Loretta says that we should be able to go back to our normal lives once the lawyer gets things straightened out with Sheriff Metzger."

I told her I was happy to help but felt the need to add, "Be patient, Coreen. It may take a little time."

Loretta reached over and squeezed Coreen's hand. "Coreen, honey, however long it takes, we are going to put this behind us."

The doorbell startled us all.

Coreen's eyes widened—not quite like those of a deer in headlights, but close.

Loretta seemed nervous as well and said, "Jessica, would you mind getting the door? Since you made the initial contact . . ."

I nodded and went to the door. I was prepared to introduce myself to Ms. Tremblay, but instead I found Evelyn Phillips on the doorstep.

"Jessica! I thought I was at Loretta Spiegel's house." Evelyn emitted a boisterous guffaw. "I must have gotten the address mixed up."

Her joking gave me just enough time to take a step forward and to the left, so that I filled the doorway, blocking her entrance without actually having to raise my hand like a stop sign.

Evelyn got the message. "So, is Loretta home? May I speak to her?"

My mind was scrambling to find a plausible reason to refuse when a striking young woman wearing a navy blue suit and carrying an expensive leather briefcase came up behind Evelyn and said, "Good afternoon. My name is Regina Tremblay. I am here to meet Loretta Spiegel."

And she held out a business card, which Evelyn promptly snatched from her hand. Evelyn took one look at the card and smiled like a Cheshire cat. "Never mind, Jessica. Tell Loretta I'll see her later."

As she pushed past Ms. Tremblay I could imagine the headline in the next issue of the *Cabot Cove Gazette*. It would read something like LORETTA SPIEGEL HIRES OUT-OF-TOWN LAWYER FOR COREEN WILSON.

I introduced myself and said how pleased I was that she was able to come so promptly.

"Is it 'Mrs. Fletcher,' or do you prefer 'Ms.'?"

"Why not call me Jessica?" I said.

She smiled. "And I am Regina. Joe stressed the urgency, and even if he hadn't, a murder charge could be pending, and that requires a speedy resolution. Before we go inside, I'd like to ask: How is Miss Wilson feeling? Her emotional state."

"Shaky, but overall, a hundred percent better than last night," I said.

"That's excellent news. In my experience it indicates that she has come to terms with the circumstances surrounding her, which will make our conversation much easier. Sometimes people think if they ignore a bad situation it will disappear of its own accord. That kind of thinking can land even an innocent person in jail."

When I introduced Regina to Loretta and Coreen, she greeted them warmly, and then asked Loretta, "Is there anything you want to be sure that I know before I meet privately with Coreen?"

Loretta responded emphatically, "I want you to know that Coreen Wilson is the most honest person I have ever met. You can be sure that whatever she tells you is the gospel truth."

"Thank you. That's good to know." Regina looked around the room. "Is there a place where Coreen and I can speak without the chance of being overheard?"

"If you don't mind sitting in my mother's old rocking chair, Coreen will take you up to the bedroom she's been using."

"Now, that sounds relaxing." Regina's laugh reminded me of the tiny silver bells we put on birthday corsages when they were in fashion decades ago. She followed Coreen upstairs, and we heard a door close.

Loretta threw herself on the sofa. "Jessica, this entire episode is going to give me a stroke. Why couldn't Nelson Penzell have gotten himself killed on a night when he didn't have an appointment to get his nails done?"

I had to admit that would have made all of our lives simpler. I sat in an armchair, and we both were lost in our own thoughts for a while. Loretta stood up and stretched her arms in front of her, and then reached high over her head. "I think I'll make some coffee. I'd rather have a glass of chardonnay, but I have to stay alert. Can I bring you anything from the kitchen? Coffee? Tea? A piece of pound cake?"

"No, I'm fine, but I will follow behind you. I wanted to tell you that when I answered the doorbell it wasn't Regina Tremblay at the door," I said.

Loretta's head swiveled and she squinted at me. "What do you mean? Who is she, then?"

"Oh, no. I didn't mean to confuse you. That young woman upstairs with Coreen is Regina Tremblay, but she arrived later. It was Evelyn Phillips who rang the bell," I said.

"Well, isn't that ducky? What on earth did she want? Oh, wait. Don't tell me she saw Regina and now knows she is a lawyer who is here to meet with Coreen. Good grief, this will be all over the front page of the *Gazette*. 'Coreen Wilson must be guilty. She hired a fancy lawyer.' Coreen will be the talk of the town."

"That isn't quite the headline I envisioned, but basically that's probably going to be in the next edition of the paper. And you know as well as I do that Coreen is already the hot topic of conversation in every kitchen and shop in Cabot Cove. Let's not pretend otherwise." I hated to be so blunt but I knew it was important for Loretta to face reality. How could she provide the emotional support Coreen needed if she didn't?

"Then you'd better get moving. Find out what happened to Nelson Penzell so everyone knows the truth before that newspaper comes out. Otherwise, oh, poor Coreen. She won't be able to show her face anywhere in the state of Maine."

Before I could reply, we heard footsteps on the stairs. Loretta poked her head through the kitchen doorway. "We're in the kitchen. Can we bring anything out for either of you?"

Coreen asked, "Do we have any more oatmeal cookies?"

I whispered to Loretta, "If she still has her appetite, things must have gone well."

Loretta nodded in agreement while saying, "Ms. Tremblay— er, Regina—can I offer you tea, coffee, or perhaps some orange juice?"

"I would love a glass of juice, and Coreen tells me that the oatmeal cookies from your local bakery are scrumptious." Regina sounded light and airy, as though she and Coreen were girl-friends rather than lawyer and client.

I crossed my fingers that her approach would keep Coreen grounded until this fiasco was resolved. We were settled around the table, munching and talking, when Regina adroitly brought us back to our current predicament. "So, Loretta, I understand that Coreen works in your beauty shop. How much of a hardship would it be for you if Coreen needed time off from work to attend a meeting with me or, say, with the sheriff?"

Loretta didn't flinch. "We are closed today and I've already canceled our appointments for tomorrow morning. Let me be up-front with you. If you believe something is necessary for Coreen's well-being, I guarantee you it can and will be done."

Regina said, "With that kind of support, I'm sure that Coreen and I will be ready to meet with the sheriff no later than mid-morning tomorrow. I am going out to my car to call the sheriff, and then, Coreen, you and I have work to do."

I was amazed when Coreen answered, "I can't wait."

*   *   *

Regina came back smiling a few minutes later. "We have a meeting with Sheriff Metzger. Ten o'clock tomorrow morning. Now, Coreen, grab one more cookie, and then let's get our strategy organized." And the two of them ran upstairs. Once again they reminded me of girlfriends rushing to the closet to pick out their dresses for the school dance.

Loretta offered to drive me home and I accepted gratefully. When she'd pulled up in front of my house she threw the gear in park and said, "Jessica, I can't thank you enough for all you're doing to help Coreen, but if you could stretch it further and use that powerful brain of yours to figure out 'whodunit,' like they say on television, then I would—well, I would stop trying to get you to let me style your hair a little poofier on top."

I said, "Loretta, if, by chance, I come across Nelson Penzell's murderer, I will hold you to that promise."

Laughing, we said our good nights.

As soon as I crossed my threshold I could hear my synopsis calling my name. I wanted to do an Internet search for the gamma camera to see if it had possibilities, and I knew the timeline of events in the story needed work. So much to do. I turned my computer on and got to work.

In spite of Loretta's repeated requests for me to try to find the truth about Nelson Penzell's death, I was sure that brains sharper than mine would solve that problem, leaving me free to spend the next few days refining my synopsis.

But, as often happens . . .

Chapter Twelve

Something was ringing and the room was dark. Then I realized the ringing was from my telephone and it was dark because I was in bed and it was the middle of the night. I looked at the clock on my nightstand. It wasn't quite the middle of the night, but at four fifteen in the morning it certainly felt like it. This whole "the telephone rings before dawn" thing was getting old fast. Assuming it wasn't Eve Simpson calling in another crisis, I couldn't imagine . . .

I yanked the phone off the receiver and mumbled, "Hello?"

"Mrs. F., I am sorry to bother you so early"—Mort Metzger sounded both tired and repentant—"but we have a situation."

"Coreen? Is she all right?"

"She's fine. This has nothing to do with, ah, that part of the Penzell case. It's . . . it's something else. It's kinda tricky. Anyway, I need your help. I am going to send Floyd to pick you up. Say, ten minutes?"

When I didn't answer he asked, "Mrs. F., are you there? Is that okay?"

I sighed. "Make it fifteen so I can at least brush my teeth."

Deputy Floyd McCallum was parked in front of my house exactly fifteen minutes later. He was a shy, respectful man who had served Cabot Cove well for many years. As I came down my front walk, he leaned over, pushed the passenger door open, and said, "Good morning, Mrs. Fletcher. It's a mite chilly, so I got the heater going full blast."

"Thank you, Floyd. It is nippier out than I expected. Of course, I never imagined I'd be up and out of the house this early. Whatever has gotten Mort in such a lather that he has us all running around at five in the morning?"

"I have to say, it was the darndest thing," Floyd started, but then compressed his mouth shut. He'd been one of Mort's deputies for many years, so I knew he was well aware that Mort and I were longtime friends. He also was party to several investigations during which I had been a help to the sheriff in solving the case. Still, loyalty to Mort prevented him from giving me so much as a hint about the reason I was being summoned to the sheriff's office in the predawn darkness. As much as I admired Floyd's fidelity to Mort, I would have appreciated being told why I had been woken from a sound sleep. It seemed, however, I would have to wait to hear it from Mort.

"You'll be happy to know that there's a fresh pot of coffee brewing at the office," Floyd said by way of apology for not telling me what I wanted to know.

When we pulled into the parking lot, I was surprised to see Mort waiting in front of the building. He loped to the car and began pulling at my door even before Floyd came to a full stop.

"I am so sorry to do this to you, Mrs. F., waking you up so early and all. Maybe you can take comfort in the fact that me, Andy, and Floyd have been working all night. And what a night!" Mort stepped ahead and opened the door for me. As soon as I walked inside, Deputy Andy Broom led me to a visitors' chair in front of Mort's desk. The second I sat down he handed me a cup of hot coffee.

Mort swiveled into his chair while Floyd and Andy stood on either side of me as though I were the emperor of Rome and they were Praetorian Guards. The excitement swirling around me was palpable, but I was still mystified, totally out of the loop.

"Mort, please. I'm not thrilled to have been hauled out of my cozy bed, and I can't help noticing that I am the only person in this room who has no idea why. What is going on here?"

"Okay, that's fair. A couple of hours ago Floyd and Andy caught a burglar," Mort said, and gave his deputies a thumbs-up.

Both Andy and Floyd grinned with delight as they smacked a high five over my head.

"That is wonderful news. You should call Evelyn Phillips. I'm sure she will print a front-page 'attaboy' story in the *Gazette*. But what has that got to do with me? It wasn't my house, that's for sure."

"Actually, it was Nelson Penzell's house." Mort tipped his chair back and folded his arms across his chest. "And these two caught the burglar climbing into Penzell's bedroom window. He was actually straddling the windowsill, one leg in and one leg out. There's no explaining that away."

"There certainly isn't," I agreed. "But that still doesn't explain why I'm here."

Mort leaned forward, his chair legs thudding against the

floor. "Yeah, that's the weird part, Mrs. F. This guy claims to know you. He says you can explain everything."

"Me? Good heavens, Mort, why would I be acquainted with a burglar?" I was astounded.

"I don't know. I thought maybe he helped with research for one of your books . . . or something," Mort finished lamely. "Okay, let's get this over with. Andy, Floyd, bring him out."

I turned toward the door to the cell block, the same one I'd watched Loretta and Andy help Coreen walk through less than forty-eight hours ago. I couldn't wait to see the faker who'd probably read my bio in the back of one of my books and knew Cabot Cove was my hometown. How far did he think it would get him?

The door opened and Andy came through. The face of the man behind him was obscured by Andy's head. What I could see of his sandy hair gave me no clue. Then he shifted his head and peered over Andy's shoulder.

"Jessica, praise the saints, you've come."

Even before I saw his face, his Irish brogue gave him away. Michael Haggerty of MI6, the British secret service.

As soon as I heard his voice a memory flashed through my mind. A few years ago in New York, Michael convinced my nephew Grady to conspire with him by not identifying me in order to keep me in an NYPD jail cell "for my own safety," and although it did turn out I was at serious risk, to this day I think they could have found a better way to handle it. *Well, Mr. Haggerty,* I thought, *turnabout is fair play.*

I took a long look, and even squinted my eyes slightly to give the impression I was studying him carefully, then said, "I'm sorry, Mort, but I've never seen this man before in my life."

Mort flicked the back of his hand toward the cell block and said, "Lock him up, fellas."

Andy and Floyd each grabbed one of Michael's arms, spun him around, and marched him back toward the door to the cells.

"Okay, now, Jess, this isn't one bit humorous. If it's New York you were thinking of, that was for your own good. This is in no way similar." Michael continued to plead until the door to the cells shut behind him and his shouting was too muffled to understand.

"Jeez, Mrs. F., I am sorry about waking you up and all, but the guy put on a good act."

I was beginning to enjoy this. "Who did he say he was?"

"First he said he was John Doubleday, Nelson Penzell's cousin from New Hampshire who'd come to straighten out family affairs. He claimed Nelson always hid a key in the old potting shed, but when he looked there he couldn't find it. What was he to do in the middle of the night without a key? He said he 'considered himself fortunate' to find an open window," Mort said.

"And Floyd and Andy discovered him." The scene I pictured was quite amusing. Michael Haggerty, who'd pulled far more dangerous antics all around the world, had been caught climbing into an unlocked bedroom window in my hometown.

"Yep, and then it got a whole lot weirder. The fellas checked the potting shed, and the door bolt was rusted and covered with grime. Probably hadn't been touched in months, never mind within the past few minutes. When they told him that, he tried to bluff his way to freedom for a while longer. Finally he realized the game was up, and he surrendered by saying. 'Okay, take me in, but then call Jessica Fletcher. She can vouch for me.' Can you imagine?"

"I certainly can." I laughed, which confused Mort further. "I may as well tell you what I do know. His name is Michael Haggerty and he works for MI6, the British secret service, and I can guarantee that is the truth," I said.

"You mean to tell me that I have a spy, an international spy, in my lockup?" Mort buried his head in his hands as if the notion was too challenging for him to comprehend.

"Exactly."

"Then why didn't you say so in the first place?" Mort was getting flustered. "You see the pickle I'm in now. What am I supposed to do with him? Call the feds?"

"I suggest you bring him back out here so we can find out what he was really doing sneaking around Nelson Penzell's house."

Floyd and Andy, who were standing a few feet away listening to all of this, looked to Mort for direction.

"Yeah, go. Bring him out." Mort pointed to the door. Then he muttered, more to himself than to me, "How do I get in these situations?"

I did feel bad about lying to Mort, even for a moment, although I was glad to have a chance to take a swipe at Michael, who marched back out from the cells so jauntily that I was almost sorry I had told the truth. Almost.

"Okay, Mr. Haggerty, you want to explain to me why a secret agent from England was snooping around the house of my murder victim?" Mort stood and folded his arms across his chest.

"Certainly. But first I have to thank Jessica for telling the truth and identifying me. You see, Sheriff, Jessica and I did have an unusual episode in New York some time ago when I left her in jail perhaps a tad longer than I should have, and, well, I hope she thinks we're even now." He looked at me with eyes pleading for forgiveness.

I shrugged, which he must have taken as tolerance, because he gave me a sunny smile; then he quickly returned to the topic at hand.

"As to your murder victim . . ." Michael stopped in midsentence, as if he needed to collect his thoughts. I hoped he wasn't using the time to make up one of his fanciful stories.

"I suppose I should call the home office, as it were, and get clearance to tell you this, but given the circumstances, I think it's best if I come clean." Michael had our rapt attention. "It's smugglers I'm after. Jewelry smugglers."

"In Cabot Cove?" Mort looked incredulous and I felt exactly the same.

Michael glanced at the mug of coffee in my hand. "Yes, there are links to an international smuggling ring right here in picturesque Cabot Cove, along with a dozen other places dotting the map." Michael settled himself comfortably in the visitors' chair next to mine and said, "Jessica, that coffee does smell good."

Mort rolled his eyes and signaled Andy, who produced a mug, filled it, and passed it to Michael, who took a deep swig and said, "Ah, that's grand, boyo, simply grand."

I was tired and irritated. Michael's dawdling along wasn't helping at all.

"Now, look, Michael. I believe you owe us all an explanation," I said.

The words were no sooner out of my mouth than Mort jumped in. "Darn right, you do. I don't care who you work for—you are still in my lockup. If you hope to get out of here anytime soon,

Jessica Fletcher & Terrie Farley Moran

you'd better start explaining what you were doing breaking into my murder victim's house."

"Of course. As the local constabulary, you are entitled to know. I've been following several threads of a group of jewel smugglers operating in Britain, Canada, and the United States," Michael said, and then stopped to sip his coffee.

I knew he always enjoyed having me struggle to get the full story out of him, so before Mort got even more upset, I asked, "And how does Nelson Penzell fit in?"

"Well, he seemed to spend a lot of time communicating with others we have on our watch list. After his name came up on more than an occasion or two, we decided to take a look at him. Unfortunately, by the time I arrived in Cabot Cove the poor man was dead."

Michael smiled at Mort with sincere innocence written all over his face, but I knew that look. There was more to the story.

Mort seemed to sense that as well. "So, with Penzell dead, you've no reason to stay in Cabot Cove. I expect you think you'll be leaving today."

"Actually, Sheriff, I've booked a room at the Hill House for the entire week. I'd like to stay on for a while. Renew my acquaintance with my dear friend Jessica and perhaps do some fishing. Unless you have an objection, of course."

Mort stiffened. "Just the opposite. I was going to suggest you stick around for a few days. You may be a superspy, but that doesn't remove you from my list of murder suspects. Andy, drive Mr. Haggerty back to the Hill House."

"Sheriff, I hesitate to mention that, much as I appreciate the lift, my rental car is parked in a side street near Nelson Penzell's house." Michael smiled apologetically.

"Fine." Mort was losing patience. "Andy, drive Mr. Haggerty to his car, and then follow him to Hill House. Check his registration while you are there and ask whoever is working the desk to make a note that we are to be notified should he attempt to check out."

Michael's smile wavered slightly, but he quickly resumed his jovial manner. "I appreciate the courtesy, and should my plans change, you'll be the first to know. Apart from Jessica, of course. May you both enjoy the rest of your day." Michael followed Andy to the front door, then turned and said, "Jessica, I will most certainly be in touch. We've got to catch up."

"What a morning," Mort said. "It is still morning, isn't it?"

"Yes, it is," I said. "And I have to go home and get ready for our next meeting."

"What meeting?"

"Coreen and her attorney are coming in a couple of hours. Have you forgotten?"

"No, that I remember. It's a meeting scheduled with you I can't recall. Oh, wait a minute. If you and Loretta Spiegel think . . ." Mort was getting frustrated.

"Calm down. Loretta knows she can't actually attend the meeting, but she would like to sit in the visitors' area while she waits for it to be over, and I agreed to wait with her. Surely you can't object to that? We'll wait in the parking lot if we have to," I said.

Mort rubbed his eyes. "Sorry, Mrs. F. I am totally exhausted. I'm trying to solve a murder and guard the boats in the harbor, and now I find out that there may be a smuggling ring doing business right under my eyes. It's like I'm tying myself in knots."

"Mort, I know you are under a lot of stress. I promise Loretta and I will not be the cause of any more of it. And I think you will find Coreen's attorney, Ms. Tremblay, to be a breath of fresh air. Some of those knots should begin to unravel quite soon."

As Floyd drove me home we watched Cabot Cove start to come alive for the day. The aroma of fresh-baked bread wafted through the open car window as we passed Sassi's Bakery. Fishermen were heading to the wharf, hoping for a good day on the water, and I saw Billy Conklin biking up and down the streets, delivering the *Cabot Cove Gazette*.

As soon as I got into the house I headed for the shower. Then I chose black gabardine slacks and a white man-tailored blouse. It was a step up from my usual jeans and plaid shirt, but I wanted to look appropriate for whatever Coreen's morning meeting would bring. I felt a great sense of relief when I came downstairs. I was nicely dressed for the day, with time to spare before Loretta was scheduled to pick me up. I hung my red blazer on the coatrack so it would be at the ready. As I headed to the kitchen to put on a pot of coffee, I noticed my computer sitting forlornly awaiting my attention. I wondered if I should turn it on and at least review my book synopsis. I half hoped that taking a quick look would jiggle loose some ideas that I was sure were in the back of my brain but just couldn't quite move forward.

My hopes went splat when the doorbell rang.

I looked at my watch. Who on earth could this be at such an early hour?

Chapter Thirteen

I pulled the door open and found Evelyn Phillips holding a copy of the *Cabot Cove Gazette*. Behind her stood a man I was sure I'd never seen before.

Evelyn thrust the paper at me. "Jessica, have a look at today's paper. Big news." Then she gestured behind her with a hitchhiker's thumb. "And it's all about him."

The man, who was wearing tan slacks with razor-sharp pleats, a white knit golf shirt, and a brown tweed blazer, blushed at the attention.

I opened the door wider and invited them both inside. "Please come into the kitchen. I was about to put a pot of coffee on the stove, unless you would prefer tea."

"Coffee is fine," Evelyn answered for both of them. "And I brought something to the party." She reached into the humongous tote she always carried and pulled out a white paper bag. "Crullers from Sassi's."

Since I still had no idea of the identity of the man was who was standing uncomfortably in my foyer, his back firmly against the door, I reached out my hand. "Good morning, and welcome. I'm Jessica Fletcher."

"Oh Lordy, where are my manners?" Evelyn said. "Jessica, this is Dan, Dan Andrews, an old friend. He's a newspaperman straight from the Big Apple. Do they still call it the Big Apple? Anyway, he used to live in New York City and now he's here." As Evelyn started walking toward my kitchen, leaving Dan and me in mid-handshake, she said over her shoulder, "And he's my replacement."

I must have looked as stunned as I felt, because Dan said under his breath, "I told her this was a bad idea."

"No," I insisted, "not at all. It's only that, well, I've had a difficult morning. You are a wonderful surprise and I am happy to meet you. Now come into the kitchen and tell me all about yourself."

He ran his hand through his hair, which was mostly white but leaned a little toward beige in some places, and said, "If you're sure. I don't want to be a bother."

I took his arm and guided him to the kitchen.

Evelyn had hung her denim jacket on the back of a chair and was already at the table munching on a cruller she'd pulled from the bag, which she'd left open on the counter, crumbs strewn in a semicircle around it. For the moment I resisted grabbing a sponge to clear the crumbs away; instead I started the coffee. Then I put the crullers on my favorite serving plate, white with bluebells dancing around the edge. By the time I finished setting the table, the coffee was ready.

As I filled our cups and passed the sugar and creamer, I noticed how uncomfortable Dan continued to be. As a welcoming gesture, I held up the serving plate to offer him a cruller, and I noticed he reached for it with his left hand.

"Oh, you're a lefty. When I was a schoolteacher some of my smartest students were lefties, but many of them had difficulties with penmanship," I said, smiling as broadly as I could. "Was that a problem for you?"

"It's hard to remember that far back." He responded to my smile with a small one of his own.

I followed up by asking how he knew Evelyn, a question made more valid by the fact that I still wasn't sure why Evelyn had brought him to my house. And I wondered what she'd meant when she said he was her replacement.

"It must have been— How long ago was it, Evelyn? Twenty-five, thirty years? Anyway, Evelyn came to work at the New York bureau of UPI, United Press International. I was already working there. That's how we met."

Evelyn interrupted. "He's too modest to tell you, but back in the day I was a rookie and Dan was my boss. I am a better reporter today because of everything I learned from him. His number one rule is, 'Hunt down the story and make sure the details are correct.'"

"Well, Dan, you must have been a terrific teacher. Evelyn is a top-notch editor and reporter. Why, the *Cabot Cove Gazette* wins statewide awards nearly every year." Praising Evelyn was something I rarely did, so these words were long overdue.

Glowing with pride, Evelyn said, "Thank you, Jessica. Coming from you, that is a high tribute indeed. And because the paper is so highly regarded, I knew I couldn't leave until I'd found the right replacement to take the *Gazette* ever higher." She finished with an upward flourish of her hand.

"Evelyn, you're serious? You are leaving the *Gazette*?"

"Not just the *Gazette*, Jessica. I am leaving Cabot Cove." Evelyn evidently had worked out the details some time ago.

I looked at Dan, who nodded his head.

"I don't understand. Why?" Between my lack of sleep and getting caught short when Evelyn showed up on my doorstep, I was befuddled.

"Jessica, I'm a rolling stone. Always have been. Ask Dan." Evelyn nodded in his direction.

"Evelyn's had a number of jobs since she left UPI. Cabot Cove seemed to have a hold on her, though. She stayed here the longest," Dan said, trying to soften the blow, giving me the impression that he was a kind man.

I turned to Evelyn. "Now what? Where will you go?"

"I have a sister living in Chicago and a cousin in Baltimore. I haven't seen either one for a while . . . not sure how long. Anyway, I will be sticking around here for the foreseeable future. I need to get Dan settled, show him the ropes and introduce him around. You can bet I'll be expecting him to garner even more awards for the *Gazette* than I ever did."

We chatted for a while and Dan relaxed enough to ask me to top off his coffee. I'd just finished pouring when the telephone rang. Aware that I had not one but two members of the press sitting in my kitchen, I hurried to the living room to answer.

Loretta began talking before I finished saying hello. "Jessica, I know it's early and Coreen's meeting at Mort's office isn't for a while, but I'm extra jumpy, and you know that's not like me."

I lowered my voice. "This isn't a good time. I will call you back in a few minutes."

"But I—"

"I have company." I was whispering, while hoping Evelyn's nose for news wouldn't lead her to the living room.

"Mort?"

"Worse. Don't *press* me." I hoped Loretta had caught my hint.

"Good grief! Evelyn Phillips?" she shrieked.

"Yes, that's right." I brought my voice back to its normal volume. "Thank you so much for calling, but I have plans for part of that day. Friends of the Library meeting. Let me check my calendar and get back to you."

"Call me as soon as she leaves," Loretta ordered.

"I certainly will. Good-bye." I hoped my tone sounded sunny and cheerful to the newshounds in my kitchen. A routine social call, nothing more.

When I returned to the kitchen there was one lonely cruller left on the platter, and Evelyn was digging in her tote. She came up with an envelope. "Here you go, Jessica. I made this copy for you."

As she held it out to me, I asked what it was.

"It's my notes on the Nelson Penzell murder. I thought you could take a look, and then we could talk. I am planning a big article on the whole sordid mess, so I'd like you to check my facts."

"Me? Shouldn't you have Mort look at this?" I put my hands behind my back to indicate that I didn't want to touch, much less see, her notes.

Evelyn dropped the envelope on the table. "Oh, definitely—he is on my list. I have plenty of copies. I am going to ask Mort, Walter Hendon, Coreen Wilson, and whoever else enters my mind to take a look."

She tapped Dan on the shoulder. "We'd better get going—we

have an appointment with the Ranieri brothers. They think I am coming to do an article on their pre-Halloween sale. You will be a surprise, Dan-o."

Dan Andrews reached for my hand and shook it warmly. "I hope our stopping by wasn't too much of an inconvenience. It was decent of you to welcome us so early in the day."

Like the tornado she often resembles, Evelyn hurried him out the door.

I walked back to the kitchen, shaking my head. Evelyn had left her envelope on my table, and I slid it on top of the refrigerator. I'd make up my mind later whether to read it.

As I cleaned up the remnants of our coffee and washed down the counter and the tabletop, I thought about Evelyn's proposal. I was positive she wasn't trying to have anyone verify her facts. It was more likely that Evelyn hoped if she talked to enough people she might somehow pick up a kernel of information that would lead to what she loved to call a "scoop." The one thing I did know for certain was that Loretta would have a complete meltdown if Evelyn so much as approached Coreen. I thought it best to put Evelyn's notes directly through my shredder and not think about them again.

I picked up the phone to return Loretta's call and chose not to tell her that Evelyn had mentioned Coreen as a potential source. We could deal with that if and when it became necessary.

Twenty minutes later I was in Loretta's car and she was driving to Coreen's house.

"Earlier I drove Coreen home to pick out her outfit for this morning's meeting. When we stopped by yesterday she packed her work smocks, jeans, and a couple of shirts, plus pajamas. Regular clothes. She is nervous about looking suitable for her meeting with Regina and Mort. As for me, I'm more worried about what she'll say than how she'll look," Loretta said. "Anyway, after we got back to my house, she decided she needed a different pair of shoes, so I dropped her off at home and told her we'd swing by to pick her up."

"Loretta," I said, "Regina Tremblay seems to be an extremely competent lawyer, and I think we can rely on her to protect Coreen from saying anything that might cause a problem for her later on. What we have to do is put together a list of people who might have wanted Nelson Penzell dead."

Loretta stopped the car in front of Coreen's apartment. "Jessica, isn't Mort going to be upset with us? Won't he resent our interfering?"

"He might," I said, "but I don't think he would object to having some help. We may not find the actual culprit, but if we can fill the field with suspects, that might make it easier for Mort to find the killer."

At that moment Coreen opened her front door and waved at us with a pair of beige kitten-heeled pumps in her hand as she came to the car.

Loretta nodded and waved back while she answered me. "Got it. We'll talk later."

When we arrived at Loretta's house, Coreen rushed to the bedroom to change her clothes.

Loretta and I were extravagant with our praise when she came down the front steps wearing a navy blue skirt with a blue and tan striped blouse. I was sure to say that her kitten heels were a perfect match for her outfit.

"Aw, thank you, Mrs. Fletcher. Coming from you that is a real comfort. You are the best-dressed lady in Cabot Cove." Coreen flushed, whether it was with pride or the awareness that she might have offended Loretta, I wasn't sure, because, stumbling on, she added, "Oh, Loretta, you always look nice, too. It's just, our work smocks . . ."

Loretta laughed. "Don't worry, Coreen. I'm not insulted. Oh, I hear a car. I thought we were going to meet Regina at the sheriff's office, but maybe I was wrong. If it is Regina, please let her in."

Coreen peeked out the window and came back into the living room in a flash. "It's that newspaper lady, and she has a man with her."

Loretta took charge instantly. "Go upstairs, Coreen, and don't come down until I call you. Perhaps, Jessica . . ."

"I think it would be best if I, too, went upstairs. There is no point in Evelyn seeing me here every time she stops by. Oh, and the man with her is a reporter. He's, ah, helping her out for a while." I thought that was the easiest explanation I could give in less than sixty seconds.

I climbed partway up the stairs and stopped, hoping to be able to hear Loretta and Evelyn. I knew they would be quite a match. I heard Loretta say this wasn't a good time for Evelyn and her "friend" to come for a visit.

Evelyn countered with "freedom of the press," and when that didn't work she said that it would be better for Coreen to talk to the local press than the Portland, Augusta, and Bangor papers and television stations, which would tear Coreen to shreds.

Instead of intimidating Loretta, Evelyn's comments infuriated her. "Get off my porch before I call Sheriff Metzger and have you and your lackey removed."

And I heard the door slam.

When I got downstairs Loretta was in the living room, scowling at the front door. She was plainly in a snit. "Jessica, how much longer are we going to have to deal with this intrusion into our lives? Coreen and Regina have to meet with Mort this morning, and I planned to open the shop this afternoon. But the salon is a public space . . . and Coreen? Should she really be at work? I thought it would help bring us back to normal, but now I'm not sure."

Before I could say anything, Coreen, who had come down the steps behind me, answered, "I can't hide forever. Regina says that as long as I tell my true story to Sheriff Metzger, I can hold my head up. And that's what I intend to do."

Coreen walked past me and gave Loretta a hug. "Don't be afraid. Everything will turn out all right. I am more than ready to go back to work and to face everyone. Besides, Regina has ordered me to never answer anyone's questions about that night, no matter who asks, unless she is with me. So I can just keep quiet."

I couldn't believe what I had heard. I felt as though I'd been thrust into one of those motion pictures where two totally opposite people are struck by some magic wand or drink an enchanted potion and—*poof!*—exchange their personalities. In this case Loretta, the strong, brave woman, was on the verge of collapse, and Coreen, the usually shaky girl, had become emboldened.

As surprised as I was at how grown-up and completely self-assured Coreen sounded, Loretta was obviously even more astonished. She took two steps back, placed her hands on Coreen's shoulders, and said, "Well, if you are ready, so am I. Regina asked us to arrive a few minutes early so you and she could talk in her car before we go inside. And after the meeting, what do you say to lunch at Mara's, my treat?"

"I say, let's go." Coreen was more confident and poised than I had ever seen her. I was grateful that Regina Tremblay had been able to instill that sureness in her, and I hoped this morning's meeting wouldn't destroy Coreen's newfound confidence.

Loretta drove into the Sheriff's Department parking lot and Regina Tremblay, dressed in a very professional dark gray suit, was leaning against the side of a blue Ford Explorer. She greeted us with a cheery smile, and then whisked Coreen into her car for what she called "a chat."

Loretta and I watched them walk across the parking lot. We were both hoping that Regina Tremblay would be able to guide Coreen out of Mort's line of vision once and for all.

Chapter Fourteen

I guess we shouldn't go inside before they do," Loretta said.

"Agreed," I said. "In fact, it might be best if we wait fifteen minutes or so after Coreen goes into the office. That will give Mort time to take them to an interview room and get settled."

"Fifteen minutes? How long do you think this meeting will take? I have clients coming in this afternoon, and I promised to buy Coreen lunch before we go to work."

I was afraid Loretta was moving into high-anxiety mode once again. I tried to reassure her. "I don't think Regina will let the meeting last for one minute longer than is absolutely necessary." Then, as a distraction, I asked, "Loretta, what do you remember about Jeremy Brewington from the last time we were here?"

"Do you mean Mr. Pompous? I remember that he barged in and demanded Mort's attention as if you and I were totally invisible. Is that who you mean?"

I nodded. "That's the one. And what else do you recall?"

"I do remember something. When he heard that Nelson Penzell had been murdered, he was even more upset than we were."

"Exactly. Mort chalked up Brewington's behavior to the old trope that big-city folks think there is never any crime in small-town USA, but I suspect there may have been more to it, that he may have had some connection to Nelson Penzell," I said.

Loretta sighed. "What more can there be? And if there is something to discover, well, neither of us knows the man."

"Think, Loretta. You and I may not know Mr. Brewington, but between us we know nearly every resident of Cabot Cove. I bet at least some of our neighbors and friends know Jeremy Brewington. I suggest that you bring his name up to everyone who comes in to get a haircut or a manicure. When small tidbits of idle gossip are strung together, you would be amazed at how they can add up."

"And you? Will you be snooping around? Who will you be talking to?" Loretta asked.

"Whoever I can. I know Brewington orders pastries from Charlene Sassi, and of course Walter Hendon would know him quite well. I suppose Gregory Leung could tell me if he is a contributor to the hospital fund-raising projects, while Julie Hecht would also know him if he is a donor to any of the many charity fund-raisers that she coordinates."

Loretta gave me an admiring glance. "Jessica, you are good at this. No wonder you write mysteries for a living."

I laughed. "I have always had a curious nature and a mind that craves organization. When those two traits mesh, lists filled with question marks start to churn around in my head and my brain doesn't settle down until I've answered every question.

Why don't we go inside and wait for Coreen's interview to be over?"

We walked into a deserted office and made ourselves comfortable in the visitors' area. Carrying some file folders, Floyd ambled through a doorway from a back room. Always polite and sociable, he waved to us.

"Hey, Mrs. Fletcher, Mrs. Spiegel. Sheriff Metzger is doing an interview right now—" Floyd stopped, possibly because he realized it was likely we were here waiting for Coreen, not Mort. "Can I get you a cup of coffee or some water? They shouldn't be much longer."

Loretta shook her head, but I asked for a glass of water. Floyd deposited the folders on the front desk, and when he brought the water to me I thanked him, and then added by way of small talk, "Mort tells me you are all working extremely hard, between the Penzell murder and the constant break-ins of boats in the harbor."

"Gorry, it's all we can do to keep up. We're all on double shifts or working extra days to try and keep everything covered." Floyd stuck his thumb in his belt and thrust out his chin, clearly proud of the job he and his colleagues were doing under adverse conditions.

"I suppose it doesn't help when someone like that Mr. . . . What was his name? Brewingham? Brewington? Yes, that was it, Brewington. When he came marching in, demanding special attention over a few scratches on a cabinet and some overturned furniture, I couldn't believe how rude he was. I don't really know him. Does he live around Cabot Cove or just sail in on that yacht of his?"

"He comes and goes. He owns a house up by the ridge; Eve

Simpson found it for him. Nice view of the harbor—really of the whole bay, right out to the Atlantic," Floyd said. "When he is in town we always know it, because the man is full of grumbles. Why, one time he came in and wanted me to go out and summons old Mr. Lawson for riding his tractor on Ragland Road and not pulling off to the side so Mr. Brewington could drive past in that fancy Corvette of his. I mean, how else is Mr. Lawson supposed to get his tractor to the repair shop down to Clementsville? Not like you can put a tractor in a suitcase and carry it—leastwise, that's what Sheriff Metzger said when he was trying to explain why we weren't going to summons Mr. Lawson, or even warn him not to take his tractor on the road again."

"And how did Mr. Brewington respond? I'm sure he wasn't polite." I gave Floyd a knowing look to encourage him to tell me more.

"Oh, no, ma'am. Between you and me, I don't think Mr. Brewington knows the meaning of the word. He likes to give orders and expects to be obeyed. Doesn't seem to know we don't work for him."

The office telephone rang and Floyd excused himself to answer it.

Loretta whispered, "You make it look so easy. A little casual conversation and we have confirmed Brewington is a man who does not like to be ignored or crossed in any way." Then she laughed. "I'm wasting my time at the beauty parlor, collecting gossip and passing it on from one client to another. With a few well-placed questions I could probably start my own blackmail business."

When she saw the look of dismay on my face, Loretta said, "I'm kidding, Jessica, kidding."

Coreen's interview with Mort took longer than I expected, so I was doubly glad that I had met Regina Tremblay and had confidence in her ability to protect Coreen. After sitting for nearly an hour, I stood and began pacing back and forth. I asked Loretta if she wanted to stretch her legs, and she shook her head. Floyd offered to refill my water and offered Loretta a drink. We both declined.

Loretta was getting jumpier by the minute. And with Floyd sitting at his desk so nearby, I couldn't distract her with conversation about other potential suspects.

From somewhere in the office I heard a door open and then close. A minute later Andy walked into the room. He guessed why we were there and gave us a cheery smile. "Good morning, ladies. The meeting is almost over. Coreen should be finished and ready to go in a few minutes."

Although we were several feet apart, I could feel the tension melt out of Loretta's body.

"Oh, Jess, she's not under arrest. Coreen is coming home." Loretta sprang from her chair and gave me a celebratory hug. "Please join us for lunch. I would like you to hear whatever Coreen and Regina can tell us. I know you understand all this stuff."

I nodded even though I was fairly certain Regina would be extremely reticent about their interview with Mort, and that she would instruct Coreen to keep mum as well.

Mort came into the room, not the least bit surprised to see us. "Coreen is lucky to have such good friends waiting for her. Ms. Tremblay asked if she and her client could use the room privately for a few minutes. They'll be right out."

"So she's done? You are finished talking with Coreen?" Loretta turned to me. "Jessica, the nightmare is over."

By the look on Mort's face I could see he was about to give her bad news. "Not exactly finished, Loretta," he said as gently as he could. "It's more like we're finished talking for today."

Loretta took a step forward, opened her mouth, and then thought better of saying whatever she was about to say. I hastened to fill the void.

"Thank you, Mort. I know you treated Coreen with courtesy and respect. We appreciate that."

He flushed ever so slightly and gave me a brief nod before he turned and walked into the recesses of the building. The upside of being a sheriff in a small town like Cabot Cove was experiencing the natural beauty of the surroundings, the friendliness of everyone you meet, and the lasting relationships you can form over time. But I understood there was a downside. Nearly every crime in Cabot Cove was committed by someone the sheriff knew, be it a casual acquaintance or even someone whom he might have considered a friend. I'm sure that often made him feel grim while he was conducting the investigative work and the interrogations and, when the criminal was definitively identified, making the arrest.

I encouraged Loretta to sit down with me again, and once we did she leaned in and whispered, "It's not over, is it? That's what Mort was telling us. It's not over."

"Loretta, we have to look on the bright side. Coreen has a competent attorney and she is not being held in a cell. That gives us time to look around at who else might have had a reason to kill Nelson Penzell. Mort has to find a killer. We don't. We only need to push a few suspects in front of him. Perhaps one will be the actual murderer."

Loretta shushed me and pointed.

Regina was holding Coreen's arm as they walked through the doorway toward us. Coreen looked tired and a little worse for wear, but she was in total control of herself and that was a major plus. Kudos to Regina Tremblay; she had clearly done her job.

As we stood to greet them, Loretta asked, "How did it go?"

Coreen stayed silent and looked at Regina, which indicated to me that she was likely following directions Regina had given her in their private meetings. Something along the lines of *When questioned, don't answer unless I tell you to do so.*

Regina's dark hair swung from side to side as she looked around to be sure there was no one within earshot, and then she said, "The meeting went extremely well. Coreen was steadfast and clear in her answers. The sheriff has no reason to continue to consider her a possible suspect except for the obvious two reasons. First, she was found near the victim, covered in his blood . . ."

Coreen visibly shuddered at the description or, more likely, the memory of what she'd endured.

"And second, there doesn't appear to be any other suspects," Regina finished.

Loretta and I exchanged a fleeting glance. We would immediately begin to work on expanding our suspect list in the hope of raising enough what-ifs that we could present it to Mort.

As a group we began to move toward the front door. Loretta invited Regina to join us for lunch but Regina declined, saying she had a work commitment.

Loretta had her hand on the doorknob and said, "Well, the next time you are in town be sure and leave time in your schedule for a meal. We'd all like to get to know you better."

I was off to the side, so when Loretta opened the door I heard the commotion, but I had to step forward in order to see that

Evelyn Phillips, the young man she often used as the *Gazette*'s photographer, and Evelyn's friend Dan Andrews were standing outside the doorway, lying in wait for Coreen.

Evelyn, in her brashest newshound voice, demanded, "Tell us everything, Coreen. Let the community know what you told Sheriff Metzger."

At the same time the photographer was clicking away. "Look this way, everybody. Don't look at Evelyn—look at me."

Dan Andrews was a couple of feet behind Evelyn, watching the entire scene, pen and pad at the ready.

Loretta went into mother-lion-protecting-a-cub mode. She pushed Coreen behind her and pointed her finger at Evelyn. "You get out of our way right now."

"Loretta"—Evelyn dropped down to her most reasonable tone of voice—"a man is dead. Coreen was on the scene and now she has been interviewed by Sheriff Metzger, with her lawyer in tow. Can't you see how that would be newsworthy to the readers of the *Cabot Cove Gazette*?"

Regina Tremblay stepped up to stand side by side with Loretta. "For the record, I am Miss Wilson's attorney, and I have instructed her to speak to no one, not even to her employer, Ms. Spiegel, about the events surrounding Mr. Penzell's unfortunate demise."

"Where does that leave the free press?" Evelyn was more curious than belligerent.

Regina looked Evelyn straight in the eye. "I can promise you—off the record, of course—that as soon as it is practical for Miss Wilson to go public with her story, she will do an exclusive one-on-one with you or your designee."

Evelyn raised her eyebrows, and her head bounced slightly. "I can live with that." Then she pursed her lips. "Just know that if you cross me, the word will get out and your name will be trash with every newspaper editor in the state of Maine."

Regina smiled as though they were discussing what they were going to wear to the Maine Press Association's annual dinner. "There is no need for coercion. My word is a sufficient guarantee. Now, if you will excuse us . . ."

Evelyn turned to the parking lot, with her photographer right behind her. Dan Andrews gave me a wave and a nod, and then followed them.

When we got to Loretta's car, Regina put her hand on Coreen's shoulder and said, for our benefit as much as Coreen's, "You did a terrific job today. You told the truth while following my directions. Your answers were concise and you didn't answer any questions without my permission. Stay the course. You will get out of this with your head held high." Then she turned toward her blue Explorer and said, "Good day, ladies."

We piled into Loretta's aging Mustang. As she backed out of her parking space, Loretta said, "Is everybody set for lunch at Mara's?"

I wondered how Coreen would answer. She'd had a stressful morning, and she was intending to go back to the beauty parlor and face her clients this afternoon. I feared the stares of other diners would be a bridge too far for a young woman who'd been more or less sheltered up to now.

Coreen didn't hesitate. "Blueberry pancakes with a side of bacon and a double shot of orange juice. Yum."

Loretta parked a few doors from Mara's, and as we walked along I noticed that crime-scene tape was still denying access to La Peinture , which brought Angus Michaud to mind. I'd have to bring him up as a topic of gossip while we ate our lunch. Coreen might have more of an idea of his relationship with Nelson Penzell than she had previously told us. Perhaps . . .

"Jessica! Jessica!" My train of thought was interrupted by someone shouting my name.

"That man is waving at you, Mrs. Fletcher," Coreen said, pointing to someone leaning across the front seat of a light gray Toyota Camry. He stretched his arm through the open passenger window and signaled for me to come closer.

Michael Haggerty.

Chapter Fifteen

I had no intention of getting involved in whatever impulsive mission Michael had in mind.

I took a few steps closer to the car so I could speak in a low voice. "Michael, whatever you want, I don't have time for you now. I have a lunch date with my friends, and then I have to get home to work on my synopsis. It's due in a few days."

Everything I said sounded completely reasonable to me but didn't touch Michael in the slightest.

"Ah, but you see, I'm in need of assistance. I find myself in a bit of a pickle." His rakish smile was set on "super charm," but I wasn't having any.

I looked back where Loretta and Coreen were waiting for me. Coreen patiently, Loretta with an impatient, perplexed look on her face. "My friends are —"

"Jess, there are lives at stake." Michael's entire face switched from charming to sincere. It was as if he'd only to push a button to shift around until he found a look that would persuade me. And if he didn't find a look that worked, he seemed sure his next sentence would. "And the reason I need your assistance is that my problem could relate to your unsolved murder."

I threw my hands in the air. Even if Michael was using Nelson Penzell's death to entice me to help him in some secret-agent nonsense that had nothing to do with the murder, for Coreen's sake I couldn't ignore him. He might be telling the truth. "Give me a minute."

I explained to Loretta that a friend had a crisis and I would be in touch later this afternoon. I gave them both a hug and told Coreen to enjoy her pancakes. Then, against my better judgment, I got into the Toyota.

Michael floored the gas pedal and the car took off like a shot.

I snapped my seat belt on and tugged to be sure it was secure. "Slow down, Michael—this is the busy part of town. You're liable to have an accident." Then, as he made a left turn, narrowly missing a milk delivery truck that had to swerve out of his way, I amended, "Or cause one."

"We have to get to Hill House as soon as we can. I need you to talk to a man," he said.

"Seriously? I already spoke to Sheriff Metzger on your behalf. That's the only get-out-of-jail-free card you'll get from me." I folded my arms across my chest. How many times could he expect me to go to bat for him?

"I don't need you to speak on my behalf. I need you to use that grand Jessica Fletcher eloquence to keep someone occupied to give me the opportunity to search his hotel room."

I was appalled. "I'll do no such thing. If the sheriff's deputies find you in another attempt to commit burglary, Queen Elizabeth herself couldn't persuade Mort to release you from the cells."

"Jessica, there's a chance—just a chance, mind you—that Clark Geddings had something to do with Nelson Penzell's murder. Don't you want me to see what I can find out? Suppose there is a connection."

But my mind had wandered further afield. "What did you say the man's name was?"

"Clark Geddings. He purports to be—"

"I know. He's a real estate agent from Boston who scours the Maine coast looking for properties for his upscale clients. My friend Eve Simpson is our local Realtor, and she ran into him at a business event very recently."

"Now, there's an opportune introduction. Listen." Michael pulled into the Hill House parking lot. "I only need a few minutes."

I wasn't warming up to the idea. "And I'm supposed to walk up to a man I've never seen before and say, 'Hi. I'm Jessica Fletcher, and you're Clark Geddings—can we chat?' Don't you think he'll wonder how I know him?"

"All taken care of." Michael slipped his hand into his pocket, pulled out a small white card, and gave it to me. "He has his picture printed on his business card. He hands them out like jelly beans at Easter. He'll never question how you know who he is, but if he does, you have the card."

It was remarkable that Geddings didn't have a card left to give to Eve at the real estate agents' event but Michael somehow managed to have one.

Inside the lobby of the Hill House, Michael maneuvered until we had a view of the dining room without actually standing in the doorway. "See, Jessica—there he is, third table along the far wall. Dark hair. Blue suit and striped tie. Now, you go and dazzle him. Get me as much time as you can. I'll stand right here when I'm finished. When you see me you can wrap up the conversation."

Michael, confident I'd go along with his plan, hurried to the staircase.

When I entered the restaurant the maître d' on duty greeted me warmly. "Mrs. Fletcher, so nice to see you again. Are you lunching alone today? I have an available table with a view of the mountainside."

"No, not today, I'm afraid, Joseph. Deadlines, you know." And I sighed as if I were carrying a heavy burden up a steep hill. "Actually, I stopped in to have a word with Mr. Geddings."

"Of course. Let me escort you," Joseph said.

When we reached Geddings's table Joseph said, "Mrs. Fletcher is here, Mr. Geddings," and before Clark Geddings could either understand or object, Joseph pulled out a chair for me. I thanked him and sat down. Geddings's face was awash with confusion.

I had devised a strategy to keep Geddings busy, but once I saw his reaction to Joseph's introduction I decided to embellish it. Jessica, who might want to sell her house and move to Boston, was replaced by J.B., who was thinking of starting a retreat colony for mystery writers in Cabot Cove.

"Mr. Geddings, I am so sorry to intrude on your meal," I gushed, "but when I saw you, well, I just had to take the opportunity to seek your advice."

A flash of impatience crossed his face, but he quickly replaced it with a forced smile. "How can I help you, Mrs.— Um, I'm sorry. I didn't catch your name."

"Gracious me. I am J. B. Fletcher, internationally bestselling mystery author. Surely you've read my books. I've been told everyone has."

"In that case, I'm sure I have. Now, if you will excuse me . . ." He signaled the waiter for his bill and put both hands on the table as if he was going to push out from it and leave.

I pressed my hand firmly on the crook of his elbow to impede him from standing. "But you haven't heard my proposal. Why, Eve Simpson told me that you were the one person who could help her make the Cabot Cove Writers' Colony a reality."

"Mrs. Fletcher, I have met Ms. Simpson and she seems to be a highly qualified real estate professional, but I am not at all sure what you are talking about." Geddings was losing patience with me and I was running out of tricks.

"Really?" I strove for haughtiness. "I am surprised at Eve. She is generally far more efficient than that. When she told me that she met you at that conference, or dinner—whatever—the other night, I assumed she'd outlined the project and you were intrigued enough to jump on board. I mean, we are talking about at least a dozen houses, possibly more."

Geddings leaned back in his chair and I removed my hand from his arm. The fish had gone after the bait, and now my hook had him.

"Mrs. Fletcher, that does sound like an extraordinary project. Perhaps you could briefly describe your proposal."

"Well, as you know, we writers require solitude and to be surrounded by beauty for inspiration. So many writers of, shall we say, my stature own homes in cities like Los Angeles, New York, Chicago, and, naturally, Boston. But when a writer needs to commune with nature to revive their muse, where can he or she go? Unless they have a cottage in the countryside awaiting them . . ."

"I see where this is going and I am definitely interested." He looked at his watch, turning his wrist so that I could see it was the inimitable Cartier Tank watch. I'm sure he wore it as an understated sign of his success. "Unfortunately, I have a meeting shortly. Please tell Eve Simpson to expect my call, and we three can have a meeting, perhaps a leisurely dinner, to discuss the possibilities."

I looked at the open doorway. Michael was nowhere to be seen.

Geddings reached across the table for the brown leather folder that held his bill. Before he could pick it up I dropped my hands on the table, and the fingers of my left hand just happened to land on the folder.

I giggled like a schoolgirl who'd finally met her favorite singer. "I can't tell you how pleased I am to have run into you completely by happenstance today. You are simply the answer to my prayers. The Cabot Cove Writers' Colony is"—Michael was waving frantically from the far side of the doorway—"going to make you very rich. Now I really must dash."

Geddings was still saying good-bye when I pushed out of my chair and hurried to the door. I did remember my manners long enough to wish Joseph a good afternoon. I would have to remember to slip him a generous tip the next time I ate in the dining room. He was far more help to me today than he would ever know.

As soon as I reached Michael he steered me toward the front door. "We have to go. Hurry."

I followed along. "Am I right in guessing you found something helpful? Something related to Penzell's murder?"

Michael tapped his key fob. His car beeped once and the locks opened. "Get in and duck down."

I had no idea what we were doing, but I sat in the passenger seat and scrunched down. Michael did the same behind the steering wheel. "We just made it. Here he comes."

Clark Geddings came down the Hill House stairs and walked purposefully to a dark green Honda CR-V. He started his engine, and Michael immediately turned his key.

"Jessica, do you know a shop owner named Roger Wilburne?" Michael asked as he pulled out of his parking space and began to drive slowly to the exit.

"Well, not personally, but his very upscale jewelry store is on Evergreen Street in Constant, one town over. Michael, where are we going? Are you following Clark Geddings?"

"Well, I am and I'm not. I found a scrap of paper on the boyo's night table that said he was to meet Roger Wilburne in his shop. The meeting time is set for a few minutes from now. So I would be following Geddings having no idea where he is going, but since I have a charming navigator by my side, we can take our time."

I had trouble keeping the frustration out of my voice. "Michael, you could have left me at the Hill House. I may not drive a car, but I do know that as soon as I told you the street and the town your GPS could have gotten you there just as well as I can. And besides, with so little traffic, we're keeping Geddings well in sight."

"Ah, but then I would be denying myself the pleasure of your company. You must confess this is a bit o' fun. Which of your many personas did you use on the unsuspecting man?" Michael asked.

"World-famous mystery writer," I admitted.

"Gets 'em every time." Michael chuckled, and then turned serious. "Thank you for your help today. I suppose you deserve to know what is going on. The smuggling ring we are tracking operates with bases in Canada, the United States, and Great Britain. Right now they are moving rare New South Wales black opals out of Australia and into countries where the market for unusual jewels makes it worth their while."

"America and Canada come to mind," I said. "What makes these black opals so special? Careful, Michael—he's slowing down. We're nearing Constant."

Michael lessened his pressure on the accelerator slightly. "Well, most opals are pale in color, but black opals have carbon and iron oxides that darken their base so that the colors within become more vibrant. I've seen some that remind me of the northern lights up in your Alaska."

"And what, may I ask, is MI6's interest in the jewels? Lovely as they may be, I don't quite understand your involvement. Oh, look—he's stopping, and there is Wilburne's shop." I pointed to a storefront across the street and halfway down the block.

Michael slid into a parking spot at the curb, and we watched as Clark Geddings got out of his car. He crossed the street and sauntered past Wilburne's Jewelry. He walked to the corner, crossed Evergreen Street, and walked back toward his car. When he reached it, he opened the passenger door and leaned inside. He appeared to be rummaging around in the glove compartment. I wondered aloud what he might be looking for.

"Not looking for—looking at," Michael said. "Should anyone be watching, he is pretending he can't find something in his car, and in the meantime he is watching for a signal from Wilburne."

At that very moment a woman and a lanky gray-haired man with a neatly trimmed beard came out of the store. They had a short conversation, and then the woman walked down the block. The man glanced around casually and then stepped inside, hung a CLOSED sign on the windowpane that filled most of the door-frame, and closed the door behind him.

Geddings stood up, locked his car door, and strode casually across the street and directly into the jewelry shop.

"It's going down right now." Michael's voice was tense yet excited. "I'd best see what the boyos are plotting. Jessica, you wait here. I shouldn't be more than a couple of minutes." He thrust a twenty-dollar bill in my hand. "But if you should get so much as an inkling of trouble, call yourself a cab and get back to Cabot Cove. I can handle this end."

"But, Michael, I don't think—" Before I could finish my objection, he was out of the car and slowly jogging across Evergreen Street. He bent to fiddle with the door lock for a few seconds, and then I watched as he slipped inside.

Chapter Sixteen

I sat in the car, my eyes glued to the front door of Wilburne's Jewelry. I was getting more fidgety as the minutes ticked by. Partly to keep myself busy, I texted Eve Simpson.

If you receive a call from Clark Geddings, do not answer him until you speak to me.

Knowing that Eve loved intrigue, I added, Top secret. Although I supposed "big business deal" would have piqued her curiosity even more. Unfortunately there was no deal, and I was well aware that I might have ruined her chances of closing any future deals with Geddings. Of course, if he was a jewel smuggler, that might have been all for the best.

I kept expecting to see cars from the local sheriff's office soaring down the street with flashing lights, their sirens hushed. I wasn't sure if Michael's trouble would come from the sheriff's deputies or the men he was spying on. Either way, I wouldn't be able to relax until he was safely in the car again.

Finally the shop door opened and Michael did his slow jog back to the car. He slid behind the steering wheel, turned the key in the ignition, and pulled away in his customary Batman style—semi-flying.

"Well? What did you find out?" I asked as he steered the car back the way we'd come.

"I overheard just enough. Bad luck to me, there was a moment I stepped on a creaky floorboard and Wilburne called out, 'Who's there? We're closed.' I ducked under a counter. He came in from the back room, checked that the door was locked, and returned to finish his conversation.

"Nerve-racking as that was, making my entrance was even more so. When I break into a store I have not visited earlier, it is stressful not to know if there is a shopkeeper's bell on the door while I am picking the lock. All in a day's work, I say, but still nerve-racking."

"Michael, enough of your silliness. What did you learn?" I asked.

"Well, in no particular order, I can now confirm that Geddings and Wilburne are part of the smuggling ring. And so was your murder victim, Nelson Penzell. The inconvenient death of Mr. Penzell has left them without a contact in Cabot Cove. Geddings intends to approach someone named Michaud but is unsure how to go about it or how the offer will be received," he said.

"Michael, we have to tell Mort. I have been struggling to come up with a name, somebody, anybody, who might have had a reason to kill Penzell, and move suspicion away from Coreen—she found his body shortly after he was killed. But she's a sweet, timid girl who wouldn't harm a—"

"Slow down, Jessica." Michael stretched his arm in front of me as if we were coming to an abrupt stop and I weren't wearing a seat belt. "Much as I'd like to help your friend, we need to keep this information between ourselves for now."

I was outraged. "Michael, you can't expect me to keep quiet about Geddings and Wilburne when one or both of them could have killed Nelson Penzell. And you already told Mort that you were here investigating smugglers. All you have to do is tell him who they are and that Nelson Penzell was one of them."

"Ah, if only life was that simple." Michael pulled off the roadway and stopped on a patch of grass next to a stand of red spruce trees. He turned off the ignition and sat with both hands on the steering wheel.

When he looked at me his face was so serious that I knew there was more complexity in his investigation than he'd told me about so far.

"Earlier you asked me why MI6 has such an interest in a jewelry-smuggling ring. And you were right to question it. Normally we would leave such criminal activity to Interpol or the local police in each involved country."

He looked me directly in the eye to be sure I was receiving his message.

"But there is more to this case than smuggling black opals," I suggested.

"Now you've got it. Some of the, shall I say, less friendly nations have taken an interest in this smuggling ring as a possible way to pass highly coded classified information along with the jewels. We're not sure if the smugglers themselves are aware of this interest, but we're certainly aware. And we're watching very, very closely."

"Michael, I do understand—really, I do—but Coreen is in danger of getting arrested for murder. I can't let that happen." My brain felt as though it were tumbling in a clothes dryer.

"Jessica, I can't promise that your friend Sheriff Metzger won't continue to suspect the young Coreen, perhaps even pester her with interrogations and the like, but I can promise she won't actually be arrested and convicted. Worse comes to worst, I'll confess to the murder myself and run them all in circles." Michael let out a hearty laugh, as if confessing to a murder he hadn't committed were the most entertaining thought he'd had in a long time. "But I have to protect my case. The security of a number of nations, including your own, is at stake."

I could feel myself weakening. "How much longer?"

"Shouldn't be long at all. I need to find out who is running the operation here. Who's the kingpin, so to speak. That's the person we want to nab, because that is the person those less-than-friendly nations will be contacting. In fact, they may have already done so. Once we can make an arrest, the kingpin will sing like a bird. They always do, if only to get the charge of espionage off the table," Michael finished, and looked at me expectantly.

"I suppose I could keep this confidential for a while longer, but, Michael, promise me you won't pull one of your disappearing acts and leave Coreen in the lurch," I cautioned.

"You're a good woman, you are. Your young friend is lucky to have you in her corner. And so am I—lucky to have you in mine." Michael turned the key in the ignition and headed to Cabot Cove.

I was so deep in thought when we reached the outskirts of town that Michael had to ask me twice where I wanted to go. I opted for home.

As I hung up my jacket, I realized I was starved. The thought of Charlene Sassi's rye bread with a nice hunk of cheese, an apple, and a cup of tea had my mouth watering. When I saw my computer patiently waiting for me on the dining table, I pushed the on button, gave it a pat, and said, "Soon, I promise, but first, lunch."

I stood at the sink, washing my hands, and made a firm decision. Michael Haggerty could spend his time looking for smugglers and spies. I was more interested in clearing Coreen.

I filled the kettle, and when I turned off the water I heard a knock on my back door. Eve Simpson was smiling at me through the glass pane. When I opened the door she twirled in, showing off a well-fitting suede vest-and-skirt ensemble over a white cable-knit sweater.

"*Très moderne*, don't you think?" Eve turned around more slowly to give me a close-up view.

"You look elegant, as always," I said, and then put the kettle on the stove. "Can I interest you in a cup of tea? If you haven't had lunch, I have plenty of fruit and cheese."

Eve pulled a chair away from the table and sat down. "I'd love a cup of tea. I stopped by because you have completely elevated my curiosity. Shortly after I received your mysterious text, who should call me but Clark Geddings?"

"You didn't—" I caught myself before I chastised her without knowing what she'd said or done.

"Of course not. I heeded your direction, but I did listen to the message he left, and that's when I realized you wanted to speak to me personally about the proposal for the writers' colony before he and I conferred. That makes perfect business sense. The idea is *magnifique*. I don't know why I didn't think of it years ago." Eve was ecstatic.

I knew I had no choice but to burst Eve's bubble. There was no gentle way, so I just came out with it.

"Eve, there is no writers' colony proposal. It is a completely made-up excuse I used so that I could speak to Clark Geddings. I am so sorry that I mentioned you to him. It was spur-of-the-moment and it was completely thoughtless of me." I was relieved to hear the kettle whistle so I could busy myself making tea to give Eve some time to absorb what I'd told her.

I set the table for our tea and placed a bowl of fruit and a plate of cheese in between us. I put a few slices of rye bread on a saucer, and then I sat down.

Eve looked at me skeptically. She was undeniably puzzled, and understandably so. I wasn't sure how I was going to keep Michael's secrets and yet explain myself to Eve, but I knew I had to try.

"You see, I was over at Hill House and someone pointed Mr. Geddings out to me," I started, not entirely sure how I would finish.

"Who pointed him out? And I have to wonder why he didn't let me know he was coming to Cabot Cove when we spoke at the dinner in Bar Harbor the other night." Eve was getting more confused by the moment.

I decided to come closer to the truth. "Eve, a person I can't name at this time pointed out Clark Geddings to me as a possible friend of Nelson Penzell's. With only a moment to come up with something to say, I—well, I used your name. I am truly sorry to have involved you. My only purpose was to help Coreen."

Eve's excitement had drained away, and I could see the disappointment creep into her face as she came to fully realize the big moneymaker she thought was on the horizon was nothing more than an illusion.

Finally she said, "I am beginning to understand. You were undercover, so to speak."

I lowered my eyes and gave a brief nod. Guilty as charged.

Eve leaned back in her chair. "I suppose I should have realized. There was one thing that struck me as bizarre about Clark's telephone message. He began by saying that he'd met the famous writer J. B. Fletcher. I couldn't imagine why he was using your nom de plume rather than referring to you as Jessica or even Mrs. Fletcher, but I glossed right over it after I heard the rest of the message."

"Eve, believe me, I am truly sorry that the phone message from Geddings got your hopes up. I intended to speak with you before you heard from him so you would know that it was all a scam. He acted more quickly than I anticipated."

Eve took a long sip of tea, then set her cup back on its saucer. "Jessica, I am disappointed that I won't be making oodles of money. But on the bright side, I didn't lose out on a project. The project never existed. So there was nothing *I did* that cost me the development."

"That's true." I folded my hands on the table and waited. I could see Eve had more to say and was figuring out how to say it.

"You said you needed to speak to Clark Geddings in order to help Coreen." Eve hesitated, then asked, "And did you find out anything that might benefit her?"

Now it was my turn to hesitate. I did find out that Nelson Penzell was involved with a ring of international smugglers, but I couldn't tell Eve. I'd already promised Michael I would keep that information secret, even from Mort, for the time being. I decided to continue being honest but evasive.

"I did learn some bits and pieces. I can tell you that much in the strictest confidence. But there are some things that don't add up, and I need to find out more before I can put all those bits and pieces together."

Eve smiled. "Jessica, if, in your efforts to support Coreen, my professional hopes get dashed, well, as I said, there was no development—not my fault." She glanced at the wall clock. "Oh heavens, I have an appointment to show a house up near the ridge to some New York socialite looking for, and I quote, 'something modern in an old-fashioned place where I can hide from my friends.' Fortunately the current owners gutted the old Taylor place, so it's Cabot Cove on the outside but definitely Fifth Avenue on the inside."

As we stood, I said, "I've been meaning to ask you: Jeremy Brewington lives somewhere near the ridge, doesn't he?"

"Near it? He lives right on top of it. Mr. Brewington bought that hideous but pristine semi-castle right at the edge of the ridge more than a year ago. For all that it cost, he doesn't spend much time there. He wanders up and down the coast on that showy yacht of his. Up the Bay of Fundy to Nova Scotia and down the coast to Boston, sometimes even New York, from what I have heard. I'm not sure why he keeps a house here at all."

As Eve described his lifestyle she gave me the kernel of an idea why the house would come in handy for Jeremy Brewington, but I kept that hunch to myself.

Eve tugged the bottom of her vest and stood tall. "And do I look like the most successful real estate agent on the Maine coast?" She was only half joking.

"You will wow them!" I said, and I meant it.

I'd closed the door behind Eve and begun to straighten the residue of our lunch when the phone rang. *What now?*

I lifted the receiver and was happily surprised when my "Hello?" was answered with a delightful Scottish burr.

"Lass, it's been too long since I heard your lovely voice."

It was my dear friend Chief Inspector George Sutherland of Scotland Yard. And he was correct. It had been too long.

Chapter Seventeen

Some years ago I had taken a trip to London at the invitation of my mentor, the long-reigning queen of British mystery writers, Marjorie Ainsworth. Over the years, I cherished her friendship and guidance. I welcomed any opportunity to spend time with her, although I will admit that on this particular visit I was saddened to see how much she had aged and that she had become confined to a wheelchair. But her personality never faltered; she remained warm and loving. Being in her home, listening to her wry humor along with her pearls of wisdom, buoyed my spirits immensely. But I was somewhat disappointed to discover I did not have Marjorie all to myself. I was merely one of a number of houseguests she planned on entertaining that weekend.

Tragically, on my first night in Marjorie's home, a strange sound woke me in the darkened early-morning hours. When I explored the origins of the sound, I was horrified to find Marjorie in her room with a dagger thrust in her chest.

I'm sure it was because Marjorie was a beloved figure of immense national importance that the chief constable for the area wasted no time in notifying Scotland Yard, and Chief Inspector George Sutherland was sent to investigate. What I remember most of our initial meeting was that George cut quite a gallant figure. He was well over six feet tall and impeccably dressed. I thought he was quite dashing in his well-pressed tweed suit. And when he looked directly at me, I confess that I found his green eyes to be captivating.

Of course, solving the murder was rather complex, but George was determined, and he was also quite willing to share information and listen to the ideas of the American writer who'd discovered the body. By the time I left England and returned to Cabot Cove it was clear that he and I enjoyed each other's company, and through the ensuing years we'd remained, well, at least friends, with something more remaining a possibility that neither of us was quite ready to act upon.

We exchanged the usual opening pleasantries and assured each other of our continued good health. Then George told me that he was going to be traveling to Paris in a few months for an international law enforcement convention.

"So, bonnie lass, I thought if I gave you enough notice I might be able to entice you to meet me in Paris for a few days on either side of the convention." George's tone was warm and hopeful, but not so much that I felt pressure.

What I did feel was unexpectedly giddy at the thought of spending a few days touring the City of Light with an appealing gentleman by my side. George Sutherland certainly filled that bill. I dug through the pile of papers next to my computer and picked up the calendar I used to keep track of my work chores: due dates, rewrites, publicity tours, and the like. "What were those dates again, George?"

As soon as I turned to the page that held the month he mentioned, I groaned. "Oh, George, I am sorry. I have a book due on my editor's desk exactly two weeks after your conference. While you are enjoying Paris, I will be knee-deep in chapter rewrites and searching for plot holes that will need to be filled."

Even as I said it, the thought flitted through the back of my mind that perhaps my "ultrabusy" work schedule was just an excuse I was using to prevent my friendship with George from progressing. Living on opposite sides of the Atlantic, we would have to force ourselves to make time to be together. Perhaps I was not quite ready to do that. *Maybe the next time,* I thought, *or the time after that.*

"Well, lass, there's nothing to be done for it. I'll be walking the streets of Paris alone while you will be filling plot holes. Tell me, does it take a large shovel and a bucket full of words to fill every plot hole you find?"

I appreciated that George's voice remained cheerful. I hoped I could take that as a sign he wasn't ready to give up on me just yet. I laughed and said, "Sometimes two or even three buckets, but never fear—I will get it done."

"Of that I have no doubt." And again I could hear the warmth in his voice, which I found comforting even with an entire ocean between us.

"You are kind," I said, and we each became quiet, enjoying the silent company of the person at the other end of the phone line. After a moment I broke the trance. "By the way, I wonder if you've run across Michael Haggerty in any of your cases that might touch on international issues."

"Can't say that I have. At least, not for several years." Then George realized there was one likely reason I would bring up Michael's name. "Don't tell me. He's there, isn't he? What is it this time? Money launderers? Gunrunners? Counterfeiters?"

"Let's just say smugglers for now. I'll tell you the rest the next time I see you."

"That's my lass, discreet about the details of someone else's case while letting me know there's hope for a dinner date sometime in our future." Through the phone I heard a polite knock on his office door. George said, "Work calls. Good-bye for now," to me, and then he was gone.

I sat with the telephone in my hand, reliving our conversation, silently chiding myself for not throwing caution to the wind and flying off to Paris. Then I pushed the idea out of my head and sat at my computer, trying to put the puzzle pieces of my synopsis together. Once or twice George Sutherland tried to creep back into my consciousness, but I soundly rejected him and focused on developing the perfect murder for my protagonist to solve. I was deep in the highways and byways of Philadelphia when I heard my kitchen door open.

"Jess, I've often told you, you should lock this door when you are not in the kitchen." Seth Hazlitt was chastising me sight unseen.

I hit SAVE on my document and called from the dining room, "In here, Seth. And yes, I know. I should have locked the door when Eve left."

"Eve Simpson was here, eh? What was it this time—her latest male conquest or some Boston millionaire making an irresistible offer for your house?" I could hear Seth pull at a chair and settle himself at the kitchen table. "Those are Eve's only topics of interest, as far as I know."

I walked into the kitchen, took the fruit bowl off the counter, and placed it in front of Seth. "Try the apples."

"Don't mind if I do." Seth picked up an apple and began polishing it on his shirt.

"Really, Seth, I would think you, as a doctor, would be more fastidious. Haven't you been wearing that shirt all day? Besides, I washed those apples when I brought them home. But if you must . . ." I took a clean dish towel out of the drawer and handed it to him.

He buffed the apple with the towel. "Are you happy now?" he asked before he took a bite.

"Yes, I am." I felt myself relax. "Oh, Seth, you know I am always happy to see you. It's just this darn synopsis. I can't quite get it together."

"Well, if that's your problem, I may have arrived with a solution in hand." Seth grinned like the proverbial cat that had swallowed the most delicious canary.

What could he possibly . . . Then I realized: "You spoke to Dr. Leung."

"I most certainly did, and Gregory is expecting us at eleven tomorrow morning for your introduction, up close and personal, to a gamma camera."

"I've been doing some research so I won't seem totally ignorant of the importance of nuclear medicine and the machines that are used in diagnosis, but for me there is nothing like hands-on, actually having a machine in front of me," I said.

"Ayuh, well, tomorrow you'll have your chance." Then Seth changed the subject. "How is everything with Coreen? Mort hasn't called me insisting that I allow him to interview her, and Loretta hasn't called me insisting that I give her some medicine to help Coreen calm down, so I am guessing you have things well in hand."

"I take no credit. Regina Tremblay, the lawyer Joe Turco recommended, has been a wonder to behold. Coreen is like a happy puppy and follows Regina's guidance without a whimper, never mind a tear," I replied. "I think Coreen senses she can trust Regina, and we are all so much the better for it."

"We can only hope for the right outcome. What I hear you say is that I can stop worrying about getting a midnight phone call because Coreen is having a flashback to the murder scene.

"Oh, look at the time. Patients will be lining up in my waiting room, and some aren't very patient." Seth laughed at his own silly pun and went on his way.

After Seth left I went over my notes about the gamma camera, which I learned is also called a scintillation camera, so I supposed the radiation makes the images sparkle somehow. It turned out that the machine itself doesn't project radiation; instead, it detects radiation that was previously injected into a patient. I still wasn't sure that I would use the machine as a murder weapon, but once I saw it I'd have enough information to figure that out.

Early the next morning I baked cinnamon-cranberry-apple muffins to take to the hospital as a thank-you to Dr. Leung and his staff for spending time teaching me about the gamma camera. Seth arrived early and poured himself a cup of coffee, and I caught him sneaking a muffin off the cooling rack while I was lining a cardboard box with wax paper.

"Only one, Seth. I have to pack the rest and bring them with us."

Seth had already taken a bite, and he nodded that he'd heard me. After he swallowed he said, "This is really tasty, Jess. If the writing thing doesn't work out for you, perhaps you should give Charlene Sassi some competition. You know, have a bake-off of some kind."

I waved him away as if I were waving at a plane aimed toward the wrong runway. "Oh no, not me. Don't you remember when Maeve O'Bannon donated a half dozen loaves of her hearth bread to the bake sale Susan Shevlin and Julie Hecht organized to raise money so the senior center could buy two new televisions?"

"Ayuh, the bread was a big hit, as I recall." Seth caught a large crumb falling from his muffin just before it hit his chest, and he popped it into his mouth. "Didn't someone mention that Maeve should begin selling it?"

"Yes, someone did. It was you, Seth. And you said it while Charlene Sassi was in earshot. Don't you remember the kerfuffle you caused?"

"Can I plead guilty and carry these muffins out to the car for you as penance?" Seth picked up the box of muffins and headed for the door.

"Careful—please hold the box straight," I said. I put on my navy blue blazer, picked up my purse, and followed him.

We were nearing the hospital when I asked Seth how Lavinia Wahl's recovery was coming along.

He hit the brakes for a stop sign, and instead of answering my question he said, "Why there is a stop sign at this corner, I will never understand. There's never any traffic over this way."

At that very second a sporty-looking yellow car turned the corner practically on two wheels and crossed directly in front of us. I decided to keep the peace by not pointing out what might have happened if we hadn't stopped at the sign. Instead, I pressed on for an answer to my question. "Lavinia Wahl? How is she doing?"

"Well, if she does her physical therapy to strengthen her muscles while those bones knit, she probably will heal with no permanent damage. But taking direction from anyone has never been Lavinia's strong suit," Seth said, and followed up with a question. "Why the sudden interest in Lavinia?"

"It's not sudden; I've known her for years. You know that." I added, "But I will admit I have been wondering how her niece has reacted to Nelson Penzell's death."

"Her niece? She's so new in town, I wonder if she even knew him." Seth went quiet. I waited for the light to dawn. When it did, he said, "The other morning. Are you telling me she didn't stub her toe on the doorframe?"

"That is exactly what I am telling you. I believe Erica had a history with Nelson Penzell, and I am determined to find out the depths of it." I didn't mention that Maeve O'Bannon had told me that Erica had been treated shamefully by a professor during her college years. After what we witnessed when we met Erica outside La Peinture, I did wonder if Nelson Penzell was the professor. If not, then I was sure that, young as she was, Erica Davenport had experienced more than one disappointing love affair.

Seth parked his car in the hospital parking lot and came around to my door. "Here, give me those muffins while you get out of the car. I promise not to eat one."

A young woman with purple hair and a friendly smile directed us to the second floor, and Gregory Leung was waiting in the hall when we got off the elevator. I handed him the box of muffins, and he raised the cover slightly at one end. "Still warm, and, oh, the smell of cinnamon . . . Jessica, you didn't have to bring us any goodies, but I am so pleased that you did."

We followed him down the hallway until he stopped at his office door to pass the muffins to his assistant and ask her to put on a pot of coffee.

"When we get to the nuclear medicine suite, Jonas Carpenter, who is our top senior nuclear medicine technologist, will be able to fill you in on all the details of how the gamma camera works and explain why we use it. Then I believe he plans to have you take a ride. You aren't claustrophobic by any chance, are you, Jessica?" Gregory asked.

"No, I'm not. And really, Gregory, this is more than I could have possibly imagined. How can I ever thank you?"

He laughed. "Cranberry-apple muffins will suffice."

Jonas, a tall man whom I judged to be in his early thirties, explained the uses of the gamma camera in diagnosing a wide variety of medical issues. The actual machine, which turned out to contain multiple cameras, was larger than I expected. Jonas showed me how the cameras were held inside big plastic-and-metal boxes that were attached to the hole of what looked like a white metal doughnut.

When it came time for me to pretend I was getting tested, I reclined on a narrow examination table and, at Jonas's direction, placed my hands over my head. The table slowly moved forward until my upper body was under the machine.

Jonas, Gregory, and Seth went into the next room, where they could watch me through a window.

Jonas asked, "Are you comfortable, Mrs. Fletcher? Would you like me to set the machine in motion for a minute or two?"

I answered yes to both questions. I am not sure what I was expecting, but the machine moved very slowly and I was completely comfortable. After a couple of minutes the doughnut started circling me extremely quickly, and then it stopped. By the time the examination table rolled back to its original position Jonas was at my side and holding out his hand to help me off the table.

I asked him a few questions and he answered with the confidence of someone who knew his facts and enjoyed his work. Then Gregory invited Jonas to join us for coffee and muffins. When Jonas declined because he had a patient coming for a test in a few minutes, Gregory promised to set some muffins aside for him.

While we sat around the small conference table in Gregory's office, munching on muffins and drinking coffee, I waited for the opportunity to ask a question or two that might help get Coreen out of her present dilemma.

Chapter Eighteen

I acknowledged to Seth and Gregory that I was certainly impressed with all the good that a gamma camera could accomplish, but I was reluctant to have my murderer force it to fall and crush my victim, for fear that some of my readers might be reluctant to slide under it if their doctor recommended using it as a diagnostic tool. That could be a major detriment to their health.

"Good point, Jess. But don't your readers know that everything you write is fiction, totally made up?" Seth said.

"Of course they do," I replied. "For example, everyone knows that standard murder weapons like poisons, guns, and knives are exceedingly dangerous. But we mystery writers often use common, everyday items to murder our fictitious victims. I have had readers e-mail me to say they never realized that this tool or that kitchen utensil could be so deadly in the wrong hands."

"I see where you are going, and I can't say I disagree. I've had more than one patient flinch at the term 'nuclear medicine,' and we certainly don't want to give anyone further reason to be discouraged," Gregory said. "Still, I am sorry that your research was for naught."

"Oh, not at all. My protagonist is a young female doctor in Philadelphia. I won't use the gamma camera as a murder weapon, but I certainly will include it in the book," I said.

"That's great news. You can help readers learn the equipment's capabilities in a totally nonthreatening way. Can I offer you more coffee?" Gregory motioned to the coffeepot.

I placed my hand a few inches above my cup. "No, thank you. I have plenty left. Before we have to let you get back to your busy day, can you tell us how the fund-raising effort is going?"

When Gregory smiled, I noticed he had a wide dimple on his right cheek. "Actually, Jessica, Julie Hecht's idea of dividing our ask into two separate donation tracks has proved exceedingly effective. Julie will be meeting—I think it's next Tuesday—with the hospital treasurer so she can be prepared to give an update report at our next committee meeting."

"Oh, that is good news. I recently learned of a wealthy gentleman who keeps a home here in Cabot Cove, not to mention a huge yacht he sometimes docks in the harbor. I was wondering if he has been a supporter of the renovations for the children's wing. His name is Jeremy Brewington."

Gregory pondered, then said, "The name is not familiar. Perhaps, unbeknownst to us, Julie is soliciting his help for this project, but I can say for sure he isn't a regular benefactor of the hospital. He does sound like a terrific lead. Wealthy people are often looking for worthy charitable causes. Donating makes the donor feel good and helps reduce their taxes."

"And wouldn't it be commendable for him to provide financial support to the children's wing of a community hospital?" I said.

Gregory laughed at my lack of subtlety. "It would indeed."

As we said our good-byes I reminded him to make sure that Jonas receive a couple of cranberry-apple muffins, and I again extended my thanks for his patience in answering my questions.

While we were walking to the car, Seth asked, "What's this sudden interest you have in Jeremy Brewington? Are you going to hound him for money for all your favorite charities, or is there something else going on?"

"The night Nelson Penzell was murdered, Jeremy Brewington burst into Mort's office, loud and self-important, blathering about another break-in on his yacht. When Mort mentioned that Penzell had been murdered, Brewington was stunned." I could still see the look on his face. "He turned pale and morphed into a fragile old man right before our eyes."

"Ayuh, shock can do that to a person," Seth said as he unlocked his car doors. I got in, fastened my seat belt, and waited for Seth to get on the road before I answered.

"After Brewington left, Loretta wondered aloud whether he knew Penzell. And Andy told us that he'd seen Brewington and Penzell arguing in the Hill House parking lot not long before."

"And your point is . . . ?" Seth stopped at the stop sign opposite the one he'd grumbled about earlier, this time without complaint.

"I don't have a point exactly, except to say that yesterday Eve Simpson mentioned that Brewington has a gorgeous and very expensive house up on the ridge but doesn't spend much time there. He floats up and down the coast in that fancy yacht of his."

"Jess. What am I missing?" Seth made another turn, and I realized we were getting close to my house.

"Seth, if you wouldn't mind, please drop me at the office Julie and Ryan Hecht share. I want to talk to Julie about the fundraising committee." Then I answered his question. "And you are not missing anything. It's just that Nelson Penzell and Jeremy Brewington are two odd ducks, both reasonably new to Cabot Cove, and Andy did tell us that he saw them arguing. Something to do with money."

Seth snorted. "Jessica, I am always amazed by the connections you make. You see A, someone mentions B, and the next thing, you've trotted through the alphabet and wind up at Z."

I couldn't dispute that. My brain was always putting snippets together, be it in real life or in one of my books. And I couldn't relax until I found a way to make the snippets fit, like the interlocking pieces in a jigsaw puzzle.

After Seth dropped me off I stood in front of the door to the redbrick office building that I always thought of as "the money building." I knew the inside was fairly large, with three rooms belonging to Ryan's accounting firm and a small office off to one side that Julie used for her fund-raising business.

It suddenly occurred to me that I had not seen Julie since I accidentally overheard her talking to Nelson Penzell shortly before he died. I could be reasonably sure she hadn't taken his murder well, but I was equally sure that she needed to hide her feelings, especially from Ryan. That must have been difficult for Julie, and I wondered if Ryan had any inkling of Julie's involvement with Nelson Penzell.

I took a deep breath and opened the door. The front reception desk was vacant, and I was about to call out when I heard Ryan's voice, sounding weary and angry. "Julie, you have to snap out of this . . . this morass you've been in the past few days. If it's about your father, if you think the nursing home was a mistake, we can bring him to live with us and I'll hire someone to take care of him while you work."

"That's sweet, Ryan, but it's not about Dad. I can't explain. I'm down in the dumps. It happens to everyone. No rhyme, no reason, but I'm sure I'll be back to my old self in a day or two." Julie added strong emphasis to her words, but to me her voice sounded as if she was about to cry.

Ryan's tone softened. "Come on, Jules. You can talk to me."

The silence was deafening, even to me. I decided to let them know I was there rather than eavesdrop any further. "Hello, it's Jessica Fletcher. Anybody home?"

Ryan came out of Julie's office. "Jessica, how nice to see you."

"Hello, Ryan. I was at the hospital with Seth Hazlitt and Gregory Leung this morning, and I had a couple of questions about the fund-raising for the children's wing. Gregory suggested I talk to Julie. Is she available?" I asked as if I hadn't heard their conversation and didn't know exactly where she was.

"Why, yes—" Before Ryan could finish his sentence, Julie leaned out of her office doorway.

"Jessica Fletcher, is that you? What a delight. Please come in."

While Ryan's office had a no-nonsense business atmosphere of sparsely adorned walls and modern office furniture, Julie's work space had a soft, homey look. Two love seats covered with a fabric bearing a design of brown, yellow, and dark green leaves sat catty-corner from each other, connected by a square yellow end table that supported a white china lamp.

The walls were decorated with arrays of photographs of the

various events Julie had helped organize. Her rather cluttered desk was diagonally opposite the love seats, and a small table with a hot plate and kettle was against the wall behind it.

I looked at some of the pictures and used them to ease my way into the conversation I wanted to have. "Oh my, the last library fund-raiser. There is Doris Ann dressed as Raggedy Ann. And isn't that you dressed in your heaviest winter gear?"

"That was a wonderful fund-raiser. So much fun. We all dressed as characters from books who shared our name or occupation or hobby. Any connection at all, really. I was dressed as Julie of the Wolves, an Inuit girl in northern Alaska. The book was written by Jean Craighead George. I believe you were out of town, Jessica. If you'd been here, would you have dressed as a character from one of your own books?"

"I sincerely doubt it. And you may not have realized that I was at the fund-raiser dressed as Jessica from the book of the same title by Kevin Henkes. In the book, Jessica is Ruthie's imaginary friend, totally undetectable by everyone but Ruthie."

Julie laughed. "And here I am, peering at the photos, trying to spot you in the background."

"Not a chance. I was wearing my invisibility cloak," I said with a wink.

I declined Julie's offer of a cup of tea, and after we settled comfortably on the love seats, she asked, "So, what brings you here today? I heard you mention the hospital fund-raiser to Ryan."

"I spent an extraordinary hour this morning with Dr. Leung. He showed me some of the modern equipment the hospital uses to diagnose a wide range of illnesses. Absolutely impressive. I am certainly going to increase my personal donation."

"Jessica, that is most generous of you. Children will benefit from this upgrade for decades. Everything will be cutting-edge, with plenty of room for the children's wing to grow and modernize as new advances come on the horizon."

Julie certainly knew how to hit all the right notes to encourage substantial contributions.

"I was wondering, though. I recently came across a man named Jeremy Brewington. According to Eve Simpson he owns a really expensive house up on the ridge, and I don't know if you've seen his yacht docked in the harbor?"

"Oh, does he own that gorgeous Bertram Convertible? It must be his. The name is *Brew's Baby*."

"That's the one. Since he is reasonably new to Cabot Cove I wasn't sure if Mr. Brewington had made it onto the hospital children's wing donor list, but I thought I should bring him to your attention," I said.

"He has made it to the top of the list now." Julie giggled. "Do you know his address, or perhaps his phone number?"

"No, no, I don't. We've never actually met. We both happened to be visiting Mort Metzger at the same time, and Mr. Brewington was talking about his yacht." I thought that was a harmless way for me to describe the chaos of the other night.

Julie's face fell, so I hurried to reassure her. "I do know he is a customer at Charlene Sassi's bakery. I am sure she has a phone number if not an address. Perhaps she could even assist you in making the approach."

"That's a real possibility. Charlene and I have worked together on a number of fund-raisers. She is wonderfully community-minded. I'm sure she'll help." Julie gratefully accepted the lifeline I'd tossed her.

Happy as I was to provide Brewington's name to Julie as a

potential donor, I was disappointed that she had no idea who he was. Then again, her relationship with Nelson Penzell had been clandestine, and it was likely their private conversations hadn't included talking about whatever the money issues between Penzell and Brewington might have been.

We chatted for a few minutes more, and then, as I was leaving, Ryan came out to say good-bye. I noticed that when he dropped his arm casually around Julie's shoulder her body tensed, just as it had when I'd seen them in Mara's the other morning. At that time I thought she was feeling guilty about putting her father in the nursing home and didn't think she deserved comfort. Now I realized the reason was more complex. I hoped that Julie and Ryan could repair their marriage.

It was sunny and more than a little breezy as I walked along the street toward the wharf. I was glad I had my jacket but wished I had thought to bring a scarf.

A maroon Jeep Cherokee pulled up beside me.

"Hey, Jessica, any news?" Evelyn Phillips stuck her head through the driver's-side window. "Have you solved Penzell's murder yet?"

"Well, reporting the news is your job, and solving crimes is Mort Metzger's job, so I'm not sure why you are asking me." I tried to be cordial but firm.

"Because everyone in town knows your penchant for crime solving, especially when someone you are fond of is involved, and I would bet Coreen Wilson fills that bill."

Evelyn certainly had that right, but I was not inclined to give in to her the slightest bit. "I am fond of Coreen, and I am sure that Mort will soon discover who actually killed Nelson Penzell, and it won't have been Coreen."

"You're a loyal friend—I give you that," Evelyn replied.

"Speaking of friends"—I changed the subject—"where is your friend Dan?"

"Oh, he's down in the morgue, catching up on back issues of the *Gazette*. It's the long-established method for a reporter to learn about the community when he starts a new job. Every newspaper keeps their back issues stashed chronologically in a morgue. Ours is in the basement, with the papers stored in metal cabinets set high on a wall in case of, heaven forbid, flooding. Of course, today we store the more recent back issues in the cloud as well."

While Evelyn talked I nodded along as if this were the most fascinating information I'd ever heard. As soon as she stopped I said, "I'm glad Dan is getting to know Cabot Cove, since, according to you, he's going to be here for a while."

"And that, Jessica, is news you can count on. See you soon." I watched Evelyn drive away, and I waited until she was out of sight before I continued my walk to the wharf. I hoped Walter Hendon wouldn't be too busy for us to have a short chat.

Chapter Nineteen

The harbor was bustling as always, with some boats coming into port and a few, even this late in the day, heading out into the bay. A charter boat had apparently docked within the past half hour or so, because more than a dozen fishermen were milling about the wharf. Many were holding their fishing poles high in the air with their catches of the day swaying in the breeze. Cameras and cell phones were recording catches of plump silver hake and Boston mackerel, which I was sure would be brought into future conversations about the fight this one put up or the massive tussle with the one that got away, which was at least twice as big.

I found Walter Hendon, wearing his customary dark blue captain's hat with a gold anchor embroidered above the beak, standing directly in front of his office door. He was talking and laughing with two old salts who were decked out in green rubber waders and jackets. I had to smile when I noticed one of the men was chewing on the stem of an unlit corncob pipe. He reminded me of the *Popeye the Sailor* cartoons of my childhood.

Walter saw me coming toward him and began to shake hands robustly with the fishermen. "See you next time, fellas. And don't forget, if it's pollack or cod you're after, shrimp and herring make the best bait."

Mr. Corncob Pipe replied, "Oh, go on, ya! Everyone knows it's squid or clams gets 'em every time. See ya again."

Walter greeted me warmly. "Great to see you, Jessica. Me and Henry have been having that bait battle for going on twenty years. It's a running joke. But I would much rather talk to you than kibitz with those two. Come on inside. Can I offer you a can of Moxie?"

Although Moxie is Maine's official soft drink, I was never particularly fond of it, so I gracefully declined. Walter opened a tiny office fridge, took out an orange can, and popped the top. He motioned to the lone cane-backed chair next to the file cabinet that took up most of the space between the door and his desk. "Have a seat and tell me how your little friend is doing. What was her name? Coreen?"

Since I knew from past experience that the chair had at least one wobbly leg, I sat gingerly and slid my feet along the floor until I found my balance. Walter's office was always damp and smelled of the sea. I delighted in being there nearly as much as being on a boat. "She is coming along. I wanted to stop in to say how glad I am, as are Loretta and all of Coreen's other friends, that you heard Coreen calling for help and came to her aid."

Walter took a long drink and wiped his mouth on his sleeve. "Ah, good stuff. Please, Jessica—and pass this on to Loretta—no thanks are necessary. I was happy to be near enough to help. The poor kid looked like the wreck of the *Hesperus*, and from what I heard she didn't get any better even after Mort called Doc Hazlitt to look her over, try to help her out. How's she doing now?"

"She is much better. Loretta can be quite the mother hen, and she has been fussing and clucking all around Coreen. It's really something to see."

Walter laughed. "Now, I'd have a hard time believing that. Loretta Spiegel is one tough cookie. Why, even back in high school—"

I interrupted before Walter's reminiscences took us too far afield. "There was an odd thing that happened that night. You left Mort's office before Loretta and I got there. But shortly after we arrived, Jeremy Brewington came storming through the front door, bellowing like a cow needing to be milked."

Walter heaved a mega-sigh. "That man is one pain in the patootie, that's for sure. What was he bellyaching about? Pirates again?"

That caught me short. "Pirates? Are you telling me Mr. Brewington thinks we have pirates in Cabot Cove? Isn't he in the wrong century? No. He never mentioned pirates to Mort. He went on and on about someone trying to break into a cabinet on his boat, and I'd previously heard he'd had an earlier theft. I thought he was referring to petty thieves or perhaps teenagers."

Walter took another swallow from his can of Moxie, then set it down on his desk. He folded his arms across his chest and said, "Let me tell you something about Brewington. He's the kind of man who, if there was no trouble, he'd invent some just so he could make lackeys out of guys like me and Mort."

I was taken aback. "You think he made up the two incidents, first the theft and then the attempted theft, just to attract attention?"

"Not everyone's attention. Honestly, Jessica, he wouldn't care whether or not you knew who he was. It's people with titles like 'harbormaster' and 'sheriff' who'd better stand up and salute when he walks in the door."

"I didn't realize—" I started to respond, but Walter cut me off.

"Why do you think he boards his crew over at Jessup's Rooming House when he docks *Brew's Baby* here? Who else do you know has a boat that size and leaves it unattended anywhere? Why isn't at least one crew member required to stay on board overnight?"

Walter continued to rave. "I'll tell you why. It's because Brewington wants to harass Mort and me. So he leaves the flashy boat unguarded, and then rants at us when something happens. And who is to say he has anything valuable on the boat anyway? Who's to say there ever was a pile of cash stolen? Or that cabinet locks were scratched in a second incident? Only Brewington. No one else. Not a single witness."

And there it was. The tiny puzzle piece that was flitting around the back of my mind jumped to the front and joined with the piece Walter had just handed me.

"Walter, that is terrible. Really awful. I am so sorry that you and Mort have been under this pressure." I stood up and stepped toward the door. "I have an engagement and I'm nearly late. I really have to go. See you soon."

The wharf was far too crowded for me to make a phone call with any semblance of privacy. I went up to the dockside but that, too, was filled with shoppers and picture-snapping tourists. I looked around and decided to ask Mara if I could use her office. Once before, when my agent called while I was having lunch with Mort and Seth, Mara hurried me into her office so I could hear over the din of the lunch crowd. This time I needed privacy for a completely different reason.

The lunch hour was long over and only a few stragglers remained sipping coffee or sweet tea and munching on desserts.

"Hi, Jessica." Mara was giving the counter a major scouring in preparation for the evening rush. "What can I get you?"

I moved directly opposite her and lowered my voice. "If it isn't too much of an imposition, might I borrow your office for a few minutes? I have to make a very important phone call and I am looking for a private space."

"Not a problem." Mara came around to the public side of the counter and led me through a back hallway to her office, which was as neat and clean as every other part of her luncheonette. Before she left me alone she said, "Just close the door behind you when you leave."

Because I didn't want to be too involved in Michael Haggerty's shenanigans, I never asked how I could reach him while he was in Cabot Cove. In fact, if I'd insisted on his cell phone number, I am not at all sure he would have given me a genuine one. I had no option but to try the Hill House. When the hotel operator transferred me to Michael's room he didn't answer, so I left a voice mail and hoped he'd get it sometime soon. I hung up and called the front desk. I was glad Margo Linwood, a young woman I'd known for several years, answered.

"Hello, Margo. This is Jessica Fletcher."

"Hi, Mrs. Fletcher. How are you? And what can I do for you today?"

"I am fine. However, I am trying to reach one of your guests. His name is Michael Haggerty. I already tried his room. Do you know if he is anywhere in the lobby or the dining room?"

"I don't know offhand, but if you hold on for a minute I will have him paged." The next thing I knew, I was listening to some unidentifiable hold music.

It didn't take long for Margo to click back on. "I'm sorry, Mrs. Fletcher, but you just missed him. Mr. Haggerty went out about twenty minutes ago. According to the concierge, he requested directions to Belfast, so I suspect he will be gone for a few hours."

If Michael asked for directions to Belfast, I could be sure that was the one place he was least likely to visit. Any clue he left regarding his comings and goings was sure to be a red herring. I tried not to sound as exasperated as I felt. "It is critically important that Mr. Haggerty call me as soon as he returns. Please take down my cell phone number."

I hung up, and when I left Mara's office I was sure to close the door behind me. Mara had moved on to scrubbing the tables in the booths along the wall. I stopped to thank her.

"Jessica," Mara said in a voice so low that I wouldn't have recognized it if she wasn't standing in front of me, "I will do anything to help Coreen. She is a sweet kid, and that Nelson Penzell was what my father would call a scoundrel. If you think of any way I can help . . ."

I gave her arm a gentle squeeze. "By giving me the privacy to make a telephone call, you may already have helped Coreen a great deal."

"I knew—I just knew—that you would be trying to clear Coreen of any wrongdoing. Remember, if you need anything, just ask. I am ready to help, and from what I hear at breakfast and lunch, so is most of the town." Mara gave me a quick nod and went back to cleaning.

I knew that I should go home and work on my synopsis, but

once I was outdoors I thought a short walk would clear my head. I decided to amble for fifteen or twenty minutes; then I would definitely call Demetri and head for home. As I passed Mellow's Notions I stopped to look in the window at a display of brass buttons I hadn't noticed the last time I was in the shop. For some time now I had been toying with the idea of replacing the old wooden shank buttons on my raincoat with brass buttons for an updated look. I'd turned to go inside when I nearly bumped into Ideal Molloy, who was walking out the door.

Ideal held up a paper shopping bag. "Jessica, wait until you see the lace trim I found for my kitchen curtains. Time to pretty up the house. Once the weather starts to get cold, I spend more time indoors. I need everything to be cheerful." Without missing a beat, she pushed her left hand directly in front of my face and asked, "Have you seen my nails?"

Rather than remind her that I was sitting opposite her in the beauty parlor when Coreen painted and decorated them, I said her nails were lovely and emphasized that I really admired the silver sparkles on her ring finger.

"Jessica, tell me the truth. Do you think there is any way that Coreen could have . . . would have . . . um, harmed that Nelson Penzell?" Ideal asked.

"Don't be silly. You know Coreen as well as I do and have known her as long as I have. She couldn't possibly hurt a fly, much less a grown man who towered over her and outweighed her by fifty pounds." I put as much confidence as I could into my opinion.

"That's such a relief. I didn't think Coreen would ever do anything like that, but, really, what do I know? You are a much better judge of character. I guess it's because of those books you write."

As with much of what Ideal says, there was no answer that easily came to mind, so I nodded in general agreement.

She looked at her watch. "Now I am running late again. I'm going to visit Lavinia Wahl. You know, to cheer her up a bit. I want to get to her house soon so we can spend some time chatting before her physical therapy hour. She told me those sessions really tire her out."

"Ideal, that is so thoughtful of you. I'm sure Lavinia is bored to tears and is ready to strangle Seth Hazlitt for confining her to a wheelchair. Do you mind if I tag along? And why don't we stop in the Fruit and Veg so I can pick up a pretty bouquet of fall flowers?"

"I'd love it. I bet Lavinia would be happy to see you. Come on—my car is right over here." She pointed a few doors down the street.

We drove the three blocks to the Fruit and Veg and I hurried inside. In ten minutes I was back with a gorgeous bouquet of black-eyed Susans surrounding a large branch of neon pink autumn joy sedum wrapped in pale pink paper with GET WELL SOON printed on it in blue, purple, and red.

Ideal gushed, "Look at that bouquet! Lavinia loves flowers, and those are gorgeous. I am so glad I invited you to come with me. I never thought of flowers."

There was no point in mentioning that I'd invited myself. And I would certainly never let Ideal know that the reason I was anxious to visit Lavinia was because I was excited to have a chance to see her niece Erica Davenport again. With Ideal along to distract Lavinia, I planned to maneuver an opportunity for a personal talk with Erica. Who knew where that could lead?

Chapter Twenty

I deal tapped Lavinia's doorbell and said, "Quick, hide behind me. You can be the big surprise. Oh, and I'll take those." She snatched the flowers out of my hand.

As ordered, I stood behind Ideal, but since I am at least four inches taller than she is, I had to scrunch down awkwardly to be even somewhat hidden. I was relieved that when the door opened there was no sign of Lavinia. Erica was standing alone in the foyer. I relaxed my shoulders and stood up straight.

"Please come in, ladies. Aunt Lavinia will be so delighted to see you." Even as she welcomed us Erica was eyeing me warily, as if she wasn't quite sure where she'd seen me before but knew it hadn't been pleasant. Then I could see the recall kick in; her eyes dropped to the floor and her cheeks turned from pink to red.

"Where is Lavinia?" Ideal asked in a stage whisper, then pointed to me. "Jessica is a special treat. I thought an extra visitor would brighten your aunt's day. And the flowers were Jessica's idea."

Ideal brandished the bouquet like a weapon, swinging it toward Erica, then toward me, then back to Erica. "Erica, you take care of the flowers. I will announce Jessica to Lavinia; then you can bring in the flowers, and that will be two lovely surprises."

"What is going on out there? Is that you, Ideal Molloy? Stop chinning with my niece and come on in and tell me all the gossip that's not fit to print," Lavinia shouted from the living room.

Erica took the flowers and went in search of a vase. Ideal pushed me to a spot next to the double doorway that led to the living room. Then she planted herself in the doorway. "I don't know, Lavinia—you are sounding awfully cranky for someone who's being treated like royalty, with that sweet niece of yours taking care of your every need."

"Royalty, ha! You ride around in this ridiculous chair and see how you like it," Lavinia snapped. She must have tried to roll forward to greet Ideal, because I heard a thump followed by the sound of metal scraping metal. "Again! I need this floor lamp when I read, especially late in the day, but every time I try to move around it some part of the chair manages to scratch the lamp's column. Wouldn't surprise me if, one day, the chair slices the lamp in two."

Ideal was still determined to get a cheerful response from Lavinia. She hid one hand behind her back and waved me forward. "And look who I brought with me as a special treat. Your favorite author."

I put as big a smile as I could muster on my face and joined Ideal in trying to placate Lavinia. "I was delighted when Ideal invited me along today. And, Lavinia, I must say, you look wonderful for someone who has been through all that you have since the . . . accident."

"Jessica, this is a treat." Lavinia leaned forward and stretched her right hand toward me, which I thought was a dangerous move. Her left leg, in a cast from ankle to hip, was supported by the wheelchair's leg rest. And when she reached out, the right side of her body tilted forward. *Too far forward*, I thought. Afraid that she would overextend and seriously injure herself, I moved closer quickly and took her hand. The last thing I needed was to have Seth Hazlitt blaming me because Lavinia broke another bone.

"Sit down, ladies. Please sit down." Lavinia seemed to remember her role as hostess and indicated a high-backed couch covered in blue sailcloth. Tucked in each corner was a throw pillow decorated with sailboats of different sizes and shapes. "Jessica, it so happens that I finished rereading *The Belgrade Murders* last night, and I still think it is one of your best efforts yet."

I felt myself blush. I generally find it difficult to accept compliments, but it is twice as hard when the compliments about my writing come from people who have known me as Jessica Fletcher, friend and neighbor, since long before J. B. Fletcher, mystery writer, ever existed.

"That's extremely kind of you to say." I grasped for something to change the topic. "And have you seen what Ideal has done to her nails?"

Ideal needed no further prompting. She stood and extended her left hand like a woman showing off her engagement ring. "What do you think, Lavinia? See how modern I am?"

"Hmm, you might think that sparkly stuff is modern, but it strikes me as gaudy for a woman your age. What made you do such a thing?" Lavinia was always one to give a forthright opinion, and it was apparent her accident hadn't changed that one bit.

Visibly hurt by Lavinia's comments, Ideal snapped back, "I'll have you know that sparkles on fingernails are the absolute latest. Decals are out. Sparkles are in. Just ask Coreen. And she should know."

As someone who was in the room at the time, I was aware that Coreen hadn't said any such thing, but I was not inclined to get involved, even if I had inadvertently started the melee.

"Coreen? Coreen Wilson, who everyone says killed that good-for-nothing who worked for Angus Michaud?" Lavinia's voice got louder with every word.

I was about to correct her multiple errors when we heard a crash and the sound of glass shattering, followed by someone crying in the hallway. Erica.

"What now?" Lavinia shouted. "Is that you, Erica? What happened out there? What did you break now?"

I hurried to the hall and found Erica on her knees in a puddle of water. She was surrounded by broken glass, and the flowers I had brought were strewn all over the floor. "Here, let me help you," I offered.

"Please, I'll be fine. Just get her to stop yelling." Erica looked at me with tear-filled eyes. "I know she's uncomfortable and cranky, but still . . ."

I nodded and picked up the large autumn joy sedum and a couple of black-eyed Susans. "I'll be back to help with the cleanup."

I held the flowers in front of me like a peace offering. "Lavinia, I am so sorry. When Ideal and I stopped for flowers I suggested that, as the driver, she stay in the car, and I went inside and found a lovely bouquet of black-eyed Susans. Then I saw this gorgeous oversized spray of autumn joy and I insisted on adding it to the bouquet."

Lavinia kept her eyes on the flowers. I moved closer and set them on her lap. She cradled them in the crook of her arm like a beauty queen.

"The store has the bouquets sized perfectly for the average vase. I may have inadvertently overweighted your bouquet when I added the autumn joy. I am so sorry," I said.

To my astonishment Lavinia waved off my apology and smiled. Then she said, "Long before we were married, during our early courting days, my late husband—you remember Albert, don't you?"

"Of course I do. He is still greatly missed." As a widow myself, I was sure we were about to hear a sweet memory.

"Albert was a hiker. He loved to go off into the woods of a morning. I was raised as a boat brat, and it was hard for me to understand that he loved the woods the way I loved the water. And I may have mentioned that to him once too often." Lavinia paused and looked from me to Ideal to be sure she had our attention.

"On a beautiful Maine day—just this time of year, it was— Albert went for a morning climb in the state park. On his way home, he stopped at my house to give me a bunch of brightly colored autumn joys. He told me that when he was in the woods, the quiet of his surroundings gave him time to think of me. He saw a field of autumn joys and they reminded him of how beautiful I was. Then—" Tears began to well in her eyes. "Then he said that, for the rest of his life, every year, sometime during the weeks leading up to winter, he would bring me autumn joy flowers from the mountainside. And he kept that promise until the year he died." Lavinia pulled a tissue from the box on her end table and began to dab at her eyes.

"That is such a romantic story," Ideal breathed.

"You hold on to those flowers, Lavinia," I said. "I'll help Erica tidy up the hall, and we will find two vases, one for the black-eyed Susans and a special one for the autumn joy."

Lavinia didn't answer. She was gazing out the window, and I was sure in her mind it was decades ago. She and Albert were laughing together and all was right in their young world. After all my years of widowhood, I still had those moments when memories of Frank took over. They might have been fleeting but they were always cherished.

Erica had piled all the flowers neatly into a bunch and was on her knees pulling paper towels off a roll. I was glad to see she was no longer crying.

"I got most of the water with those." She pointed to some sopping-wet towels heaped in a plastic tub. "Now I'm trying to be sure I got every bit of broken glass with these." She wadded the paper towels and wiped the floor. "The larger shards were easy, but it's the tiny pieces I worry about. One could get caught in Aunt Lavinia's wheels and wind up scratching her floors or tearing a hole in one of the rugs. I would never hear the end of it."

I bent down and examined the entire area. "Well, you certainly did an excellent job. Why don't you put the towels in the laundry room? And I will bring the flowers to the kitchen. Where did you find that vase?"

"On the bottom shelf of the china closet in the dining room. I heard what you said to Aunt Lavinia. You tried to take the blame for my clumsiness. That was very kind of you," Erica said. "Aunt Lavinia has been very . . . I guess the word is 'difficult.' She is not good at being tied down."

"Oh, I imagine she isn't. Lavinia has been an outdoor girl all her life. Confinement doesn't suit most people, but it really doesn't suit someone like Lavinia. She sails, works in her garden, volunteers at the elementary school, sings in the church choir; I believe she still goes horseback riding, although you'd have to check with her on that. My point is, Lavinia is not the type to be content to sit in her living room."

For the first time since the morning she stopped in to make an appointment at the beauty parlor, I saw a smile flit across Erica's face. "Oh, I know. I've spent so many happy summers here. Each year as school was ending, my friends would begin bragging about going to specialty camps for crafts, or boating, or sports. Coming to stay at Aunt Lavinia's was so much better. She taught me how to do all those things and more. Did you know she taught me how to play soccer? And I played in a travel league all during high school. There was nothing I couldn't learn from her."

She tossed the paper towels into a nearby wastebasket, then stood and picked up the plastic tub. "Let me get these in the washer, and I'll meet you in the kitchen."

Lavinia had several lovely vases in her china closet. I thought a fluted crystal vase would hold the black-eyed Susans nicely. And when I saw a white china vase with mountaintops painted on the front, I knew it was perfect for the autumn joy.

By the time I'd rinsed the vases and begun to arrange the flowers, Erica came into the kitchen. She held up the china vase. "I wish I had seen this earlier. Oh, but I didn't know the story of Uncle Albert, the mountain, and the flowers, so I wouldn't have known the significance."

She opened the refrigerator door, took out a pitcher, and set it on a tray alongside some glasses. "We have iced tea, and let me check the pantry. I know we have chocolate chip cookies. Aunt Lavinia complained that they are 'store-bought, not from Sassi's Bakery,' but she's been nibbling on them ever since."

I knew I was running out of time to ask the questions that were rattling around in my head. While Erica was arranging cookies on a serving plate, I looked directly at her so that I could judge her reaction.

"Erica, I was sorry to hear about the death of your friend Nelson Penzell. Had you known him long?" I hoped I sounded more consoling than inquisitive.

The cookies she held in her hand dropped helter-skelter. Some landed on the serving platter, some on the countertop. Her head snapped up and she glared at me. Then her anger melted into sorrow. "How did you know?"

"When I saw you come out of La Peinture the other morning, you called him Sonny. I was under the impression that was a special nickname."

"And I guess it was obvious things between us ended a long time ago." Erica walked around to my side of the counter and lowered her voice. "I don't want Aunt Lavinia to know. I mean, she knows—the entire family knows—I had a romantic problem at school. Hard to hide when I dropped out for a semester. But she doesn't know that he turned up here in Cabot Cove."

I nodded and clucked sympathetically. "You must have been surprised to find him here."

Erica continued. "It was a lovely day for some fresh air, and I was pushing Aunt Lavinia along Main Street, window-shopping, you know? Not a care in the world, and then I saw him, crossing the street about a block ahead of us. I hadn't seen him in nearly three years but I still remembered the slope of his shoulders, the tempo of his gait. He was there, and then he disappeared into a storefront. But those few seconds brought it all back. I asked around, found out he owned La Peinture, and wandered in casually, like any tourist would. He was rude—nasty, even—and ordered me out of the store. That's when you saw me . . ." Her voice trailed off.

I needed either to satisfy myself that she was a potential suspect or to cross her off my list. Hard as this was for Erica, I persisted. "How did the relationship end?"

Erica laughed bitterly. "Badly. In one word, it ended badly. The short version is that I was a dopey college junior who fell in love with her art history teacher, the debonair Mr. Penzell. When he noticed my interest, he, er, asked me to call him Sonny. He stressed that we needed to keep our relationship a secret because he was up for tenure and the college had a strict rule against teacher-student dating.

"The day the semester ended, he stopped returning my calls and texts. It was as though I no longer existed. When I finally confronted him, in the school library of all places, he told me to go away and grow up. I skipped the next semester, and I heard from my friends that he hadn't gotten tenure and was leaving. When I returned to school the following semester, he was gone."

I chose my words carefully. "Erica, you might want to have a quiet talk with Sheriff Metzger. I'm sure he will be investigating Nelson's past, and it would be better if he finds out about your, um, connection from you."

Erica stared at the floor while twirling her hair for a few heartbeats. "I suppose you're right. I can't hide from the past, no matter how hard I try."

I patted her shoulder. "No, you can't, but please don't bury yourself under a mountain of guilt. Nelson Penzell used his position as a professor to lure you into a short-term relationship. It's likely that was his habit each semester. As a former teacher, I am totally angry at his violation of the code of conduct that all teachers must follow. Promise me you won't let this one incident with a predatory professor affect your life going forward."

Erica gave me a small smile. "I promise. And, Jessica, thank you."

I smiled back. "Now let's get the party started. If you can carry the tray with the iced tea and cookies, I'll bring the vases."

The afternoon went by pleasantly, and it was nearly dusk when Ideal dropped me off at home.

As soon as I walked down the steps from my foyer to the living room, I noticed the kitchen light was burning. I moved closer to the kitchen and heard a noise.

The shape of a man filled the doorway between the kitchen and the dining room. Because he was backlit, I couldn't make out his face, but there was no mistaking that voice.

"There you are, Jessica. I've just now put the kettle on. Can I interest you in a cuppa?"

Michael Haggerty.

Chapter Twenty-One

I've had enough tea for today, thank you, Michael, but what you can do is explain to me exactly what you are doing in my kitchen. Breaking into houses in Cabot Cove seems to be your latest specialty." To say I was annoyed would be putting it mildly.

"Oh, come now, and wasn't it yourself who's been looking for me?" Michael flashed the pretty-boy smile that he seemed to think would always absolve any infraction. "I've an informal arrangement with the concierge at the Hill House. Whenever someone inquires as to my whereabouts, he sends them off to Belfast, which, as far as I am concerned, is in Northern Ireland, but your American map does in fact show it to be on the coast of Maine as well."

I folded my arms across my chest and began to tap my toe to send him the message that my patience was wearing thinner by the second.

"I check in with him periodically to see if he has directed anyone to visit Belfast, and he said that Mrs. Fletcher had called. Well, I know you are too smart to go off on a wild-goose chase, so I thought I would find you at home, and now here you are. I might ask, if you weren't expecting me, why would you leave your kitchen door unlocked? Anyone could wander in." This time he added a wink to the smile.

"Michael, really, when you saw I wasn't home, why didn't you simply decide to come back later? Why is it always cloak-and-dagger with you?"

"Jessica, Jessica, must you take the fun out of everything?" Michael held up his teacup. "Would you happen to have a biscuit or two that I could enjoy with my tea? And then please sit down and tell me why I'm here."

I'd half a mind to tell him that the reason he was here was because he broke into my house, but since I'd already said that and it didn't bother him in the least, I took a deep breath and pulled out a chair. "I'm sorry, but I am all out of treats. However, I can tell you why I called earlier today."

Michael patted his stomach and said, "Just as well, I suppose. I could do without the biscuits, but not without the news."

"You suspected there was a connection between Clark Geddings and Nelson Penzell. When Geddings met with Roger Wilburne, everything you overheard confirmed that Penzell was indeed part of their smuggling operation—am I correct?" I asked.

"You are right on the money, as always," Michael affirmed.

"What, then, is the missing piece?" I asked. "We have Geddings, a real estate agent whose travels supposedly done in the name of his business would never draw suspicion. Then there is Wilburne, a jeweler who trades in the kind of merchandise that you suspect the group of smuggling. And finally we have Penzell, an art dealer with the ability to attract high-end clients, and who, I recently learned, also had credentials as a professor of art history. Again, who is missing?"

Michael tipped his head back and stared at the ceiling. Then he turned to me and said, "I believe we are missing two people: One is the moneyman who bankrolls the operation and takes the biggest cut of the profits, and the second is the traveler who is able to cross borders numerous times without suspicion. I have been unable to locate either of them. I had hoped Geddings was the traveler, but it looks as though he limits himself to the New England coast, with an occasional foray into New York. I've no idea as to who the moneyman might be."

"And suppose, just suppose, there was a strong possibility that person one, the moneyman, and person two, the international traveler, are actually the same person. I believe I know the name of the kingpin you've been searching for." I slapped my hand on the table and felt all the delight of saying "Gotcha."

I withheld Jeremy Brewington's name while I explained to Michael in great detail everything I'd learned about the potential kingpin over the past few days, particularly from Eve Simpson and Walter Hendon. The more impatient Michael grew, the more I dragged out my explanation.

Finally I took pity on Michael and began to tie it all together. "So, you see, he is a man of great wealth who keeps a home here but rarely uses it, at least according to my real estate source. And my friend who follows the goings and comings at the harbor insists that no one who has a sixty-foot yacht would leave it docked without any crew members on board for security. Why, the sleeping quarters on that kind of boat are quite luxurious, or so I'm told, and yet he routinely pays for the crew to bunk at a rooming house that is probably less comfortable than his yacht in order not to leave his crew on board without him for great periods of time. Is it possible he doesn't trust his crew members? Perhaps he fears one or two might get curious about what the boss stores on the yacht or takes with him on his travels."

When I stopped speaking, Michael motioned with his hands as if trying to pull more information out of me.

"Well, don't you agree that the pieces fit?" I asked, and then leaned back confidently, as if I had imparted life's great secret to happiness.

"All right, my girl, you've had your fun. If I agree that your 'pieces' have produced a fine lead, would you kindly provide me with a name?"

"In a moment. Let me finish. Our potential kingpin sails up the Bay of Fundy, which as you may know is a wondrous tourist attraction. Not only does it consistently have the highest tides in the world, but its marine life and geological finds—think whales and dinosaur fossils—bring visitors back time and time again," I said.

"It's the link." Michael grew excited. "The Bay of Fundy could easily be the link between the United States and Canada for the smugglers. Even if customs from either country examined the ship, black opals are relatively tiny, easy to secrete. And if these smugglers become foreign assets, microchips are even smaller."

"Yes." I nodded. "The Bay of Fundy is straight up the Maine coast. One minute a boat is in the Gulf of Maine, and the next it is in the Bay of Fundy, nestled between New Brunswick and Nova Scotia, with access to all of Canada. What could be easier for him?"

"And 'he' would be . . . ?" Michael asked, clearly impressed that what I surmised had real possibilities.

"Jeremy Brewington, of course."

Michael's stare was so blank that I knew at once he hadn't yet run across Brewington in his investigations.

I continued. "Brewington first came to my attention when, after Penzell's murder, one of the sheriff's deputies mentioned overhearing the tail end of an argument between Brewington and Penzell. Deputy Andy said it sounded like the topic was money."

"So Sheriff Metzger is keeping an eye on this Brewington?" Michael asked.

"No, no. I doubt it. Brewington happened to come into Mort's office while Loretta and I were waiting for Coreen the first time Mort tried to question her. After Brewington left, Andy mentioned the argument. It was meaningless gossip until you showed up with your smuggling investigation, and then I began to—"

"Say no more. I know. You snooped around, and then you put the pieces together, as you like to say," Michael said. "Well, I must admit, you've done a fine job. Now let's go over this again. I need every scrap of information you can give me about our kingpin."

I went into the dining room and pulled a blank paper from my printer. I wrote down everything I had told him, including the location of Brewington's house on the ridge. I confessed I had no idea of the address.

"Ah, it's not like you to miss a detail," Michael said.

When I gave him a look that said *Don't push it* he quickly added, "But, under the circumstances, you've done an admirable job. And it occurs to me that I have been hard to reach, and now, with this new information, I may become harder still. There's only one thing for it. Let's trade cell phone numbers to avoid a repetition of the unfortunate events of this afternoon."

I put my cell number in Michael's phone. After he handed me back my phone with what looked like a legitimate phone number, I asked, "And exactly how long will I be able to reach you on this number?"

Michael said, "It's evident you know me too well. I can almost guarantee that the phone number should last until I tidy up this gang of smugglers, or perhaps would-be spies. Of course, disastrous things can happen to a cell phone, but I will do my best."

"I'm sure you will. And if I find out anything more about Brewington, I will—"

"See, there's where you've gone wrong. You've done more than your share." Michael folded the paper with my notes, then stood and put it in his jacket pocket. "Best leave the smugglers to me, and if one turns out to be your murderer, well, then I'll let you know. And I did notice that pile of papers by your computer in the dining room. It looks like you've plenty of work of your own to keep you busy."

Well, that was certainly true.

Michael slipped out the back door and I locked it behind him, giving the lock an extra-hard turn. First Seth, now Michael. Why did these men walk through an unlocked door and then complain that I hadn't locked it?

I decided to have a light dinner before I settled down to work. I knew that I'd been distracted by my talk with Michael, and I was sure that I needed a few minutes for my mind to transition from murder and smugglers to my book synopsis. The thought made me laugh to myself. The synopsis had at least one murder;

maybe a few smugglers would spice it up. What could they smuggle in a hospital? Certainly not black opals, but narcotics—now, there was a possibility. Could my protagonist inadvertently stumble upon an intricate interstate drug-smuggling ring? I'd have to see.

I'd made a pot of vegetable soup with a pumpkin base earlier in the week. I poured some into a saucepan to heat while I tossed together a salad. I had my head buried in the refrigerator, looking for the goat cheese, when I heard the kitchen door rattle too loudly to be the effect of a blast of wind.

By the time I turned, Seth Hazlitt was tapping on my window with an insistent knuckle. I unlocked the door, and he began complaining before he'd even walked into the kitchen.

"Woman, can you tell me why the kitchen door is locked when here you are, not ten feet away from it?"

I threw up my hands. "No, Seth, I can't tell you. Apparently it doesn't matter whether I keep that door locked or unlocked. Whichever I do, some man has something to say about it."

And I turned back to searching for my goat cheese.

"Sorry, Jess. Obviously I hit a sore spot." Seth put his medical bag on a chair, went to the sink, and began washing his hands.

"I'm sorry, too. I shouldn't have snapped at you. My day out was longer than I'd intended. I got home only a few minutes ago, and I am hungry and tired."

Seth pulled a dish towel off the rack and began drying his hands. He wrinkled his nose in an exaggerated sniff. "Something sure smells good."

"Oh my." I rushed to the stove, picked up my slotted spoon, and stirred the soup. "Thank goodness, I caught it just in time. I don't like soup to boil on the reheat. Boiling tends to turn the vegetables to mush. Would you like some? It's pumpkin vegetable."

"I suppose there's no meat to be had?" Seth was forever telling me that, no matter which vegetable soup I made, it would be vastly improved if I weighed the recipe down with large chunks of stew meat or poultry.

"There's not so much as a shred. But I do have some of the rye bread you like." I opened the bread box and put a couple of slices on a plate.

"And butter?" Seth asked expectantly.

I opened the refrigerator door. "And butter."

"Well, that's a meal, then, isn't it?" Seth said. "And rather than sing for my supper, which no one would enjoy hearing, I've brought you something you are going to find extremely interesting."

I had wondered in passing why Seth had brought his medical bag into the house when he generally left it in his car. I got my answer when he opened the bag and pulled out a manila folder.

"You may want to wait until after dinner to look at this. It's the autopsy results for Nelson Penzell. I warn you, it's gory, even in medical-speak."

I paid no attention to his warning. I took the folder and scanned the pages quickly. "Seth, what is a subarachnoid hemorrhage? It's listed as cause of death."

"That is the primary cause. The arachnoid membrane is the . . . I guess you could call it the cushion that protects your brain. Below that, the subarachnoid space is where the cerebrospinal fluid circulates, and in a case of assault like this, in order for the subarachnoid space to hemorrhage, the trauma to the victim's head has to be extremely severe. We see that injury quite often in victims of serious car accidents."

I felt a glimmer of hope. "Seth, to you as a doctor, what would define 'severe'? Suppose someone was trying to fend off an attacker. Would one defensive blow with a heavy brass candlestick cause this degree of injury?"

"Based on everything in this report, I can tell you with absolute confidence that someone grabbed the candlestick and pounded Nelson Penzell's head repeatedly and with great force. There were similar injuries on the back of his neck, which also would indicate repeated blows."

My conviction was growing. "That doesn't sound like anything Coreen could possibly do, no matter how insistent Nelson's advances became. Even if she summoned the courage to hit him once to make him stop, I'm certain she is too emotionally fragile to strike him multiple times."

"And I can pretty much assure you that she doesn't have the physical strength to inflict such severe wounds," Seth concurred.

"So this autopsy is evidence that Coreen is innocent. I've got to call Loretta." I'd taken a few steps to the telephone when Seth stopped me cold.

"Jessica, the autopsy only proves the cause of death. It proves *how* Nelson Penzell died, not *who* killed him."

"But, Seth, you said, based on the severity of Penzell's injuries, Coreen couldn't have attacked and killed him."

"Ayuh, and that is my professional opinion. The person whose professional opinion you have to change is Mort Metzger."

Chapter Twenty-Two

Seth made small talk all during dinner, but he could tell I was totally distracted. "Jess, it's bad enough that you are not laughing at my entertaining stories, but you are pushing that salad around your plate like a child whose mother cooked lima beans for the third time this week."

"Lima beans? There are no lima beans in my salad." I knew I hadn't been the most attentive company, but I wasn't sure how lima beans had become a topic of discussion.

Seth tossed his napkin on the table. "Never cared for 'em myself, but you know what I do like? Mara's apple pie. I say we hop in my car and run right down to the docks for some apple pie à la mode."

I started to protest. "No, Seth, really, I've had a long day, and I have a ton of work to do this evening."

"Nonsense. I'll drive and Mara will serve up dessert. Nothing for you to do but show up. I insist. Now, I'll clean off this table, and you go put on your face, or whatever it is you women do before you go out on the town. Be back here in ten minutes ready to roll." Seth began to clear the table.

When I stood and picked up my soup bowl, he pulled it away from me and shooed me out of the room.

As always, Mara's was cheerful and homey. People clustered in booths or around tables, enjoying the delicious food as well as one another's company. Seth and I sat in a booth next to the broad windows overlooking the harbor. During the day the view was glorious, with boats constantly sailing in and out. From Mara's windows patrons could see far out to the horizon, where the bay met the ocean. The evening view was more peaceful. The lights from the wharf cast a glow that reflected on the ripples of the water. The only movement was the swaying of the boats docked for the night.

When I turned away from the window Seth was smiling at me. "Jess, all you needed was a change of scenery and a piece of Mara's apple pie."

"Seth's got that right." Mara was ready to take our order. "That will be two apple pies? Ice cream, cheddar cheese, or both? How about coffee or tea?"

"Mara, you read my mind. I'll have a slice of cheddar on my pie, and a nice cup of decaf coffee," I said.

"Woman, are you insane? Why would you ruin a perfectly good piece of pie with cheese? I'll have vanilla ice cream, and if you wouldn't mind, Mara, top it off with a dab of whipped cream." Seth gave me the same defiant look that he used when I criticized how much butter he spread on his pancakes.

Mara said, "How about a cherry on top, Doc?"

"That'll do fine, along with a cup of tea."

Mara stepped back to let a customer pass by. When I saw who it was I reached out, waved, and said, "Good evening, Angus. Would you care to join us?"

Seth went bug-eyed, but I was not going to miss an opportunity for a chat with Angus Michaud.

"How do, Jessica, Seth? But no, thank you. I'm only waiting for a takeaway. I thought Mara's fried chicken would hit the spot this evening."

"I believe her chicken would hit the spot anytime," I said. "And I am glad to see that you are taking care of yourself during what must be a difficult time for you."

For a brief second Angus looked like he wasn't at all sure what I was talking about; then he realized I must have meant Nelson Penzell's murder. "Truth be told, I am at sixes and sevens. Sheriff Metzger won't let me open my shop. Only let me go inside one time, for two minutes, to pick up my fishing rod and check our phone messages. And he sent a deputy with me to make sure that was all I did. I mean, it's not like I was going to steal something. I own the store, for pity's sake."

"Angus, how terrible for you to be treated that way. Like a common criminal." Hopefully, I sounded sincere.

"Danged right, Jessica. And that's when I saw that those law people had spread powder and chalk all over and left a big mess behind. When are they going to clean up and let me open? A man's got to make a living."

"True. True," I agreed. "And have you found out yet who your new partner will be?"

"What are you talking about? Not to speak unkindly of the

dead, but I didn't like working with a partner, and now that Nelson is . . . gone . . . well, I'd just as soon go it alone," Angus said.

I scrunched my eyebrows and pursed my lips as if I were mystified. "But surely Nelson Penzell had an heir—a brother, a cousin, a friend—someone who will inherit his estate. I assumed you and he had some sort of an arrangement. I mean, none of us lives forever."

Angus's weather-beaten face turned a deathly white. "It's early days. Nelson come from away, and who knows anything about family and such? I'd best check on my chicken."

And he fled.

Seth looked at me. "You really unnerved the man. What all is going on?"

"That is exactly what I was trying to find out."

Mara brought our pie and drinks. "I gave you an extra sweet there, Doc," she said, and pointed to the two bright red cherries atop his pie.

"Mara," I asked, keeping my voice as low as possible, "what is the story on La Peinture? I mean, without Nelson, can Angus manage?"

"Jessica, that is the talk of the docks. No one knows. Some lady from Boston looking to open a dress shop was in here with Eve Simpson earlier today. Apparently Eve had been showing her around town, but the lady was being all hard to please. Didn't like this; didn't like that. When they came in for lunch, the lady took one look out my window and said to Eve, 'This is what I want, a view like this for my shop.' From what I hear, Eve is getting ready to approach Angus, since he has the only storefront on the dock that might become available."

As soon as Mara moved on to help other customers, Seth said, "That Eve Simpson is something else. She is to real estate agents what ambulance chasers are to lawyers. Do anything for a dollar."

"Oh, Seth, don't be so hard on her. She has to make a living," I chided.

"Ayuh, but how she makes it is often questionable."

I didn't bother to respond to Seth's criticism of Eve's business practices. My mind had already moved to the possibility of speaking to her in the hope of learning any information she had gathered about the finances and ownership of La Peinture. Anything that might give Angus a motive to rid himself of his partner would be of great help to Coreen.

Mara refilled my cup from the orange-topped carafe that held decaf coffee. "Tell me, Jessica, how is Coreen doing? She seemed tired and didn't talk much when she was in here with Loretta. I made sure to tell them in no uncertain terms whose side I was on. Why, you and I both know that girl couldn't swat a fly."

"Well, there's the man you have to convince." Seth nodded toward the door. Mort Metzger and Floyd McCallum had come in and were walking our way. As they passed under the fluorescent ceiling lights I realized that although I had always considered Floyd's hair to be auburn, it was very similar in color to Erica's ginger.

"Hey, Mrs. F., Doc. Mind if we join you?" Mort glanced at my plate. "What is that you have on your pie? Is that a slice of cheese?"

"Mort, my pie is delicious. On one of my early trips to England, I discovered the combination of apple pie and cheddar cheese. I rarely order it here at home, but today Mara mentioned it, and so . . ." As I answered Mort, I realized that Michael Haggerty's showing up in Cabot Cove and George Sutherland's recent phone call had brought England, its people, and its food to the front of my mind.

As soon as they sat down Mara was at the edge of our booth, her order pad in hand and menus tucked under her arm. "I know you're always in a hurry, Sheriff. Do you need menus, or are you ready to order?"

Mort and Floyd exchanged a look. Mort said, "I'll have a burger, medium well, and a root beer."

Floyd ordered the same.

Seth asked, "So, what are you boys up to tonight? Are you going to sit and wait until you trap some poor, unsuspecting driver who blows through that useless stop sign out toward the hospital? I've been telling everyone it serves no purpose. Didn't I just say that, Jess, when we went to see the gamma camera?"

"The who camera?" Mort asked, ignoring Seth's complaint about the stop sign.

"A gamma camera is a piece of hospital equipment that I am hoping to use in one of my books. Dr. Leung was kind enough to let me see one and have an extremely knowledgeable technician explain its intricacies," I said.

Mort nodded. "So are you going to use this camera to murder someone, or maybe to record the killing in real time?"

Seth said, "Now, Mort, it's not that kind of camera."

As soon as Mara set plates in front of Mort and Floyd, Mort lost interest in anything we had to say. He picked up his burger and bit into it with gusto.

"Oh, now, there's a man's burger. Eat up, Floyd," Mort said between bites.

"I'm waiting on the—"

"Looking for this?" Mara placed a bottle of relish on the table. After Floyd thanked her, Mara stood by. I thought she was checking to be sure we had everything we needed. But she was obviously waiting for Mort to have a mouthful of burger, because as soon as he took his next large bite, she said, "Now, you listen to me, Mort Metzger. That Coreen Wilson is a sweet little scaredy-cat who wouldn't have the gumption to talk back to anyone, much less kill a man. Go find yourself another suspect."

Then she stomped away, leaving us all speechless until Floyd held up the relish bottle and asked, "Any for you, Sheriff? It's mighty tasty."

Mort waved him off and said, "I am getting tired of this. Everywhere I turn, there are members of the Coreen Wilson defense team badgering me."

"And yet you came in and decided to sit here?" Seth asked, and pointed to me.

"Aw, come on, Mrs. F. You'll let me eat my dinner in peace, won't you? Then we can wrangle if we have to," Mort pleaded.

"Of course, but don't eat too slowly," I teased.

Mort always ate quickly. I assumed it was one of the hazards of his job—catching meals on the run, being interrupted to respond to a call, that sort of thing. Tonight, however, he seemed to slow down, taking time to enjoy his meal. At long last he took his final bite.

"Okay, Mrs. F., have at it. You don't believe Coreen could possibly commit a murder. She is a wonderful human being." Mort used that singsong tone people sometimes use when they are repeating something they have heard a thousand times but don't quite believe.

"No need to get testy, there, Mort," Seth said.

"Sorry." Mort ran a hand through his hair, as he frequently did when he was frustrated. "I wish I had another suspect, but Coreen checks all the boxes. For one thing, she was right there, screaming like a banshee."

"But, Mort, if she deliberately killed him, why would she scream for help?" I asked.

Mort started ticking off reasons on his fingers. "She was covered in his blood, and her appointment with him was scheduled very near the time of death. And that appointment was no secret. It was in Penzell's date book, and Loretta knew about it. No way could Coreen pretend she wasn't there. We're still trying to determine if anyone knows the exact time she went into the shop. If her timeline changes by only a few minutes, that will clinch the deal." Mort looked down, and then looked straight at me. "I wish I could see it differently . . ."

"What about the autopsy results? Surely you don't think Coreen—"

Mort cut me off. "What do you know about the autopsy results? Oh, I get it. Doc, you managed to get your hands on the file and shared with your good buddy."

Seth was quick to admit, "Ayuh, I did."

"Now, don't blame Seth. You know that if I had asked you if I could see the autopsy report, you would have allowed me to do so," I said, and suppressed a smile when Floyd nodded almost imperceptibly in agreement.

"True," Mort acknowledged, "but I didn't see anything in the report that would definitely eliminate Coreen as a suspect."

"The report indicated that Penzell was severely bludgeoned. What is that injury called, Seth?"

"Subarachnoid hemorrhage."

"That's the term I was looking for. Mort, it isn't likely that a person of Coreen's weight and stature could have inflicted the severe wounds that were found on Nelson Penzell's head and neck," I said.

"You'd be surprised," Mort countered. "When people get enraged and the old adrenaline starts pumping, they can—"

"Metzger!" Jeremy Brewington started shouting as soon as he came through the front door, and he chugged directly toward us like a steam engine. "The harbormaster's office is closed. Lights out and everything."

Mara stepped in front of him, very much in charge, even though the top of her head barely reached his shoulder. "Walt Hendon is responding to a family emergency and had to leave for a while. And I expect you to either mind your manners or leave my restaurant. Your choice."

Brewington gave her a brief glance and mumbled something that must have satisfied her demand, because Mara stepped aside and let him continue to our booth.

In a tone that was temperate but filled with anger, Brewington asked, "Would you mind telling me who is guarding the wharf while you're in here feeding your faces?" He motioned from Mort to Floyd and back again. "Exactly who is watching my boat?"

I put my hand on Mort's arm and leaned across him. "Mr. Brewington, surely you have crew members aboard to prevent intrusion? Why, if I had a yacht that grand, I would make sure she was always occupied to keep her protected."

Brewington glared at me and said, "I was speaking to Sheriff Metzger."

Before I could offer a sassy retort, Mort said, "Mara told you Walter had an emergency. Floyd and I are on our meal break. Now, if there's nothing else . . ."

Brewington's words could barely seep through his gritted teeth. "Next time."

We all watched as he bounced off the edge of a booth, hit a couple of chairs, and slammed out the door.

Seth observed, "Now, there is a man destined to have a heart attack."

"Nah, when it comes to heart attacks, I think Brewington's a carrier. He'll give 'em by the dozen before he ever has one himself." And Mort gulped down the last of his root beer.

Chapter Twenty-Three

I woke the next morning with renewed energy. Seth had been absolutely right. What I really needed last night was an hour at Mara's with good friends and apple pie. While I was doing my morning stretches I remembered what Mara had told me about Eve's latest client, and I decided that talking to Eve would be high on my to-do list today.

I put on my sweat suit, determined to have a good long run. I'd realized long ago that exercising my body was generally the best way to energize my brain. While I was focused on moving, my mind was super busy sorting out all the notions, ideas, conclusions, and suppositions that were jumbled together. I was sure that by the time I came home I'd have my synopsis concepts neatly tied together, and any thoughts connected to Nelson Penzell's murder would merge into a batch that I could share with Loretta, to be passed on to Regina Tremblay.

I stepped out the kitchen door. Sunshine was burning off the morning fog, and the sky was getting brighter by the minute. The scent of the sea was especially invigorating, so as soon as I walked through my gate I began a slow jog.

Maeve O'Bannon was sweeping her front walk and called out as I passed. "Early morning to you, Jessica."

I waved and headed toward my favorite path, alongside a grassy field overlooking the harbor. I jogged to the flagpole at the end of the path and was pleased to see that Ray Jones had already hung the American flag high, as he did each morning, barring snow or pelting rain. I circled the flagpole and started back toward home. Halfway along the path I saw an unfamiliar gray Trek bike coming toward me. Between his helmet and sunglasses I didn't recognize the rider until he pulled up alongside me and took off his sunglasses.

"Good morning, Mrs. Fletcher. It's nice to see you again."

It was Evelyn Phillips's colleague Dan Andrews. His Kelly green windbreaker and the clips that cuffed his pants told me he was a serious rider.

"Hello, Dan. You are out early this morning. And as I recall, we decided you would call me Jessica."

"We did"—Dan reddened ever so slightly—"but after that gimmick of Evelyn's, trying to interview Coreen Wilson coming out of the sheriff's office, well, I wasn't sure how you felt about us."

"Evelyn has a job to do, and so do you, either working with her or, from what she claims, taking her place—although I can't imagine Evelyn leaving Cabot Cove." I looked at him for any hint of what the future might hold.

"Evelyn's plans to leave are definite." Dan was emphatic. "She's not quite sure where she is going or what she will do when she gets there, but once the wanderlust is upon her, Evelyn Phillips is the original rolling stone. But don't tell Mick Jagger I said so."

I returned his smile. "So then, you will be the new editor of the *Gazette*. Will you be telecommuting from New York?"

"Cabot Cove is now my home. Since I arrived I've been spending a lot of time on my bike because a good reporter knows every nook and cranny of his territory." Dan looked at the rocky hillside. "And there are certainly a lot of nooks and crannies."

"Oh, have you settled on a residence?" I was surprised the grapevine at Mara's or Loretta's hadn't already spread the word about the new man in town, right down to his shoe size. I supposed speculating about Nelson Penzell's murder was taking up all of the town's available gossip time.

"I leased a small cottage a block from Main Street. It is comfortable, and from that vantage point I will be able to get to know the town quite well in a short period of time," he said. "The only thing is . . ."

"You miss the hustle and bustle of New York City?" I guessed.

"Oh no. Nothing like that. My one problem is a Realtor named Eve Simpson, who keeps calling with invitations for me to look at houses. And does she ask questions! Do I want a fireplace? What about a two-car garage? Large front yard or small? She seems like a nice person, but to be honest, I need time to get my bearings. It will be a long while before I know whether I want to live in the heart of town or on the outskirts. As a city dweller my entire life, I can't imagine living farther out in the land of fields and meadows—you know, the farm country—but nothing is impossible. I made this move, and now that I am here, I want to take my time, get to know the people, become familiar with the places, and then find my long-term Cabot Cove house. I have tried to tell her that I am in no hurry, but every time I decline to look at a house, Ms. Simpson acts as though I am rebuffing her personally. Then, within a day or two, she is back on the phone, with another place that she insists I've 'just got to see.'"

I understood completely. "That certainly is my friend Eve. She is persistent if nothing else. Perhaps I can help."

Dan looked at me hopefully.

"Would you like me to talk to Eve? I could explain that you are not avoiding her but simply need more time to learn about your surroundings and decide exactly where in Cabot Cove you belong," I said.

"Do you think she would listen to you? I've tried but I can't seem to get through to her. But if you think you could . . ."

"Dan, Eve and I have been friends for years. I'm sure she would listen to me. I may have to add that when you are ready to settle in a permanent home you will give her the first opportunity to find you a house. Would that be all right?" I hoped I hadn't overreached.

I was relieved when Dan laughed.

"Mrs. Fle— Jessica, that would be perfect. After all, I already have her phone number on a wall calendar and two refrigerator magnets, so she'll be easy to contact." He looked at his wristwatch. "I'd better get moving. I'm meeting Evelyn in an hour. See you soon, and thank you for any help you can give me with Ms. Simpson."

I watched him pedal away. *Oh no, thank* you, *Dan, for giving me an excuse to speak to Eve Simpson.* Once I got her talking about real estate, I could segue into the possibility of La Peinture's becoming available for sale or rent, and find out if she'd learned anything about the business relationship between the two partners. As I jogged home, I was pleased that the day appeared to be filled with possibilities.

After I showered and changed into jeans and a shirt, I sipped a cup of coffee while I popped a piece of bread into the toaster and poached two eggs. I'd taken only a few bites when the telephone rang.

"Good morning, Jessica. Doris Ann here. I hope you haven't forgotten about the Friends of the Library meeting."

"Oh, of course not," I said, "I have it written on my calendar. You can mark me as a definite."

"I know that's normally the case. Once you respond I can count on your attendance, but with so much of your time spent working with Coreen Wilson's defense team, well, I thought I would tell you that the committee members know what a sweet girl Coreen is, and men, well, sometimes . . ." Doris Ann trailed off uncertainly. "Anyway, if you are too busy helping Coreen's lawyer and can't attend the Friends of the Library meeting, we would certainly understand."

"Doris Ann, Coreen has an extremely capable attorney who is representing her splendidly with absolutely no help from me. You can be sure that nothing is going to prevent me from attending the meeting. I will see you this afternoon."

My eggs were getting cold and starting to congeal. I considered heating them in the microwave for a few seconds, but I feared that might do more harm than good. Luckily they tasted better than they looked.

I'd barely swallowed the final bit of egg when the telephone rang again. I realized that after this call I was going to have to turn on my voice mail if I was going to get any work done today.

"Hi, Jessica. It's Loretta." There was a catch in her voice that set off alarms in my head.

"Loretta, is everything all right?"

"That's just it, Jess—I'm not sure. Regina Tremblay called a few minutes ago. It seems that Mort wants to what Regina called 'interview' but I call 'interrogate' Coreen again. Mort asked them to come in today, but Regina told him that both she and Coreen would have to rearrange their work schedules to accommodate him. I love that word, don't you? If the situation were reversed, can you imagine Mort accommodating anyone? Anyway, he said that tomorrow morning would do. Jess, this can't be good." The anxiety in Loretta's voice was growing more obvious with every word.

"Stay steady. I agree that it would be best for Coreen if Mort stopped considering her as, well, whatever he considers her to be," I said.

"You mean, he might think Coreen is a person of interest, like on *Dateline* or one of those other television shows?" Loretta got even more agitated.

"No, if the evidence had gone that far in Mort's eyes, he would not have acquiesced to Regina's request to reschedule the meeting from today to tomorrow. In that case I'm sure he would have ordered them to meet at his convenience, not theirs." I hoped I was right, but even if I wasn't, I heard considerable relief in Loretta's voice.

"You're right. I didn't look at it that way. You would think, with all the true-crime shows I'm always watching, that I would know the procedures by now," she said.

"Don't be too hard on yourself. It's totally different when the case involves you or someone you care about," I said gently.

"You got that right. Thanks for the pep talk, Jessica. I have back-to-back clients this morning, but maybe later on we can put our heads together and come up with something, anything, that will make Mort back off."

"Let's see how the day goes. I'll check in with you later," I said noncommittally.

I hung up the phone, set it to voice mail, and poured myself another cup of coffee. After my conversation with Mort last night, I knew that Loretta was right to be, if not worried, at least concerned. I slid a piece of paper out of my printer and began to make a list. Mort was set on Coreen as his number one suspect. I needed to encourage him to look in other directions. The most obvious person to me was Angus Michaud. By all accounts he and Nelson Penzell appeared to have had a rocky partnership. Who knew what kind of issues could have caused friction between them? Financial issues came to mind. And last night Angus definitely sounded as though Nelson's death was more a blessing than a curse.

Then again, it wouldn't be hard to envision Jeremy Brewington, with his domineering and quick-to-anger personality, bludgeoning anyone to death. If only I knew what his financial connection to Penzell was. At some point I would have to nudge Andy. Perhaps, that night in the Hill House parking lot, he heard more than he mentioned to us.

And I kept Michael Haggerty's smugglers top of mind. I couldn't see Wilburne the jeweler closing up his shop one evening, driving to Cabot Cove, and pounding Nelson Penzell to death. Although I have to admit that stranger things have happened. I thought it more likely that Clark Geddings, who was staying at the Hill House, could easily have done the deed. That theory was flawed, because Michael overheard their conversation and Penzell's death had clearly interrupted their current plans, not to mention left a hole in their chain of connections for future smuggling operations. Still, if I went with Mort's in-the-heat-of-the-moment theory, one of them could have done it.

Julie Hecht, who had no business having a lover at all, was extremely jealous when Penzell became visibly flirtatious with other women. I could see her lashing out if she was triggered by a combination of hurt and anger. But in spite of Mort's insistence that an adrenaline rush could give anyone superhero strength, I had a hard time seriously considering her capable of beating someone to death.

Then there was Ryan Hecht. I had no idea if he had any suspicions about Julie's affair. If he did, surely he would address that with her and not with the man involved.

I couldn't forget that Nelson Penzell had wielded his power as a professor to seduce Erica Davenport and seriously damaged her self-esteem when he abruptly ended the affair, but I was sure that Erica was far too sensitive to hurt, never mind kill, another human being. Even as I wrote down her name, I was certain she really didn't belong on my list at all.

And in my past experience there was often a Mr. X, an unknown suspect existing completely under the radar, laughing at everyone.

I looked at the clock. Today was going to be a busy day. I called Demetri to arrange for him to pick me up in a couple of hours. Then I turned on my computer, determined to wrestle my synopsis into shape. I'd work on pretend crime for now and try to find answers about true crime later.

Chapter Twenty-Four

Demetri was leaning on the fender of his taxi just outside my front gate. As I came down the walk, he opened the passenger door and waved me inside with an exaggerated flourish. "Your carriage awaits, Your Highness."

"Thank you," I laughed. "I feel like royalty."

"Ah, well, my brother Constantine and his family are visiting for a few days. His four-year-old granddaughter, Anna, is at that princess stage that all little girls seem to love. Yesterday she made me a knight. I am now Sir Demetri, at least within the family. Children are always so much fun. You said you were going to Eve Simpson's office?" he asked.

"Yes, I am. I have a few errands to run, and then a meeting at the library. I may call you to take me home. I am not yet sure how the day will go," I said. "Now tell me more about the little princess Anna."

In a few minutes I was standing in front of Eve's office. I

hadn't called ahead, because I didn't want Eve to push me off to a later time or day because she had business appointments. I'd decided to drop in casually, and if she was with a client or out of the office I would continue on to my other errands and circle back to speak with her later. Angus Michaud was too high on my suspect list for me not to be persistent in ferreting out whatever Eve might have discovered about the finances and ownership arrangements of La Peinture.

Before I opened the door and stepped inside, I turned my cell phone off to make sure a call didn't interrupt us. Eve was sitting alone at her desk with her phone to her ear. She waved me to a visitors' chair.

I heard her say, "Next Thursday it is. I'll see you then."

She hung up and began clapping her hands gleefully. "Oh, Jessica, I can't believe it. I have a nibble on the Barkley house. A Boston Realtor sent me a serious buyer who's coming to view the house on Thursday."

"That is wonderful news. Did the Realtor happen to be Clark Geddings?" I asked.

"Oh no, once I told him that the writers' colony is temporarily on hold due to an encumbrance on the land . . . well, I don't think I'll ever get a referral from him."

"I am sorry about that, Eve. I do know it was my fault for making up such an inane story on the spot." I still felt guilty about using Eve's connection to Geddings as I had, but if Michael could work his usual magic, it wouldn't be long before Geddings would be in a jail cell and Eve would be quite happy that she had no real estate ties to him.

"And I feel worse still because I've come to ask a favor," I said.

"Anything, Jessica. You know that." Eve beamed. "Old friends are the best friends, I always say."

I crossed my fingers mentally in the hopes that Eve's positive frame of mind would make my two matters mere blips on her screen. I went with the simpler one first. "Actually, I ran into Dan Andrews today on the jogging path."

"Oh, please tell me he is ready to buy. I have at least three listings that would be perfect for him," Eve said, and then she got up and came around her desk carrying file folders.

I held up my hand, stop-sign fashion. "Quite the opposite. He is determined to stay in his rental for the foreseeable future; however, he did mention in passing that you have been so kind and so professional that when he is ready to buy, you are the only Realtor he will consider."

Eve dropped the folders back on her desk, stood up straight, and touched her hand to her heart. "*N'est-ce pas agréable?* Isn't that nice?"

"It is," I said. "So you can safely tuck him away in the 'definite, just needs time' file until you hear from him again."

"Thank you so much for letting me know. I am buried under a mountain of work, and being able to take even one person off my call list frees me to do other things." Eve raised and dropped her shoulders as if tossing a great weight off them.

"I have heard that you're extremely busy. Mara told me about your new client, the woman interested in opening a dress shop here in town," I said with a tinge of curiosity in my voice.

"Oh my, yes. Jane Kealy Keating. She's one of the Boston Keatings, you know. What an asset she and her shop will be to Cabot Cove. Mrs. Keating and her daughter like to, shall I say, dabble in clothing. Right now they own a high-end dress emporium in Boston, and since so many Bostonians summer in this area, they picked Cabot Cove as the site for their latest venture. They plan to open a moderately upscale dress shop that will carry some apparel the locals can afford. During tourist season they intend to fill the shop with more upmarket clothing for the weekenders and summer residents. Wait until you see the line of dresses. *Très chic.*" Eve bunched her fingertips together and kissed them.

"Mara said that you were looking for a storefront on the dock. I hope that's not a deal breaker; I know dock space is hard to come by." I furrowed my brow. "Of course there's La Peinture, but who knows what the status of that place is? With Nelson Penzell dead it could be tied up for months."

Eve's grin got so wide, she looked as if she would explode if she didn't tell me her news within the next minute. "Well, I can't risk anyone finding out and spoiling my potential deal, but since I know you are the most circumspect person in all of Maine, I can trust you to keep what I say strictly confidential. And I am dying, absolutely dying, to tell someone.

"I hired an out-of-town attorney who I've used before for discreet inquiries and requested that he find and contact Nelson Penzell's attorney. No easy feat, but he managed to do it. As it turns out, Angus and Nelson had one of those clauses in their business agreement that if one of them died, the other got the entire business lock, stock, and barrel. Nelson's attorney told my attorney that he advised Nelson not to agree to those terms, but Nelson said that he was so much younger than Angus, he was sure that becoming the sole survivor was a safe bet."

"And," I said slowly, "instead of being the survivor and sole owner, Nelson has become a murder victim and Angus Michaud is now the sole owner."

Eve stood perfectly still and a look of terror crossed her face. "Jessica, don't tell me. Please, please don't tell me that Angus Michaud murdered Nelson Penzell. Why, if he did, it would have a disastrous effect on my opportunity for a sale."

It took longer than I expected for Eve to calm down. I assured her several times that no one had a whit of evidence that Angus was in any way involved with Nelson's death. No matter what I said, Eve appeared to have visions of thousands of dollar bills flying out the window instead of into her bank account.

Her telephone rang, and when she saw the caller ID she said, "Hot lead. I have to take this."

I recognized the opportunity that presented itself. I waved good-bye and slipped out the door before she could stop me. My next stop was Charlene Sassi's bakery. I was nearly there when I noticed Evelyn Phillips's Jeep Cherokee parked at the curb. I took a quick look around and saw her coming out of the drugstore.

"Are you staking out my car?" Evelyn joked, and then she shrugged. "I guess this is payback for my staking out Coreen Wilson's meeting with Mort Metzger."

"And that stunt of yours drove Loretta absolutely crazy," I said.

Evelyn laughed. "Who could have known that tough-as-nails Loretta Spiegel would turn into a mama bear guarding her cub as soon as the press showed up? It's like she never heard of the First Amendment to the United States Constitution. Didn't she ever take civics in high school?"

"Now, Evelyn, you can't put all the blame on Loretta. It would have been kinder for you to ask for an appointment to speak with Coreen," I said.

"Hold it, Jessica. You know darn well that not one of you—not the lawyer, not you, and especially not Loretta—was going to voluntarily let me talk to Coreen. So I took a chance and tried to get a picture and a few words. And my efforts paid off. I got a promise from the lawyer for an exclusive. That's worth something. And I will hold her to it."

Rather than continue squabbling, I changed the topic. "I met Dan this morning. He is quite the bicyclist. He rides in some of the same places I jog, so I suspect we will be running into each other quite often."

Evelyn unlocked her car door and placed her package on the rear seat. "If you are fishing, Jessica, I will give you this one for free. Truth is, I will be leaving Cabot Cove for parts unknown fairly soon. Once I'm gone, Dan Andrews will be editor in chief, running the show at the *Gazette*. You may have noticed that Dan has a gentler, kinder persona than I do. He is soft-spoken and always courteous. But do not mistake his kindness for weakness. He is dedicated with a capital 'D' to the people's right to know and the press's obligation to find and present accurate facts. You can take that to the bank."

I was flabbergasted trying to decide how to answer, and finally I decided on the truth. "Evelyn, I wasn't fishing for information. I mentioned that I saw Dan because I was going to say that he seems to be settling in quite happily."

"Even so, everything I told you is the truth. And you would do well to remember it. Before I drive off, do you need a lift anywhere?" she asked.

I was so blown away by her lecture that even if I did need a ride, I would have called Demetri rather than risk getting into her car. I could imagine Evelyn launching into a full-fledged sermon that would lead me to jump out of a moving Jeep.

I walked over to the bakery and stopped outside for a moment. I took a deep breath, enjoying the sweet fragrance of fresh baked goods. Through the front window I watched two small children dancing around their harried mother while she made a valiant attempt to search through the pictures in the book of cake decorations, looking for the exact right cake for whatever festive occasion was coming up for the family. As soon as Charlene reached across the countertop and offered the children cream-filled chocolate cookies, they stopped dancing, then stood quietly eating their cookies. The mother smiled at Charlene and began picking out her cake decorations in earnest.

I waited outside until the mother completed her order and hustled her little ones out the door.

As I entered, Charlene was cleaning the cookie crumbs from the floor with a handheld vacuum.

"Hi, Jessica. I saw you watching through the window. Believe me, it is so much easier to give children cookies and clean up the debris afterward than it is to try to keep their mother focused selecting what she wants while they do their best to distract her." Charlene laughed. "Just give me a minute. I have your Friends of the Library order all packed and ready to go."

"Please don't rush on my account. I'm running a bit early," I said. "And I do want to ask you about Jeremy Brewington."

"That old creep. What about him?" Charlene looked baffled.

"Nothing much. It's only that the last time I was here he telephoned an order, and when you got off the phone, he'd clearly upset you. I wondered if he is like that all the time." Of course, I already knew firsthand what Brewington was like, but this question was the opener for what I really wanted to know.

"Bossy, loud, and impatient. That about sums him up," Charlene said.

"Is he like that when he comes in to pick up his order?" I asked. "There are people who are rude on the phone but behave quite differently when they have to speak to someone face-to-face."

"Come into the store? Not likely. A man like Brewington couldn't be bothered. He expects his pastries to be brought to him. If he wants something outside our normal delivery hours, luckily I have an arrangement with the Fruit and Veg, so their service will pick up from me and drop off to my customers."

"I had no idea. That certainly is convenient. Local merchants helping one another," I said. "I suppose Mr. Brewington wants his food delivered to that gorgeous house he lives in up on the ridge."

"Strangely enough, he doesn't," Charlene said. "Every order I have ever prepared for him, be it large or small, has been delivered to his yacht in the harbor. I sometimes wonder why he ever bothered buying the house. Now let me go in the back and get your order."

I had to wonder why Jeremy Brewington had his bakery order sent to the yacht. He could have been treating his crew, or perhaps he was holding meetings of some sort. I'd have to ask Walter if he'd noticed a lot of comings and goings on *Brew's Baby*.

Charlene came out with two paper shopping bags. "I packed your treats in two bags, balanced by weight so you can carry one in each hand. There is a plastic zip bag with candles and a book of matches right on top."

"You are so thoughtful," I said. "The library isn't that far away, but if you'd loaded everything in one bag I might have had difficulty carrying it."

I paid Charlene, and as I got to the door Ryan Hecht pulled it open. Julie was on the sidewalk just behind him.

"Come ahead, Jessica," Ryan said.

I walked outside and he let the door close behind me.

Julie said, "Jessica, don't think I have forgotten your brilliant suggestion. I do intend to ask Charlene to help me reach out to Mr. Brewington for the fund-raiser for the children's wing of the hospital, but right now we're here for pastries to bring to my father. The nursing home called. He had a particularly difficult night."

Her eyes filled with tears and Ryan put his arm around her. Once again I noticed that she stiffened. This time Ryan drew her closer, wrapped both arms tightly around her, and said, "Don't worry, honey. I think he'll be happier when we can hang a large, bright seascape in his room on the wall opposite his bed. He can see it first thing in the morning and last thing before he falls asleep at night. He will also have a nice view of the painting when he sits in the lounge chair by his window."

I nodded. "I'm sure that will be a great comfort to an old sailor like your father, Julie. When I am away from home, any reminder of the sea brings me right back to Cabot Cove in my mind."

Ryan nodded, kissed Julie's cheek, and said, "Honey, I'm really sorry that we can't buy a seascape yet. But you know that, with Sonny dead, the This and That Shop is still sealed off with police tape."

He smiled at me. "Instead, we decided some of Charlene's delicious cream horns might cheer Dad up. Certainly better than showing up empty-handed."

Abruptly, Julie pulled away from Ryan. "We're running late. Take care, Jessica."

And she hurried into Sassi's.

"You'll have to excuse Julie. She's anxious to see her father. That phone call this morning has her deeply upset. The social worker from the nursing home told Julie that her dad had begun searching the hallways, looking for her mother, who died eight years ago. Can you imagine? I'd better go. Maybe I can talk Julie into buying me a whoopie pie." Ryan chuckled and opened the bakery door.

I started out toward the library, and I had walked only halfway down the block when I heard someone call my name.

"Jessica. Jessica Fletcher. Over here." And there he was again. Michael Haggerty had stopped his car in the middle of the street and was waving frantically. If I'd learned any lessons from the past, whatever Michael wanted me for, it would likely seriously interrupt my plans.

Chapter Twenty-Five

I was tempted to ignore him and keep walking to the library, but there was one slight problem. He had stopped his car in the exact spot where it would block traffic in every direction. Not one car could move along the street, and several drivers had begun to honk their horns. I heard one man yell, "Pull over, you idiot!"

I walked a few yards along the sidewalk until I was next to an empty parking spot. I signaled Michael to use it. As soon as he guided the car to the curb, he began his usual patter. "I'd almost given up. I called. There was no answer on your house phone. I tried your cell phone but my call went straight to voice mail. I have been looking for you everywhere. I started at your house. I will say, it was grand to discover that this time you locked your kitchen door when you went out."

"Michael, whatever you want, I have to tell you I don't have the time. I am on my way to an important meeting." I was unequivocal.

He leaned his head out the car window and checked the contents of my shopping bags. "And I suppose the topic of the meeting is 'Baked Goods I Have Known and Loved.' Your packages smell delicious."

"I'm going to the monthly Friends of the Library meeting. Our community librarian, Doris Ann, is celebrating a special birthday, so I am bringing refreshments. And I really must hurry."

I turned to leave, but Michael stopped me cold when he said, "The time has come when your sheriff could make a fine arrest. Wouldn't it be grand to see the good Sheriff Metzger's picture on the front page of every newspaper from Cabot Cove to London in the east and Canberra in the west? That's what will happen when he breaks this smuggling ring wide open. The shame of it is, even if I offer assistance, he's not likely to take any information seriously if it comes from me. It is a bit awkward for me to admit, but I'm confident that I find myself on his 'Not to Be Trusted' list."

I looked at my watch. "I have a very few minutes. What exactly is it that you want me to do?"

"Please, Jessica, get in the car and come with me to talk to the sheriff. It will be much simpler if I have you by my side to vouch for my truthfulness," Michael said.

"How would that help you? Mort knows you are MI6. If that isn't enough to persuade him to listen to what you have to say, I am not sure that anything I offer could add to your credibility." I shifted from one foot to the other. The pastry bags were starting to weigh heavily.

"Jess, please. Get in the car, and I'll explain as we go. Then I'll drive you to your meeting, if need be." He sounded desperate, a rarity for Michael.

Knowing I still had more than a few minutes to spare before the library meeting, I said, "Michael, this is entirely against my better judgment. I will give you no more than fifteen minutes. In exchange, you promise that you will drive me to the library so that I am not late for my meeting." I used my sternest schoolteacher voice from days gone by.

"Jessica, you have my word." Michael leaned over and opened the passenger-side door.

I slid onto the seat. My packages were cumbersome in my arms. I nudged one to the floor and held the other on my lap.

As soon as Michael pulled away from the curb he said, "I've been following Clark Geddings without fail each time he leaves the Hill House, be it day or night. This morning he wound up in that restaurant on the dock for breakfast."

"Do you mean Mara's Luncheonette?" I asked.

"That's the very place. And who do you think he was there to meet? None other than Nelson Penzell's old partner, Angus Michaud. They were in a booth, nice and cozy. Unfortunately, I couldn't get a seat close enough to hear their conversation, but I could see them from my table, and each one kept quite a serious look. Those two were all business.

"Then Geddings walked back to the restrooms. When he'd been gone for what I thought was an unusually long time, I wandered back there myself, and he was nowhere to be found. I saw the back door and knew I'd been foiled. Although I don't think he was onto me. I believe that, like any good thief, he was being extra careful."

"Michael, I don't have time to help you search all of Cabot Cove for Clark Geddings," I said.

"Ah, but that is not my intention at all. As I walked back to my table Angus Michaud signaled for his check, and I did the same. I stood right behind him at the register, so I was only a minute behind him out the front door—"

I interrupted. "He was gone. Disappeared from view."

"You are a sly one, Jessica Fletcher. That is close, but not quite what happened. As I set foot on the dock I watched Angus Michaud duck under the police tape crisscrossing the entrance to La Peinture, and then he disappeared right into the shop."

"That shouldn't be a surprise," I said. "The last time I saw Angus, he was complaining about Mort keeping the store sealed. Angus wanted access to the store without a time limit and without a deputy sheriff as an escort."

"And did you think there was something specific he wanted to retrieve, or was he merely irritable about the situation at large?" Michael asked.

"Now, that would have been hard for me to discern. Angus is known to be generally crabby, so people tend not to pay attention, myself included. I honestly couldn't tell if he was whining his usual 'poor me' or something more. What happened when he came out of the shop?"

"That's just it. He never came back outside. I waited, and then I realized that all the stores on the dock probably have rear doors similar to the one in the luncheonette."

"And you were right," I said.

"I decided to risk my cover and knock on Michaud's back door," Michael said. "But I was too late, for all the good it did me. I knocked, waited, and knocked again, and when there was no response I began banging with both fists and yelling, hoping that would lure him outside to see what the racket was all about."

Michael made a left turn into the Sheriff's Department parking lot and pulled into an empty space.

"And what happened?" I asked. "Did Angus come out?"

"Not a peep from him, but after a few minutes the shopkeeper next door came out to tell me to quiet down, go home, and sober up. I did a bit of tipsy walk away from the door to play into his assumption. But I realized that if the shopkeeper couldn't stand the noise, Angus was probably long gone, or he would have yelled at me even sooner."

"That's a fascinating story, Michael, but let's get to whatever you need me to do before I am late for my library meeting. Would you please explain what we are doing at Mort's office?" I asked. "More precisely, explain what I'm doing here."

"My superiors have confirmed that a multimillion-dollar shipment of black opals destined for the Canadian city of Winnipeg was trafficked from Brisbane, Australia, to Grand Forks, in your great state of North Dakota. 'Twas a sad day for the traffickers when they were nearly discovered during a routine border patrol exercise. For some reason they either decided to or were ordered to come all the way east and pass the gems to colleagues who consistently use this alternate route to cross the border and would transfer them to associates who would double back to Winnipeg. Normally this route is only used for deliveries to or from Quebec City and Montreal and the surrounding areas."

I was astonished. "Are you telling me that the demand for black opals is so great that the smugglers have designed passages to and from specific towns and cities all over the map?"

"Not quite. What I am telling you is that the group that organized these routes has used them to move dozens of valuables both into and out of Canada, the United States, Australia, and England. Right now the Australian black opals happen to be popular," Michael said. "And it was the success the team has had in moving the black opals that caught the eye of an espionage organization from a certain unfriendly nation."

I sat back for a moment; then I said, "I understand your assignment, but I am not quite sure where I fit in, or even how Mort comes into it. He's the local sheriff, not the commissioner of the United States Customs and Border Protection Agency."

"Now, you see, that is exactly the point, my girl. It is because Metzger is the local sheriff that I need him to make the arrest. This must look like it was business as usual for Small Town, USA, criminals who got a bit messy, what with the murder and all, and thus came to the attention of local law enforcement." Michael furrowed his brow, as if deep in thought. He must have made a decision, because he continued.

"It would be best for all concerned that there be no inkling that we are onto the likelihood of this crowd moving up to espionage. If any federal agencies are involved, it could serve as an alarm and endanger the mole who first brought us the information. In his own country he'd be hanged for a traitor, possibly after a lengthy torture session."

I winced. "I understand completely. You need Mort to arrest the smugglers so that it looks like he discovered they were trafficking illegal goods while he was investigating Nelson Penzell's murder."

"Yes. And I need you to explain to the sheriff that he should help me, because I am the employee of a foreign government and have no legal standing here. We need never mention espionage, and he need be none the wiser. Plus, you will have to convince him, just as you convinced me, that this Brewington fellow is the kingpin." Michael looked at me as if the future of democracy were sitting on my shoulders.

What choice did I have? As a warning more to myself than to him, I said, "Michael, don't make me regret this."

As we got out of the car Michael said, "Why not let me put your packages in the trunk? They'll be safe, and we won't forget them when I drive you to your meeting."

The thought of leaving the food for Doris Ann's birthday celebration in Michael's car gave me shivers. I was familiar with his penchant for disappearing due to some emergency that I would never know was real or imagined. And I didn't want the birthday festivities to disappear with him.

When I said I'd rather take the packages with me, Michael said, "Of course. That's fine, too. At least let me carry them."

Floyd McCallum was standing behind the counter. He gave me a cheery hello, and then his blue eyes did a double blink when Michael Haggerty walked through the door behind me. Without taking his eyes off Michael, Floyd leaned back, turned his head slightly, and called, "Sheriff, you're needed at the counter."

Mort came through the doorway from the cells. "Hey, Mrs. F. Something smells real good in here."

Michael lifted up a bag of pastries. "It's Doris Ann's birthday cake or some such."

Mort looked confused. "Haggerty. What are you doing here? And what's in the packages?"

"Mort, let me explain. I am on my way to the Friends of the Library meeting, and the committee is celebrating Doris Ann's birthday with the muffins, doughnuts, and pastries that Michael is carrying." I pointed to the bags. "By chance I met Michael as I was coming out of Sassi's Bakery. He has some information, and I think you should listen to what he has to say."

There was a tense silence before Mort responded. It's possible that his distrust of Michael was grappling with his confidence in me. He waved us to follow him to his desk.

Once we were seated the office became eerily quiet, as if everyone was waiting for someone else to speak first. Mort took charge. He clenched his jaw, gave Michael a stern look, and said, "Well?"

"Sheriff, you may recall that when we first met, I mentioned an international smuggling ring that I thought might be operating in this very area. I am now certain that the ring exists, it is quite close by, and your murder victim had a role in it," Michael said.

Mort leaned forward, elbows on his desk, and inquired, "May I ask how it is that you became so certain?"

Michael hesitated but quickly decided to reveal as much as he could. "A man named Clark Geddings, a Boston Realtor, came into the British government's vision a few months ago. He seemed to have a connection to known traffickers of items of value on the international market. However, he never leaves the United States. In fact, he rarely leaves Boston, unless it is to come to coastal Maine on 'business trips,' but we could not be sure exactly what business he attended to on these trips. Several days before his most recent trip, to Bar Harbor and then here to Cabot Cove, he made several phone calls to Nelson Penzell."

Michael let that point hit home before continuing. "Bar Harbor was the site of a massive awards event held on the same evening Penzell was killed. I've confirmed that Geddings remained among the real estate agents and brokers until the wee hours."

I broke in. "In fact, Eve Simpson was there and spent some time with him, so she can vouch for his attendance."

"Of course she can." Mort raised his eyes skyward as if beseeching heaven for patience. "So, if we know this fella Geddings has an alibi for the murder, why is he of any interest to me?"

Michael said, "Because he can lead you to the rest of his cronies. When you lock them up you'll shut down a major international smuggling ring that is trafficking Australian black opals throughout the United States, Canada, and Great Britain. You may become the most famous sheriff in the state of Maine."

Mort laughed. "And wouldn't Evelyn Phillips love that! She'd zip right in here demanding the first interview."

Michael looked perplexed until I said, "Editor of the local newspaper."

Mort pursed his lips. "Tell me, how does this become my collar? If you have it all nailed down, why aren't you locking them up?"

"I'm an agent of a foreign government. I have no real authority here. My original plan was to gather intelligence and, if I came across an arrest possibility, turn it over to the local authorities. In this case, I believe that's you."

"And who am I supposed to be arresting, and for what crime, exactly?" Mort asked.

This is where I expected the conversation to get a bit dicey. And I was right.

"I overheard a conversation between Clark Geddings and another partner in crime, Roger Wilburne."

"Any relation to the jewelry store over in Constant?" Mort asked.

"He's the owner. In fact, that's where he and Geddings had the tête-à-tête that confirmed for my superiors that they work together in transporting goods illegally and that there is now a hitch in their system. They need to replace Penzell."

"And you overheard this conversation while you were in the store without Wilburne's knowledge? I don't suppose you had a warrant?" Mort asked.

"Now, where would I get a thing like that on this side of the Atlantic? Possibly Canada, I suppose, but that would be of no use here." Michael raised the palms of his hands as if that explained everything.

I decided it was past time for me to intervene.

Chapter Twenty-Six

I f I could clarify a point or two, we could all get on with our day. I have a meeting to attend, and I know each of you is usually quite busy."

Both men turned and looked at me as if they'd forgotten I was in the room.

Michael leaned back in his chair and looked at Mort, who said, "Have at it, Mrs. F."

"What Michael will eventually get around to telling you is that this morning he observed Clark Geddings having breakfast at Mara's with Angus Michaud. I suspect they were discussing how Angus could take Nelson Penzell's place in the organization."

I looked at Mort, who nodded for me to go on.

"Geddings slipped out the back door, and then Angus left Mara's, ducked under the crime-scene tape at his own shop, and went inside. When, after a few minutes, Angus hadn't come out,

Michael checked and saw that La Peinture has a back door, just as Mara's does."

"So you lost 'em both." Mort gestured toward Michael, who simply shrugged his shoulders.

"No, Mort, that's where I think you are off the mark. Michael didn't lose them. It was merely that he didn't realize where they were going. If I were you, I would call Walter Hendon and ask him if he has noticed any unusual activity on *Brew's Baby*." I indicated the telephone on his desk.

"Seriously, Mrs. F.? You think these smugglers have been tampering with Brewington's yacht?" Mort was incredulous.

"Not at all. What I think is that Jeremy Brewington is the mastermind, or kingpin, which is the term Michael uses, of the entire trafficking gang. Think about it. He is rich enough to afford the outlay to start up an operation and keep it going. He's so obsessed with privacy on his boat that he doesn't even allow his crew to sleep aboard when he stays at his house. And what clinched it for me is that he spends an inordinate amount of time riding up and down the coast, straight into Canada, via the Bay of Fundy, and back again."

Mort got that look in his eyes, a kind of spark that always told me he thought I was onto something. He picked up his phone and hit speed dial.

"Walter, it's Mort. Is *Brew's Baby* still docked? Good. Tell me, have you seen anything unusual going on around the boat? Really? When? Hang steady. We'll be right there." Mort's voice boomed with authority. "No, don't you do anything until we get there, unless anyone tries to leave the boat. Hold 'em. Grounds? Tell them . . . tell them that I'm on my way and may have a few questions because we are following up on Jeremy Brewington's complaints about break-ins."

By the time he hung up the phone, Floyd and Andy were standing by the door. Floyd asked, "One car or two, Sheriff?"

"Better make it two, Floyd. We may have company coming back." Mort grabbed his hat from the coatrack and said, "Walter Hendon saw Angus Michaud climb aboard *Brew's Baby* a little while ago. Most likely after he slipped away from you." Mort couldn't resist flashing a tiny triumphant smile in Michael's direction as he followed his deputies out the door.

Michael said to me, "And wasn't I the smart one to wheedle you into speaking to the sheriff on my behalf? With any luck he'll bust the lot of them, and we will have prevented an international crisis. The world owes you a great debt."

"Which you can pay right now by driving me to the library." I looked at the wall clock. "The meeting has already started, and here I sit with the refreshments."

Michael picked up the bags. "I've been meaning to ask—the scent is so tantalizing—do you think your committee members would notice if a doughnut or two went astray?"

I opened one of the shopping bags and pulled out a small waxed bakery bag. "Let me see . . . Aha, brownies. What do you think?"

"Splendid," Michael said, and reached toward the bag, which I promptly set down on Mort's desk.

"I'm sure, however things go on *Brew's Baby*, a snack would not be amiss for Mort and his deputies when they return," I said.

And I started for the door, with Michael behind me saying, "It's a cruel woman you are, Jessica Fletcher."

When Michael pulled up in front of the library, I hesitated before getting out of the car. It was likely that once he confirmed Mort had rounded up the smugglers, Michael would disappear as quickly as he had first appeared.

"Take care of yourself, Michael. Don't let MI6 lead you down too many dangerous paths." I smiled and patted his hand.

"You're not quite done with me yet. I'll be around for the next little while, in case your sheriff needs a hand with my smugglers. Besides, you haven't identified Nelson Penzell's murderer. I wouldn't want to miss that grand finale."

In all the excitement, I'd nearly forgotten that there was another, more serious puzzle piece to be found, but for now my focus was on the meeting that had surely started without me.

I stopped at the circulation desk and asked if I might use the break room to set out the food I'd brought. When I explained that it was in celebration of Doris Ann's birthday, Edward, the library aide, offered me a rolling book cart so I could, as he said, "wheel the birthday celebration to the meeting in true library fashion." With his help, it took only a few minutes to have everything set out on the plastic trays Charlene had put in the bottoms of the bags.

"Candles?" Edward asked.

"Right here. And I have matches," I offered.

"No need. We have a lot of birthdays to celebrate around here, so we have— Let me see . . ." Edward opened a cabinet drawer. "Here we are, not one but two of those wand lighters. One or the other is bound to work." And he put them both on the rolling cart.

We wheeled the cart behind the stacks just outside the meeting room and lit the candles. Then Edward held the door open, and as I pushed the car into the room he began to sing, "Happy birthday to you . . ."

Everyone joined in, and Doris Ann's cheeks turned a happy pink. When we were done singing she clapped her hands and said, "Jessica, what a lovely surprise. Thank you so much."

Ideal Molloy quipped, "Doris Ann, you'd better jump up and blow out those candles so we can all celebrate with a muffin. Oh, and do I see doughnuts? Are there any chocolate crème?"

Soon everyone had at least one sweet treat on a paper plate, and the committee members settled back in their seats.

Doris Ann said, "Jessica, before you came in—"

I couldn't help but say, "I am sorry to be late, but it was unavoidable."

"I think I speak for the entire committee when I say all is forgiven." Doris Ann held up a chocolate chip muffin with a candle stuck firmly in its center. "Feel free to be late anytime you want to stop at Sassi's on your way to one of our meetings."

When the laughter settled down, she went on. "We resolved one piece of business. We have decided to move the annual book sale forward a few months so that we can participate in the fundraiser for the children's wing at Cabot Cove Hospital. We've all agreed that, rather than compete with the hospital, we would like to help sustain their efforts."

"Oh, that is so thoughtful. I wholeheartedly agree," I said.

"Maybe we could contribute children's books when the new wing opens," added John Martinez, a young, dark-haired man with a serious addiction to reading Westerns and thrillers.

"That would be wonderful," I said. "I am not sure if we can afford new books. The hospital doesn't accept used toys, books, or games because of the germ factor."

There were murmurs of "Understandable" and "Completely reasonable" around the table.

Doris Ann looked at Lorna Mason, the committee treasurer, who nodded and handed over her treasury report.

After reading it Doris Ann told us how much was left in the kitty and how much she thought we could safely spend on children's books without endangering our other projects.

There was general agreement around the table. Doris Ann asked John Martinez if he would head up the purchase committee, and when he agreed, several other members volunteered to work with him.

I was always so proud of how generous my friends and neighbors were with their time and their money. And because Dr. Leung had asked me to serve on the entertainment subcommittee for the children's wing project, I asked Doris Ann to add my name to the purchase committee, explaining that I could be the connection between the two groups.

"Next order of business," Doris Ann said, "is to plan out what types of books will occupy our Friends of the Library corner for each of the next three months. As it happens, we have received an e-mail with a suggestion from a library patron. It seems he was looking to reread an old favorite, *The President's Daughter* by English thriller writer Jack Higgins. You may remember Higgins wrote the classic *The Eagle Has Landed*."

Doris Ann was pleased that, although the book was written decades ago and its story referred to an even earlier moment in time, *The Eagle* struck a chord with even the youngest committee members.

She continued. "Our patron, Mr. Nguyen, decided to do an Internet search for *The President's Daughter* and was astounded when he found nearly a dozen books in multiple genres with that very title. And he recalled that within the past few months we had books with 'daughter' in the title as our Friends display."

Several members nodded, and someone said, "I think we also had 'daughters' as our display about two years ago. It is a popular title hook."

Nancy, a newish committee member I didn't know well, reminded us, "*The Alchemist's Daughter* by Katharine McMahon won a lot of awards. And don't forget *The Bonesetter's Daughter* by Amy Tan."

John Martinez said, "I bet Mr. Nguyen is upset because the Jack Higgins book has been overshadowed by the James Patterson book of the same title. And Patterson wrote his book with an actual former president as coauthor."

Doris Ann laughed and held up a printout. "When I received this e-mail I looked up the book Mr. Nguyen mentioned, and I was surprised to learn that 'Jack Higgins' is the pseudonym of an English gentleman named Henry Patterson. As far as I can tell, he is no relation to James."

After we all had stopped laughing, Nancy asked, "So is that what we are going to display next month—books written by anyone named Patterson?" And, of course, that was followed by gales of laughter.

"Settle down, everyone. This is a serious discussion." Doris Ann was still chuckling herself. "Mr. Nguyen has suggested that, in honor of men everywhere, we devote a month to books with 'son' in the title. What do you all think?"

The woman in the seat next to mine said, "A few months ago my book club read *Not My Father's Son: A Memoir* by, you know, the actor Alan Cumming or Cummings. It was awesome."

Nancy answered, "His last name is Cumming, and I love when he does the introductions to *Masterpiece Mystery!* on the public television station."

Someone else mentioned *Notes of a Native Son* by James Baldwin.

"That's a classic," Doris Ann agreed.

John Martinez threw in a ringer. "Then there are books with the other 'sun' in the title, like *A Thousand Splendid Suns* by Khaled Hosseini.

Leave it to book lovers, I thought, *to present variations on a theme.*

Ideal, who'd been mostly silent throughout the meeting, said, "I only just noticed, it doesn't matter whether you spell it 's-o-n' or 's-u-n'—once you add an 'n' and a 'y,' you will always have 'sonny' or 'sunny.'" She giggled. "That can be helpful on a gloomy day."

Everyone at the table laughed and two people clapped.

Pleased that her contribution was appreciated, Ideal continued. "I think we should use both spellings and alternate the shelves. Put 's-o-n' on the odd-numbered shelves and 's-u-n' on the even-numbered shelves. Let's give the readers a choice and a challenge."

Lorna Mason said, "Isn't the whole point of the Friends of the Library to encourage people to read more? I am not so sure we should challenge them. That might confuse the readers."

Around me everyone was talking at once, each person strongly presenting their views on the matter. But my mind had drifted elsewhere.

Doris Ann rapped her knuckles on the table and pulled me from my reverie. "Jessica, what do you think? Jessica?"

At that moment the final puzzle piece fell into place. I realized it had been right in front of me all along. I snapped my fingers. "Of course. Why didn't I think of that? Will you all excuse me? I have to make a phone call."

Before I could get out of my seat, Doris Ann said, "Jessica, what do you think of Ideal's proposal?"

"I vote yes," I said. Then I stood and hurried outside, dialing my cell phone as I went.

"Sheriff's Department. Deputy McCallum speaking."

"Floyd, it's Jessica Fletcher. I know you are extraordinarily busy, but would it be possible for me to have a few words with Sheriff Metzger?" If Floyd was answering the phone, they must be back from their investigation on *Brew's Baby*. I wondered whether it had been a successful mission.

"Mrs. F., I owe you big-time." Mort's voice contained a mixture of elation and fatigue. "It's going to be a long night, but I promise that tomorrow I will take you to Mara's for as many slices of apple pie covered with cheese as you can eat."

"So it went well?" I asked.

"It sure did. Would you believe the three wise men, Brewington, Geddings, and Michaud, were sitting around the kitchen table having a cup of coffee and discussing their next venture while—get this—a dozen of those opals Haggerty described were sitting on a saucer in the middle of the table? We searched the yacht for the rest and found not one but three safes, two in walls in the master suite and one in the floor of the salon."

"And were there more opals in the safes?" I asked.

"Don't know. I suspect the major stash is in one of them, because Brewington refused to open any of them. I called in two other deputies and left them, along with Walter Hendon, guarding *Brew's Baby* while Floyd and I brought the three crooks in here, and I sent Andy to the courthouse for a warrant. He should be back any minute. And thanks to Haggerty's tip-off, I called the sheriff in Constant. She is bringing Wilburne in for questioning. Oh, and thanks for the brownies. Definitely no meal breaks for any of us tonight."

"Mort, I have something urgent to discuss with you. I know this is a busy time but I don't think it can wait."

"Can you give me an hour? Maybe a bit more?" Mort replied.

I heard Floyd say something in the background, and then Mort said, "Brewington's lawyer just walked in. Gotta go."

"But, Mort—" I was too late. The line went dead.

Chapter Twenty-Seven

I was totally flummoxed. Happy as I was that Mort had smashed the smuggling ring, I was more concerned with solving Nelson Penzell's murder. I needed Mort to hear what I had to say, and then, if he agreed, we could eliminate Coreen as a suspect once and for all.

I stood in front of the library with my phone in my hand, deciding what to do next. Then I hit speed dial for Loretta's Beauty Parlor. Coreen answered, and she sounded nearly as cheerful as her old self. When I asked for Loretta, Coreen put me on hold, and then came back. "If you can give her a minute, she'll be right with you."

"Thank you, Coreen. And how are you feeling?"

"Regina—that's Ms. Tremblay, my lawyer—says I am the perfect client. I do exactly what she tells me to do, and I don't let myself be bothered by anything that anyone else says to me or about me."

Coreen sounded quite proud of herself, as well she should have been.

I was awed by the personal strength Coreen had shown since she had gotten past her initial shock. I was in the midst of telling her how impressed I was by her resilience when she said, "Here's Loretta. Bye, now."

"Jessica? What's up? I have a cut and blow-dry in five minutes," Loretta said.

"I won't keep you. I just wanted to know when you will be finished with work for the day."

"This next client is the last one on the schedule. Say forty-five minutes. An hour, tops."

"I'm at a meeting at the library. I may have good news about Penzell's murder. Ideal Molloy is here, and I'm sure I can get her to drive me to see you when our meeting is over," I said.

"Well, that sounds worth waiting for. I'll be here." Loretta's voice dropped to a whisper. "Should I say anything to Coreen?"

"Although what I can tell you may be very good news indeed, I can't say for sure that the murder has been resolved yet. Decide how much you think Coreen can handle, and we'll play it by ear."

"See you later—my cut and blow-dry is coming through the door." And Loretta hung up.

I spent the rest of the Friends of the Library meeting on pins and needles. When Doris Ann announced that the meeting was adjourned, I got up so quickly that I nearly knocked my chair to the floor.

"Careful there, Jessica. You could break either the chair's leg or, worse, your own." John Martinez had grabbed my elbow, preventing me from falling. "Are you okay?"

"Thanks, John. I'm fine. It's only that I am in a dreadful hurry," I said, involuntarily looking at the wall clock.

"Do you need a ride home? I'd be happy to give you a lift. It's right on my way."

When I told him I was going to Loretta's Beauty Parlor, he said that was not a problem in the least. With that assurance, I jumped at his offer. Unlike Ideal, John would not be the least bit curious as to why I was going to Loretta's, nor would he want to come inside.

It was somewhat daunting to climb into the front seat of John's pickup truck. The cab was higher than I was used to, and I was glad I'd worn pants rather than a skirt. John graciously put an arm around my waist and helped with a gentle push. He was also gentlemanly enough to get out and assist me in getting down again when we reached Loretta's.

I waved good-bye as John drove away, and then I stayed rooted to the spot, organizing my thoughts. When I had my plan ready I opened the beauty parlor door just as a woman with a neatly styled blunt cut was leaving.

Loretta was standing just inside the door and holding both hands up, indicating that I should stop right there. She leaned in and whispered, "Coreen is in the back doing laundry. I don't want to get her hopes up. Tell me what's going on."

It took me a few minutes to get Loretta to understand what I was thinking, but at last she agreed that it could lead to a solution. My next step was to call Mort. I looked at the digital clock on my cell phone and noted that it had been more than an hour since I had last spoken to him. I hoped he had time for me now.

When he got on the phone Mort was positively gleeful. "Mrs. F., the opals were in the floor safe, which pretty much nails Brewington. It's his boat. And the other two are singing like canaries. Do you know how I could reach Haggerty to thank him? According to the Hill House he went to Belfast. For a second I thought the concierge meant Northern Ireland, what with Haggerty's brogue and all."

"No, but we can find him later. Listen to me. I have something to tell you about Nelson Penzell's murder."

When I'd finished, Mort said, "I get it. I'm not as sure as you are, but it is certainly worth a try. I'll set the wheels in motion. When do you think you and Loretta will get here?"

"Soon. We have one stop to make." I hung up, gave Loretta the thumbs-up sign, and picked up the phone again to call Mara's and order a platter of hamburgers and some side salads.

Mara asked with a dash of lightheartedness in her voice, "Are you having a party without me, Jessica?"

"Hardly. It's for Mort and his deputies. They're having a busy night."

"So I heard. The whole town is abuzz. Fancy jewels smuggled from Australia, and there's Mr. Jeremy 'Self-important' Brewington stuck in the midst of it. Serves him right. I do feel kind of sorry for Angus, though. He's just a greedy old man. He never gave a thought to what he was getting himself into, I'm guessing. Do you think one of them killed Nelson?" Mara asked.

"I suppose it is possible," I said.

"Well, I hope it wasn't Angus. And as to your burgers, if I were you I'd go light on the salads and add French fries. And if you've a mind, Andy Broom does like his poutine."

I laughed. "Mara, when it comes to food, you know best. Pack up whatever you think they will enjoy. For once I am not going to worry about healthy diets."

Loretta and I dropped off Coreen at home, and then stopped at Mara's to pick up the burgers. When Loretta parked in the visitors' section of the Sheriff's Department parking lot, I said, "Let me go in and make sure there isn't a big hullabaloo, with lawyers and clients clamoring for justice all over the waiting room."

When I opened the door, I was surprised to find the visitors' seating area deserted. On the other side of the counter, Floyd was sending a fax. I waved to him, and then signaled Loretta to come ahead with the food.

When I turned back, Mort was coming around the counter, his face serious, his demeanor businesslike. "We are all set, Mrs. F., and we're lucky. Evelyn Phillips and that new guy, Dan, came in for a statement about what Evelyn is calling 'the *Brew's Baby Bust*.'"

"Catchy," I said.

Mort laughed. "Evelyn thought so. I gave them as much information as I could, so they shouldn't come barging through the door at the exact wrong time."

Then he noticed Loretta coming in carrying bags and boxes, and he called Floyd to give her a hand. Mort whisked me to his desk at the far end of the room and asked me in hushed tones, "Are you sure this will work?"

"Yes, I am. Have a little patience, and you may be known as the Maine sheriff who solved two major cases in one day."

Floyd came over with a cardboard takeaway box and put it in front of Mort. "Mrs. Fletcher and Mrs. Spiegel brought us dinner from Mara's. Your burger, just the way you like it, and some fries on the side." He turned to me. "Can I get you something? There's plenty."

I declined, saying I had snacked at the Friends of the Library meeting, but the truth was I knew I was too nervous to eat. Perhaps I'd consider having something after we confronted the killer, but not now.

Loretta came out of the back room and joined us. "Jessica, to whoever thought of ordering the poutine, Andy says thank you. Me, I never saw the point of covering fried potatoes with gravy and tossing in cheese curds."

Mort said, "Loretta, when I first moved up here from Brooklyn I thought the same, but I've grown to like it." Then he raised his voice to be sure Floyd could hear him. "But I never did get the idea of relish on a burger."

"You don't know what you're missing, Sheriff," Floyd answered.

Mort had finished his meal and cleaned up by the time the front door opened and Ryan and Julie Hecht came in. Ryan had his arm locked firmly around Julie's shoulder.

When Ryan saw Loretta and me sitting with Mort, he said, "I hope I'm not disturbing you, Sheriff, but you did say it was important, so I came as quickly as I could."

Mort stood up and walked around his desk. "And I thank you for doing so. Come on in."

"Julie and I were visiting her father, and both of our phones have been blowing up with the news about the jewelry smugglers. That is an impressive arrest, Sheriff. Congratulations."

"Thank you," Mort said.

"I suppose you need an accountant to help record the value. Did you recover cash as well? I'll be happy to be your witness when you count it up."

Mort said, "I appreciate the offer, but that's not what I wanted to talk to you about."

I noticed that as soon as the Hechts came around the end of

the counter and into the main room, Floyd moved behind them, effectively blocking their path back to the door.

Ryan looked bewildered, and automatically drew Julie closer. "Well, then, Sheriff, I'm not sure how I can help."

Mort said, "Actually, what I wanted was for you and me to have a conversation about your relationship with Sonny. Particularly about how it ended."

Julie turned pale and began biting her lower lip.

Ryan said, "Who? I don't know any Sonny."

I'd sat by, hoping that my only role would be to listen, but at that point I knew I would have to intervene. "I'm sorry, Ryan, but that's not true. Earlier this afternoon when I met you and Julie in front of Sassi's Bakery, you mentioned that you couldn't buy your father-in-law a seascape because La Peinture, which you called by its former name, the This and That Shop, was still closed because Sonny was dead."

"Nelson—I'm sure I said Nelson." Ryan looked at Mort. "I already told you I don't know any Sonny."

I wasn't about to let him get away with a barefaced lie. "On the contrary, I am certain that Nelson Penzell insisted his paramours call him by the pet name 'Sonny,' and I am just as certain that you had reason to know that."

Julie slipped out from under Ryan's arm, and tears welled in her eyes. As they began to flow down her cheeks she looked at her husband and said, "Oh, Ryan, what did you do? Please, no, don't tell me."

Ryan turned to Julie and said in a hushed tone, "You left your phone in the office. Remember that? When I got home you asked me if I had seen it, and I pretended that I hadn't, but I had. It was on the counter in the office kitchen."

Julie looked stricken. "A careless mistake."

Ryan continued. "I picked it up and saw you had a text. Without thinking, I automatically tapped on it. He, that pig, wrote, 'I can't wait to taste your sweet lips again.' It was from Nelson Penzell."

He stopped and leaned on the counter. "Maybe, if I could have a seat?"

Mort nodded, and Floyd immediately pushed a visitors' chair toward Ryan. At the same time, I took Julie by the arm and led her to the chair I'd been sitting in earlier. Floyd brought each of them a paper cup filled from the watercooler.

Ryan took a long drink, and then said, "Well, I knew his reputation with the ladies, but I was still thinking, or maybe hoping, he'd sent it to Julie in error. I scrolled through their previous texts, praying I would find only business conversations."

He was silent for a few moments, leaving us to imagine what he did find.

"Instead I found a string of texts, including many where my wife . . . *my wife* proclaimed her love for 'Sonny.' I guessed that was her pet name for Nelson Penzell, who was clearly her lover."

Julie reached out to touch his arm, but he yanked it away and said to her, "Why did you save all that filth? If only you hadn't saved those messages."

Mort, his voice soft but firm, said, "Ryan, do you want to move on to telling us what happened the evening you went to Nelson Penzell's store?"

Ryan nodded. "I deleted the text and put the phone back on the kitchen counter, exactly where Julie had left it. Remember, Julie? You found it there the next day. Anyway, I was at a loss. I couldn't figure out what to do. If I confronted Julie, well, suppose she chose him over me? I couldn't have that.

"It took me a couple of days to decide that my only course of action was to tell Penzell to stay away from my wife. The first night I drove to the dock, the store was closed, which increased my frustration but made me more determined. I decided I would drive by every evening until I found Penzell alone, and then I would have it out with him.

"A few nights later the shop was open, but the only person I saw inside was Angus. My rage was building. I began to run on the treadmill in our basement every night to relieve my stress just so I could sleep.

"Finally, on the night you want to hear about, I saw the store lights were dim. Through the window I saw Nelson flitting around. At the same time I opened the door, he turned off the one lamp that was lit. When he turned to the door and saw me, he told me the shop was closed, that I would have to come back the next day. He didn't even realize who I was."

He stopped talking and looked like he thought he was finished. Mort waited patiently, and then said, "Ryan, we need to hear the rest."

Ryan heaved a deep sigh. "There he was, the man I was afraid was planning to steal my wife from me, and when I looked past him at the candles and the wine, well, I knew Julie was home, so it was clear he was waiting for another woman. In that moment I realized Julie was nothing more than a toy, a plaything, to him. How dare he treat her that way? I snapped."

Julie began sobbing. I took a packet of tissues from my purse and pressed it into her hand.

Ryan continued. "I raised my arms and pushed him as hard as I could. He lost his balance, and as he stumbled backward, Nelson said something about, if I was a thief, I could have the cash—just please don't hurt him. Hurt him! Hurt him! The man destroyed my life, and he didn't want me to hurt him. I picked up a candlestick and hit him. He fell down backward against the table, then landed facedown on the floor. I kept bashing his head until he stopped moving. After that I went home to dinner. One thing I knew for sure—there would be no more texts between my wife and Sonny."

Between sobs, Julie cried out, "This is entirely my fault. Ryan, I am so sorry."

Mort signaled Floyd, who tapped Ryan on the shoulder, and when Ryan stood, Floyd led him to the cells.

Just before the door closed behind them Julie called, "I'll get you the best lawyer I can find."

I was afraid she was offering too little, too late.

Chapter Twenty-Eight

A few days later, I was in Loretta's chair and she was standing over me with a blow-dryer in one hand and a round brush in the other.

Before she turned on the blow-dryer, Loretta said, "I want you to know, Jessica, that I intend to honor my promise. You successfully helped Coreen, so I will never, ever again try to talk you into letting me poof your hair higher or wider than you would like it to be."

"I plan to hold you to that." I laughed.

"Tell me, will I see you Saturday night at the going-away party for Evelyn at the community center? It's hard to imagine Cabot Cove without Evelyn Phillips nosing into everyone's business. She is meddlesome and often cantankerous, but I like her anyway. She has spunk." Loretta began winding a section of my hair around her brush.

"I wouldn't miss Evelyn's going-away party. I like her, too. And I think she chose her replacement wisely," I said.

"Really? I don't know. He seems a bit too quiet for the job. This town is used to Evelyn's bluster." Since she was moving the blow-dryer back and forth just above my right ear, Loretta lowered the speed setting so I could hear her more easily.

"Well, according to Evelyn, Dan Andrews may appear more low-key than she is but he is ferociously dedicated to investigating the news and presenting it truthfully. I believe her exact quote was that we shouldn't 'mistake his kindness for weakness.' I took it as a warning—underestimate him at your own peril." I didn't add that my own sense of Dan agreed with Evelyn's description.

In the mirror I watched Coreen gather up a basket of used towels and take them into the back room, presumably to launder them. When she left I asked Loretta how Coreen was doing.

Loretta put the blow-dryer on the highest setting and placed it on the counter to cover our conversation. She lowered her voice and leaned in closer to me. "She seems fine. I am having trouble accepting how well she is doing. I keep waiting for her to crash, but so far, nothing. For example, we met with Regina Tremblay yesterday, and she has been extremely kind regarding her bill. The amount is far less than I expected and her payment plan is definitely reasonable. With a little help from me, Coreen will be out from under it in no time. What surprises me most is that Coreen seems to have grown up during this entire ugly incident, and she took the payment plan right in stride. I expected crying and 'woe is me'-ing, but not so much as a sniffle."

"I suspect when you find the battered and bloodied dead body of someone you know, as Coreen did, everything that comes after that adjusts to scale," I said. "I saw her exclusive interview in the *Gazette* and I thought she sounded composed, very grown-up."

"I'm sure it helped that Regina Tremblay sat by Coreen's side the entire time, and Evelyn took a soft approach. After all, by the time they spoke, Ryan Hecht had already confessed," Loretta said. "So, the morning after the arrest, instead of being interviewed by Mort as a suspect, Coreen was interviewed by Evelyn as a witness."

"When you mentioned Regina's fee, it sounded like you and Coreen haven't heard that Mara has set out an old gallon jug with a sign that says 'Coreen Wilson Legal Fees' right next to her cash register. I've seen plenty of folks drop money into the jug. Why, even Seth Hazlitt managed to part with a few five-dollar bills, and you know what a skinflint he is." I laughed.

I was surprised to see the glint of a tear in Loretta's eye, but I knew better than to mention it. She brushed it away and said, "I think I'll surprise Coreen by bringing her to Mara's for a bite to eat when we close up shop. Let her see for herself how much her friends and neighbors think of her. Isn't Cabot Cove a great place to live?"

I nodded my head. On that we would always agree.

The front door opened and Ideal Molloy came in, making figure eights in the air with her left hand. "My sparkles were a huge success, except with that bad-tempered old Lavinia Wahl, but what does she know? I am thinking of taking my nail decorations a step further." She stopped and looked around. "Where's Coreen?"

"Right here, Miss Ideal." Coreen hurried out from the back room. "You don't think I would miss our nail appointment? And did I hear you say the sparkles were popular?"

"Popular with all the right people. You know, the younger crowd. Why, just yesterday I met Lavinia Wahl and her grand-niece coming out of the Fruit and Veg. Instead of 'Hello,' Lavinia sniffed and said, 'I see you still have that shiny stuff on your hand,' but Erica jumped right in and told me not to mind her aunt. She said that, as a nail biter herself, she was jealous of how gorgeous my nails are."

Coreen said, "You know, when Erica came in for her haircut, I gave her some hints to help her stop biting her nails. I wonder if she's tried any."

"What kind of hints?" Ideal asked.

"Easy things," Coreen said. "Like keeping her hands busy, doing something like knitting or crocheting so she doesn't absentmind-edly put her fingers in her mouth."

"From what I've seen, Lavinia wouldn't approve of Erica re-laxing with a pair of knitting needles and some colorful yarn. Lavinia is go, go, go." Ideal plainly thought Coreen's plan was a nonstarter.

"No problem. If Erica can't keep her hands busy, chewing on a stick of gum will keep her mouth busy. Now come sit over here and let me get your nails ready for today's spectacular polish. I have a few ideas."

As she walked past me, Ideal said, "Jessica, I read in the *Gazette* that Sheriff Metzger brought a worldwide smuggling ring to justice. He found it right here in Cabot Cove, and the article mentioned that you were involved. That sounds like something you would write about in one of your mystery books."

"Believe me, Ideal, Mort Metzger and his deputies did all the important work. Cabot Cove is lucky to have such hardworking law enforcement officers."

"Speaking of law enforcement, has anyone heard how Julie Hecht is doing?" Ideal asked. "What a tragedy. Didn't I tell you all, didn't I warn Eve, that Nelson Penzell was nothing but trouble?"

"Well," Loretta said, "Julie's sister came up from New Hampshire, and Joe Turco helped them find a topflight criminal attorney for Ryan. Still, it doesn't look good. It will be really hard to get past that confession he made."

"I don't care who Joe Turco recommends; the only criminal lawyer I will ever use is Regina Tremblay. She is the best." Coreen sounded so adamant, we all burst out laughing.

Loretta said, "Coreen, I agree Regina is highly competent, and she took great care of you, but it would probably be best if you never needed a criminal attorney again."

Coreen's cheeks reddened. "Well, yes, but you know what I meant."

"Yes, Coreen, we do. We also know that you are a very loyal person, and that is a wonderful way to be." I wanted Coreen to know that we appreciated that what she said was not exactly what she meant.

The door opened and Eve Simpson twirled into the room. She was wrapped in a dark gray cloth with a light gray border. She spun around twice more, and then stood still. "Well, what do you all think? Isn't it gorgeous?"

Apparently we were supposed to say, *Yes, it's gorgeous.*

But Loretta and I were not fast enough. Ideal said, "It's very pretty. Did you inherit your grandmother's shawl?"

"Really, Ideal! How can you say such a thing? This is a very modern ruana, a wrap made for warmth and style. And"—Eve ran her hand across her shoulder—"it is one hundred percent cashmere. Isn't it *enchanteur*? Enchanting!"

"It is stunning," I said.

Loretta chimed in. "You look ravishing, Eve."

Pleased with our comments, Eve continued to preen. "That is exactly the look I was going for. I have a meeting in an hour with an extremely wealthy gentleman who is interested in a summer home on the Maine coast. He called the statewide Maine Realtors Association, and because I made such a hit at the dinner in Bar Harbor, Jonathan Kimbrough, the president of the association, recommended me highly."

"That's wonderful, Eve. And what spectacular houses are you going to show this well-heeled client?" Loretta asked.

"Of course, I generally show my second- and third-best listings to warm up the client, and then shoot for the moon, but in this case I am going right to the top. I will show him the Brewington place up on the ridge. Why, the notoriety alone . . ."

I raised my eyebrows. "Eve, do you actually have that listing? I would suspect Jeremy Brewington has a lot on his mind right now. Have you signed him as a client?"

"Isn't Mr. Brewington in jail?" Coreen asked.

"No, he isn't in jail. He and Clark Geddings were released on bail. Angus took a little longer to secure a bail bondsman, but I am sure he is out and about by now. And, yes, Mr. Brewington is my client. I signed him yesterday and promised him top dollar for that lovely estate."

"You mean the house?" Loretta asked.

"Well, yes, the house, but 'estate' sounds chic, don't you think? It gives the property a certain aura. However, none of that is why I am here. I need a favor from Coreen, and, I suppose, from Ideal."

Loretta and I exchanged glances. This was going to be good.

Coreen, unaware of what was coming, said, "Ms. Simpson, if you can wait a few minutes, I'll be happy to help you with whatever you need as soon as I finish with Miss Ideal."

"Coreen, if I was willing to wait my turn, well, then I would hardly need a favor, would I?" Eve huffed.

"I suppose." Coreen was uncertain.

"Look." Eve wiggled the index finger of her right hand at Coreen. "I split the top of this nail. I need a patch and paint right away so I will look *de tout beauté* when I meet with Mr. Givens. You wouldn't want me to look slovenly?"

Ideal said, "So you want to interrupt my manicure for a broken nail?"

"No, Ideal, it's not for the *nail*—it's for the *sale*." Eve was getting exasperated.

Loretta and I were transfixed. We had stopped pretending that Loretta was working on my hairdo, and we were barely able to contain our merriment. Nothing was as much fun as listening to Ideal misunderstand while Eve explained.

Ideal said, "But you do want Coreen to stop working on my manicure so she can work on your one little nail."

"That's the point, Ideal. It's only one nail. Coreen can fix it in a jiffy."

Then Coreen said, "Actually, it will take a few minutes for the patch to dry. Then I have to reapply your polish. I hope I still have a bottle of the color you chose last week."

Eve was staring at Coreen as if willing her into total silence, but Coreen didn't notice.

The finale eroded into blackmail, with Ideal demanding that Eve treat both her and Coreen to breakfast at Mara's the next morning.

When Eve agreed, Loretta whispered to me, "Show's over." Then she said more loudly, "So, tell me, Jessica—how is work coming on that . . . What do you call it? The summary for your next book."

"In publishing it's called a synopsis. When I go home, I am going to give my synopsis one final read and send it off to my editor. Then tonight I will celebrate. I'm going to have dinner at the Hill House with an old friend who, I am sure, is about to leave town."

Chapter Twenty-Nine

I was delighted that Joseph was the maître d' on duty when Michael and I entered the Hill House dining room.

"Mr. Haggerty, your table is ready." Joseph turned to me with a broad smile. "And, Mrs. Fletcher, it is always a pleasure to see you."

"And you as well, Joseph. I have been meaning to stop by to thank you for escorting me to meet Mr. Geddings the last time I was here. You were an invaluable aid to the cause."

Joseph blushed. "I am always happy to serve. I did, as Ms. Phillips often says, 'read all about it' in the *Gazette*. And, Mrs. Fletcher, even before I read the article, I suspected instantly that your fine hand was part of the solution. Cabot Cove was the center of a high-stakes smuggling ring. Who could ever have imagined?"

Michael, completely without sarcasm, said, "I certainly would not have guessed such a thing was possible."

Joseph led us to a quiet corner table. "Your waiter for the evening will be Shane. Please signal me if anything is not to your satisfaction, and I will see that it is corrected immediately. Enjoy your dinner." And he withdrew.

Shane was young and dark haired, and had a pleasant manner that made me feel like I was at a private dinner party rather than a table in a public place.

I sat back in my comfortable plush chair, thankful that the chaos that had enveloped Cabot Cove, and me, in the recent past was finally over.

Michael tapped his fingers on my hand. "You look a little too relaxed. I fear you may fall asleep before dinner is served."

"I am never so relaxed that I would skip dinner." I laughed. "In fact, I am looking forward to hearing what the chef has prepared specially for this evening."

Michael turned to Shane, who stood at the ready. "Anxious as we are to hear the daily specials, please arrange for a bottle of Taittinger Brut La Francaise to be brought to the table."

"Really, Michael, do we need an entire bottle of champagne?" I asked. "It would be unusual for me to finish more than a glass. I'd hate to see such an elegant drink go to waste."

"Jessica, you helped bust an international smuggling ring wide open, and managed to catch a murderer in the bargain. Why not simply enjoy the fruits of your labor?" Michael teased.

"And did I, by any chance, prevent an international spy ring from becoming an operational reality?" I raised a questioning eyebrow.

"Now, that would be telling, wouldn't it? Let's just say we can all sleep better, safer, tonight. And here's the very man." Michael smiled at the sommelier, who, after holding the heavy green bottle for Michael's inspection, expertly popped the cork and poured about an ounce of champagne into Michael's glass so he could taste and approve.

Michael swirled the champagne in his glass, sniffed, and then took a sip. "Excellent. Please pour for the lady."

He held up his glass and said, "To Jessica. It is, as always, a delight to be in your company."

Shane waited until we finished toasting, and then described the dinner items that were not on the standard menu. He finished with his particular recommendations.

I wondered if our choices of entrée reflected our basic differences in personality: I ordered the baked salmon, and Michael ordered a porterhouse steak and asked for it to be served "near bloody."

Dinner was perfect, and quite filling, so I protested when Michael asked for dessert menus.

"How many times must I remind you? Tonight we are celebrating. Think of all those miners in Australia whose wages won't be negatively impacted by the price of black opals dropping through the floor because of these dastardly smugglers. We must be as decadent as possible on their behalf." He gave me a gleeful wink.

I decided to humor him and began to scan the menu for a dessert that would do as little damage as possible, but I soon realized I was not likely to find one.

"Look at this, would you? Isn't it some sort of a violation of interstate agreements for us to eat Boston cream pie here in Maine? How did it even get on the menu? Jessica, if I am going to indulge, please point out a local dessert that will tempt my taste buds." Michael put down his menu, waiting for my suggestion.

"Well, blueberry pie is the official Maine dessert," I said. "At least according to an edict the Maine state legislature passed some years ago."

"Then that's what we'll have." He signaled Shane, who was hovering discreetly nearby. "Shane, boyo, we'd like to taste your home-state blueberry pie and two cappuccinos. Now, what is that annoying noise?"

The buzzing was clearly coming from Michael's jacket pocket. He pulled out his cell phone and tapped a button. I was quick to notice that it was not the same phone he had been using when we exchanged phone numbers a few days ago. I assumed that once a job was complete, Michael would have a new phone at the ready for whatever might come along next.

"Jessica, I am sorry. I have to return this call. If dessert should arrive, please begin without me. I'll be back momentarily." Michael pushed his chair away from the table and stood. For a moment he looked as though he had more to say, but then, perhaps thinking better of it, he gave me a hasty salute and hurried toward the lobby.

I waited for a few minutes after Shane served the pie and cappuccino, but finally, tired of waiting for Michael, I began nibbling my slice of pie.

I'd eaten nearly half the slice, had pushed the plate away, and was sipping my cappuccino when Joseph came to the table. He leaned toward me and, in a voice so soft it was nearly a whisper, said, "Mrs. Fletcher, I am sorry to inform you that Mr. Haggerty has asked me to make his excuses. He must attend to an emergency. He asked that you accept dinner with his compliments."

"Thank you, Joseph. This is so typical. I wonder where he's

gone this time," I mused more to myself than to Joseph, but he answered nonetheless.

"I'm afraid Mr. Haggerty didn't say." Joseph looked so apologetic that I had to laugh.

"Wherever Michael's gone, Joseph, we can be sure that he is off on another bold adventure on Her Majesty's service."

I took out my phone to call Demetri. I was going to need a ride home.